Gone
Gull

Gone Gull

A Meg Langslow Mystery

Donna Andrews

Minotaur Books

A Thomas Dunne Book
New York

A THOMAS DUNNE BOOK FOR MINOTAUR BOOKS.
An imprint of St. Martin's Press.

GONE GULL. Copyright © 2017 by Donna Andrews. All rights reserved. Printed in the United States of America. For information, address St. Martin's Press, 175 Fifth Avenue, New York, N.Y. 10010.

www.thomasdunnebooks.com
www.minotaurbooks.com

The Library of Congress Cataloging-in-Publication Data is available upon request.

ISBN 978-1-250-07856-8 (hardcover)
ISBN 978-1-4668-9088-6 (ebook)

Our books may be purchased in bulk for promotional, educational, or business use. Please contact your local bookseller or the Macmillan Corporate and Premium Sales Department at 1-800-221-7945, extension 5442, or by email at MacmillanSpecialMarkets@macmillan.com.

First Edition: August 2017

10 9 8 7 6 5 4 3 2 1

Acknowledgments

I continue to be grateful for all the great folks at St. Martin's/ Minotaur, including (but not limited to) Hector DeJean, Jennifer Donovan, Melissa Hastings, Paul Hoch, Andrew Martin, Sarah Melnyk, Talia Sherer, and especially my editor, Pete Wolverton. And thanks again to David Rotstein and the art department for another beautiful cover.

More thanks to my agent, Ellen Geiger, and the staff at the Frances Goldin Literary Agency for handling the business side of writing so brilliantly and letting me concentrate on the fun part.

Many thanks to the friends—writers and readers alike— who brainstorm and critique with me, give me good ideas, or help keep me sane while I'm writing: Stuart, Elke, Aidan, and Liam Andrews, Chris Cowan, Ellen Crosby, Kathy Deligianis, Suzanne Frisbee, John Gilstrap, Barb Goffman, David Niemi, Alan Orloff, Art Taylor, Robin Templeton, and Dina Willner. Any passage of police procedure that I got right is wholly due to Robin Burcell's expert guidance, and if I got it wrong, clearly it's something I should have asked her about. Thanks for all kinds of moral support and practical help to my blog sisters and brother at the Femmes Fatales: Dana Cameron, Laura DiSilversio, Charlaine Harris, Dean James, Toni L. P. Kelner, Catriona McPherson, Kris Neri, Hank Phillippi Ryan, Mary Saums, Joanna Campbell Slan,

Marcia Talley, and Elaine Viets. And thanks to all the TeaBuds for two decades of friendship.

And of course, Meg's adventures would not continue without the support of many readers. I continue to be delighted and humbled by how many of you tell me that Meg's adventures often prove to be a comfort in dark and trying times. Thank you!

Gone
Gull

Chapter 1

Monday

"Wow, you could kill someone with that thing! Doesn't that worry you?"

I counted to ten before looking up from the anvil, where I'd been about to start hammering on an iron rod. I'd only just finished heating the iron to the perfect temperature for shaping it. If I was working in my own barn, I'd have ignored Victor Winter's remarks.

But I wasn't in my own barn. I was at the Biscuit Mountain Craft Center being paid—quite handsomely—to teach Blacksmithing 101. And however annoying I found Victor, he was a student. If ignored, he'd start muttering again about complaining to management. I didn't want him doing that. Management was my grandmother Cordelia, owner of the center, and I didn't think she needed the aggravation today.

So when I'd reached ten I put my hammer down, set the rod safely on the anvil, and pushed up my safety goggles. Then I smiled, and did what I could to turn his question into a teaching moment.

"Yes, Victor," I began. "You could kill someone with this metal rod—even if it wasn't heated to its present temperature of approximately a thousand degrees Fahrenheit."

This generated a few titters from the other eleven students. I deduced that I wasn't the only one in whom Victor provoked the occasional brief homicidal fantasy. Victor, coshed on the head with a ball peen hammer. Victor, skewered through the heart on the pointed end of the rod I was turning into a fireplace poker. Victor, doubled up and stuffed through the door of my forge, like Hansel at the mercy of the wicked witch.

"That's why we spent so much time this morning learning all about proper blacksmithing safety," I went on. "Do we need to go through all of that again?"

Several of the other students groaned—understandably. After just one morning, they were already tired of hearing safety lectures. I understood how eager they were to start working iron, but I was not about to turn twelve beginners loose with hot metal rods and two-pound hammers until I was absolutely sure that they understood the dangers. And even more important, that when I barked out an order, they'd obey.

"No, I'm good." Victor smirked as if he'd said something clever.

I caught several of the women students rolling their eyes. They probably realized as well as I did that all the safety lectures in the world couldn't guarantee that Victor—already referred to behind his back as "The Klutz"—would make it to the end of our weeklong class with all his digits intact and without third-degree burns. I worried, just for a moment, about whether Cordelia had a signed waiver on file from Victor. And then I reminded myself that of course she did. An important detail like that would not have escaped her eagle eye. If there was such a thing as a gene for organization, Cordelia was definitely the one I'd gotten it from. And even though she was in her eighties, some days she made me feel like a slacker.

Though the waiver probably wouldn't protect the center if I slaughtered Victor, no matter how annoying he was. So I took a few of the deep, calming breaths my yoga-savvy cousin Rose Noire would have recommended and went back to my lesson on how to determine when your iron was hot enough to be worked.

My students—five men and seven women—watched with keen interest. Even Victor. A few of them took notes, but most merely drank in everything I did and said with rapt interest and peppered me with questions.

"Okay, I think we're ready for one of you to try it," I said at last.

In my peripheral vision I could see Victor waving his hand frantically, like a first grader in dire need of a bathroom break. I pretended not to notice him. I called on one of the women and let her be the first to try hammering iron.

The morning crept along. One by one, each of my fledgling blacksmiths—even Victor—had the chance to heat an iron rod in the forge and hammer it on the anvil for a bit, while I gave helpful comments. I was a nervous wreck, trying to keep them all from hammering their hands, inflicting serious burns on themselves or their classmates, or impaling each other with the rods. When the bell rang to announce that the morning session was over and lunch was available in the dining room, I breathed a sigh of relief.

"Thank you, class. We'll reconvene at two this afternoon."

As the students filed out, I busied myself with tidying the studio and getting things ready for the afternoon session.

"Ms. Langslow?"

"Just Meg," I looked up to see three of the women students clustered in the doorway. "We're pretty informal here at Biscuit Mountain."

"Would you like us to save you a place at our table?"

They looked so eager. Suddenly, I found myself remembering how in high school who sat at your table during lunch period could make or break your social standing. Back then I didn't recall anyone soliciting my presence with such fervor. It made a nice change, and I wished I could oblige them. Maybe later in the week.

"Rain check?" I said aloud. "Because I have no idea if I'll make it to the dining room for long enough to sit down and eat today—always a lot of administrative stuff to do on the first day of a session. But if I do get there, I'll look for you and pull up a chair."

"Great!" "Hope you can make it!" "Okay!"

They hurried off, smiling.

"What's up?" My friend Amanda Walker was standing in the doorway, resplendent in an African tribal-print dress that I suspected was her own design. She was teaching weaving this week in the fiber arts classroom across the hall. "I thought mingling with the students was part of the job."

"It is, and you should go and mingle," I told her. "I'm going to go around and check on all the studios and classrooms and meet with my grandmother briefly before I go to lunch. Where I, too, will mingle if there's anyone still there to mingle with."

Instead of heading for the dining room, she stepped into the studio and shut the door.

"I will," she said. "But first, since there aren't any students here at the moment, you want to fill me in on whatever problem it was you were trying to hint at last night? Because after the long drive up here from North Carolina, I was too exhausted to figure out what the heck you were talking about."

"Sorry," I said. "I should have just waited till this morning to tell you. Last week we had some problems with vandalism."

"In the studios?" She sat on one of the benches that formed the tiny classroom area at one end of the studio.

"Mostly in the studios." I perched on the next bench. "For example—someone left a bunch of windows open one night in the room the watercolor class was using." We both glanced over at the huge wall of nearly floor-to-ceiling windows that made the studios such wonderful work spaces. "And the rain that blew in ruined a bunch of very nice student paintings."

"Could have been an accident." She frowned as she studied the windows. "Whoever was working in there last could have opened them to get the breeze."

"Yes, but Cordelia and I knew the thunderstorm was coming. We made sure all the windows were closed before we went to bed. They were definitely closed at midnight, and yet at six a.m. we found the ones in the watercolor studio wide open and the whole room was soaked."

"Damn." She shook her head so all the little bells woven into her long cornrow braids tinkled, their cheerful sound at odds with the somber tone of our conversation. "And here I thought this was going to be a peaceful, restful week."

"We're hoping it will be," I said. "So far, nothing has happened this week. With any luck, whoever did it was only here for last week's classes. So lock up anything it would break your heart to have stolen or broken, keep your eyes open, and try to have a nice time anyway."

"You don't ask much," she said. "I was going to skedaddle over to the dining hall, but I think I'll go back and tidy up my studio first. And maybe lock it up till the afternoon session's about to start."

"Good idea." I wished more of the instructors would get the point this quickly.

"By the way." She had stopped with her hand on the door-knob. "Is it true that you gave up your room here in the inn to me? Please tell me it's because you and Michael found someplace even better. Or since I seem to have your dad and your grandfather down the hall and your cousin Rose Noire next door, maybe the room was a little too close to family?"

"More a case of being too far from the family we needed to be near," I said. "Did you see the painted Gypsy caravan out back?"

"I did indeed," she said. "If someone's teaching a class about making one like it, I just might abandon my students to enroll."

"It belongs to a friend of ours—Caroline Willner, who runs the Willner Wildlife Refuge. She's here this week helping Grandfather with the nature photography class. When the boys saw the caravan, they begged to sleep in it, and Caroline jumped at the chance to move into a room with real plumbing."

"So now you and Michael are sleeping with the boys in the caravan."

"Actually, Eric, one of my nephews, is sleeping with the boys in the caravan," I said. "We drafted him as babysitter for the summer—in addition to serving as Michael's intern for all the children's theater classes. He's a busy kid. But even with him there we were a little nervous about having the boys so far away, so Michael and I are in a tent near the caravan. Away from the main campground, but still—a tent."

"I'll be sure to thank Ms. Willner for tempting the boys with that caravan," Amanda said. "And if you change your mind about sleeping in the tent—"

"We wouldn't try to kick you out."

"And you wouldn't succeed if you tried." She shook her head and chuckled. "But you'd be welcome to lay out your sleeping bags in my studio. You could guard my stuff."

"If we change our minds about the tent, we'll lay out our sleeping bags in *my* studio, to guard *my* stuff." I put on my sternest expression, which only made her giggle.

"You're no fun," she said. "Well, I'd better go do what I can to protect my studio. Later."

I went back to doing the same thing in my own studio and then made a quick trip up and down the hallway. There were six huge studios on this floor, three with a view of the front lawn and three overlooking the valley over which the center was perched. I peeked into all the rooms—at least the ones whose doors were open. Several of the instructors had locked up for lunchtime—probably, apart from Amanda, the ones who'd survived the previous week's incidents. Gillian Marks, the returning pottery instructor, was eating lunch in her studio. She glanced up with a frown when I peeked in, and then, recognizing me, waved and returned to her sandwich and her book. Ever since the vandal had turned up the temperature in her kiln, ruining a lot of nice student pots that were firing overnight, she'd been diligent about guarding or locking her studio.

Baptiste Deshommes, Grandfather's staff nature photographer, had locked his studio. I didn't have to nag him—not after the vandal splashed half a dozen of his best twenty-by-thirty-inch photo enlargements with a mixture of soy sauce and ketchup.

Valerian Eads, the returning leatherworker, hadn't been a victim, but he'd been methodical about locking up even before the incidents began.

The door to Edward Prine's studio was standing open, as usual. Even after the vandal had splashed red paint all around his studio, ruining one of his paintings along with a lot of his students' work, Prine had continued to be careless about locking up. Unless he, like Gillian, was eating in his studio. I stuck my head in to find him standing, brush in hand, frowning at a canvas and running his free hand through his disheveled mane of gray-streaked hair. Difficult to say whether he really was so absorbed in his art that he didn't notice me or whether he was posing. Knowing him, my money was on the latter. And it was probably a good thing if he painted through the lunch break. Prine considered himself quite a ladies' man, and unfortunately seemed oblivious to the distinction between flirtation and sexual harassment. The dining hall was always more peaceful without him.

Nothing seemed amiss in any of the studios, so I hurried downstairs and did a quick inspection of the three studios there—only three, because we considered natural light a prerequisite for a proper studio. The rooms on the valley side had light, but we'd set up the equally large rooms built into the side of the hill as storage rooms—storage rooms plus my grandmother's office. Everything was in order and locked up tight, so I dashed into Cordelia's office.

She was sitting at her desk with a plate in front of her, waving a forkful of lettuce at Grandfather and Dad. Dad was munching away at something from his own plate, which held Caesar salad, some slices of roast chicken, and some crusty French bread with butter. Grandfather paced up and down, occasionally snatching a bit of food from Dad's plate. From the look of relief that crossed Cordelia's face when I walked in, I suspected my diplomatic skills were needed.

"There you are, Meg. I had Marty send up lunch. For three, actually," she added, glaring at Grandfather.

"I'm not staying to eat," Grandfather said, through a mouthful of chicken.

"Looks as if Marty sent enough for ten, as usual," I said. Playing referee for Grandfather and Cordelia was turning into a full-time job.

"Your father tells us he may have spotted our first incident of the week," Cordelia went on.

So much for our hopes that the vandal was gone.

Chapter 2

"How bad is it?" I remained standing in case I needed to dash off to inspect the damage.

"Sit." Cordelia indicated a chair beside her desk. "You need to eat. Only a minor incident, and already taken care of. And not destructive. You know how we strung up clotheslines in the children's rehearsal room, so they can use the clothespins to hang up what they do in the art sessions as the week goes on? Well, at some point last night or this morning, someone put up his own display there."

"A good thing Michael went over early to get the room set up," Dad said.

"Why?" I asked. "What would the kids have seen if he hadn't?" Our eight-year-old twins, Josh and Jamie, were among the students in their father's children's theater class, so I was particularly unhappy to hear that someone was pulling dirty tricks in the kids' section of the center.

Dad took a large bite of buttered French bread and began to chew it rather slowly, obviously so Cordelia could be the one who answered my question.

"Lingerie," she said. "And pretty tawdry lingerie if you ask me. A leopard-print corset with pink marabou feathers. Red lace panties that don't perform the basic function you'd think panties were invented for. Some rather Marquis-de-Sade leather accessories."

"Do you suppose they brought the stuff in especially for the purpose of shocking people?" I asked. "Or is it possible that they stole the garments from one of the guests?"

"Dear me—I hadn't thought of that last possibility, and I certainly hope not," Cordelia said. "But I suppose I should make a discreet announcement. Though what I'll say is beyond me. I can't just announce 'Will the pervert with the fetish for cheap lingerie and bondage gear please report to my office to claim your stolen belongings?' And of course then everyone would know that someone was vandalizing us. Well, this is more of a prank than vandalism, but still—not something we really want to advertise."

"We could blame Spike," I suggested. "Since only Michael has seen the lingerie hanging in the art room, why not gloss over where we found it." The Small Evil One, as we called our eight-and-a-half-pound canine fur ball, had already come in handy as a scapegoat for some of last week's damage. Though Spike wasn't completely alibied for every night, we were reasonably sure he had never left his comfy berth in the caravan with the twins, the only human beings he had never been known to bite.

"I could say that someone unwisely let the dog loose, and fortunately the only mischief he committed was dragging a few undergarments out of someone's suitcase or bureau," Cordelia mused. "Anyone missing any items can reclaim them by describing them to me, and please, everyone, be careful with the dog gates. Yes, I think that would work."

I watched with approval as she wrote something in the small flower-covered binder that was her equivalent of my notebook-that-tells-me-when-to-breathe. Tasks that made it into that flowered binder didn't get overlooked.

"Great idea!" Dad beamed with approval now that the problem seemed well on its way to solution. "And when you come down to it, this latest problem is an improvement, right? Really just a silly prank—so that's good news!" He sounded pleased. In fact, now that we'd stopped discussing risqué lingerie, he was beaming with enthusiasm—until he noticed that the rest of us were scowling. "Isn't it?" he added, more tentatively. "I mean, now we can narrow down our pool of suspects—we can eliminate anyone who wasn't here both this week and last week, right?"

"Actually, we were hoping to eliminate the vandalism it-self," I said. "Preferably by figuring out the culprit before the first week of classes ended. But I could have lived with never knowing who was responsible if the problems had stopped when last week's faculty and students went home."

"I agree," Dad said. "But since they're still continuing—" He stopped, and I realized that the main reason he was so excited was that he hadn't been here last week, and had thus missed the chance to try his hand at solving the mystery. "But at least now we're that much closer to figuring out the cul-prit," he went on. "It's one of the people who came back this week. That's a much smaller number. We can narrow down our suspect list. Let's figure out who was also here last week."

"I already did." I realized it was time to trot out my statis-tics. "Fourteen students returned to take new classes this week, four faculty members are teaching again this week, and the eleven staff who made it through all of last week are still around."

"But that's assuming an individual is responsible," Corde-lia said. "And I'm not at all sure that's the case. I could name several groups who might have good reason to target Biscuit Mountain."

"Nonsense," Grandfather said. "It's pretty obvious to me who their target is—me! I can think of any number of people and organizations who would love to cause me problems.

Greedy developers! Corporations with heinous environmental track records! Individuals with—"

"Then if you're so all-fired certain you're the target, why don't you do something about it?" Cordelia demanded.

"Like what?" Grandfather snapped.

"Like leaving!" Cordelia shot back. "If you're the target and Biscuit Mountain is just collateral damage, then you could solve our problem by going away."

"And what about my class?" Grandfather asked. "We have twenty students signed up for this week's nature photography class with Baptiste and me. What happens to them if I just run away?"

"Baptiste can do the class just fine without your help," Cordelia said. "And James could lead the nature walks on his own." Dad cringed, as he usually did when caught in the crossfire between his parents. "For that matter, Caroline's here to help you this week—she could handle it."

"Nonsense!" Grandfather bellowed. And then, since even he realized that of course Dad and Caroline and Baptiste, the photographer, could handle both the class and the nature walks just fine, he cut the conversation short by storming out of the office, slamming the door behind him.

"Oh, dear." Dad looked back and forth between the door and us, as if unsure whether to dash after his father and calm him down or stay in his mother's office to continue with one of his favorite pastimes, discussing crime and detection.

"I do hope he doesn't really decide to leave," he said finally.

"Don't worry," I said. "He'll be fine once he cools off."

"And if you think he's likely to give up the chance to lecture to a captive audience all week, you don't really know him," Cordelia added. "Getting back to what I was saying— what if it's a group behind this rather than an individual?"

"Oh, I see!" Dad exclaimed. "You mean that they could have sent in one operative last week, and a completely different one this week! How diabolical!"

I'd have called it merely sneaky, myself, but I didn't want to spoil Dad's enjoyment of the situation.

"That's right," Cordelia said. "So Meg's list of who was here last week and came back again this week—well, it's interesting data, but it doesn't really narrow down our suspects that much, does it?"

"I can understand why a lot of dastardly groups might want to target my father." Dad looked thoughtful. "I'm afraid I'm not as up to date with who might have it in for Biscuit Mountain."

"What a very polite way of suggesting I'm not as important as your father." Cordelia smiled as she spoke, but I could tell the idea rankled.

"I didn't mean—I wasn't—" Dad spluttered.

"You're not as infamous, certainly," I said. "But I'm sure that developer who wants to buy Biscuit Mountain to build a luxury resort hates you just as much as Grandfather. Possibly more."

"Smith Enterprises," Cordelia said, for Dad's benefit. "And yes, the guy who runs it certainly doesn't much like me. You'd think I'd stolen something from him, instead of just saying a polite "No, thank you" when he asked to buy my land. But I think he's still trying to work through legal means. And I'm not at all sure a slick outfit like that would resort to such petty tricks. No, if you ask me, the Jazz Hands people are at the bottom of this."

"Jazz Hands people?" Dad echoed. "That's a choreography term, right? You suspect the students in the dance class?"

"The Jazz Hands Art Academy is an arts and crafts learning

center outside Charlottesville," I explained. "Calvin Whiffletree, the owner, seems to view us as his archrival."

"No, he seems to view us as upstarts who have pirated his
idea," Cordelia said. "Never mind that there are any number of places all over the country that have been doing the
same thing for even longer than Jazz Hands. There's Touch-
stone in Pennsylvania, Arrowmont in Tennessee, Haystack,
Pilchuck, Penland, Peters Valley, The Crucible—"

"As you can see, there are quite a lot of them." Cordelia's
memory was good enough that she could easily recite the
whole list if not sidetracked. "I've taught at a few over the
years, and before starting up Biscuit Mountain, Cordelia
took classes at several, to say nothing of interviewing the
people who ran them."

"And none of them were anything but welcoming and
helpful," Cordelia said. "Except for Whiffletree and his
wretched people at Jazz Hands, who seem to think I'm copying everything they do. I'd be the first to admit that I was
studying them to see how they operate—them and all the
others, so I could figure out what the best practices were.
And Jazz Hands was absolutely the bottom of the barrel—a
more disorganized, customer-hostile, and utterly awful place
you've never seen. But if Whiffletree sends any spies—and
I'm sure he will, if he hasn't already—he'd figure out that
we're making considerable efforts to do just about nothing
the same slipshod, inefficient way he does."

She'd also spent a considerable amount of money to support her goal of doing things properly at her center. Was
Cordelia merely irritated at Jazz Hands, Smith Enterprises,
and whoever was vandalizing Biscuit Mountain? Or was she
worried—even scared? Michael and I had done enough
renovating over the years to have an idea how much money

she had to have spent on Biscuit Mountain. What if it was more than she could afford to lose?

I filed that away as something to figure out later.

"Getting back to the vandalism." Time to change the subject. "If it's going to start up again this week, maybe it's time to call in Stanley." Stanley Denton, the leading—well, and only—private investigator in our hometown of Caerphilly, had already indicated that if we needed his help he'd clear his schedule and dash up here to Riverton within the hour.

"And how are we going to explain away his presence?" Cordelia asked. "To find out anything he'll have to snoop around and ask questions. Aren't people going to wonder about the balding, middle-aged student who shows up a day or two late and then starts asking nosy questions?"

"They might already be wondering when we're going to do something about the vandalism," I said. "At least the ones who have noticed it. Hiring Stanley would at least be something. And what about installing a security system?"

"Good idea." Dad beamed his approval. "After all, what's the use of having a son who's a cyber whiz if you don't let him help you with things like this?"

I was tempted to point out that my brother, Rob, wasn't a cyber whiz. He merely had a gift for coming up with ideas that could be turned into highly profitable computer and video games. Well, that and the good sense to hire people who knew what they were doing to take care of the small details like programming the games and running Mutant Wizards, the company that sold them. But I bit my tongue. If thinking it would be Rob who installed her security system instead of his highly skilled (and paid) staff helped convince Cordelia that she needed one . . .

"Like all those the computers and cameras your grand-father has at his zoo?" Cordelia said finally. "I hate the idea of spying on people. So . . . Big Brother."

"How interesting," I said. "That's just what Grandfather said when Caroline suggested that he install a security sys-tem." Cordelia bridled slightly at that, as I knew she would. Not for the first time, I wondered how she and Grandfather had ever gotten along well enough, however briefly, to pro-duce Dad. And, for that matter, what would have happened if Grandfather had been nearby when Cordelia discovered she was pregnant, instead of off on the Galápagos Islands and unreachable by post. Odds are they would have married—it was what one did, back then, in such a situation. Would they now be an elderly divorced couple, still squabbling over the same things that had ended their marriage? Or would one of them have done the other in out of sheer exasperation?

"I'll talk to Caroline," Cordelia said finally.

"Good," I said. "She can tell you all the things Grand-father should have done with his system to make it first rate."

A slow smile spread across her face. One-upping each other was one of Grandfather's and Cordelia's favorite hob-bies. I made a mental note to brief Caroline, so she could work that angle and close the deal on a security system.

"Incidentally," Cordelia said. "You'll notice that the Slacker is back."

"Yes." Not welcome news—at least not to me. "I can't help wishing he'd changed his mind."

"The Slacker?" Dad repeated.

"A student who started off in Gillian's pottery class last week," I explained. "Then Tuesday morning he informed us pottery wasn't his thing, and asked if he could switch to the papermaking class."

"Where he lasted a day and a half before hopping over

into the watercolor class." Cordelia's tone left us in no doubt what she thought of the Slacker's fecklessness.

"He can't possibly have learned much that way." Dad shook his head in disapproval.

"No—that's why we call him the Slacker," Cordelia said.

"Perhaps *dilettante* would be a more accurate word," I suggested.

"He seems more interested in the meals and the social life than in the classes." Cordelia seemed to find this strangely annoying. I figured as long as he paid his tuition, he could be as lazy or as diligent as he liked.

"Maybe he just likes hanging out with creative people." I'd had this conversation with my grandmother before. "And the meals and the social life are well worth it."

"He was originally signed up for a second week of Gillian's classes," Cordelia said. "Clearly that wasn't going to work. Since I more than half suspect him of being the Jazz Hands spy, I wouldn't have minded giving him a refund."

"Surely a spy would make more of an effort to blend in," I said.

"I suggested he switch to the nature photography class," Cordelia went on. "Any fool can point and shoot a camera. Doesn't make you a real photographer, but I imagine it's easier to muddle on with that than pottery or watercolors. He bowed out, though, when he heard about all the hiking. Not for the faint of heart, hiking with Monty." She sounded—well, affectionate would be an exaggeration. Proud of Grandfather.

"So where did the Slacker end up?" Dad asked.

"Rose Noire's herb class."

"They have hikes, too." Dad frowned. Was he miffed that the Slacker had scorned the class he was helping out with?

"Her herb-gathering expeditions aren't exactly hikes." Not

by my definition, anyway. "They drive a mile or two up the mountain until they find a nice pretty spot and then they set out the picnic baskets and wander around for a few hours within sight of the van, harvesting stuff. That's just his speed."

"But he's a suspicious character," Cordelia said. "Tell her to keep an eye on him."

"Will do," I said. "We should also keep an eye on Victor the Klutz if you ask me. Granted, he wasn't here last week, so he couldn't be solely responsible for our problems, but I've already started wondering what the devil he's doing here. Never have I seen anyone with less natural aptitude for blacksmithing."

"We will keep our eyes on him as well," Cordelia said. Dad nodded his agreement.

"And now I'm going to the dining hall." I stood up and stretched.

"There's plenty of food left." Cordelia waved at the spread. "In spite of your grandfather."

"I was planning to set a good example by mingling with the students," I explained.

But as I strolled down the hall, double-checking the studio doors along the way, just in case, I pulled out my phone. When I was upstairs again, well out of earshot if Dad or Cordelia stepped out of her office, I put in a call to my nephew Kevin, Eric's older brother, who actually *was* a cyber whiz.

"I have a job for you," I said, when we'd finished with the social amenities.

"One that actually pays?"

"Only in goodwill."

"Rob actually pays me for the consulting I do for him."

And probably very handsomely, given Eric's skills.

"That's true," I said aloud. "But for him it's a business expense. There's also the fact that by helping me you might help keep some creep or creeps from putting your great-grandmother's craft center out of business before you even get the chance to come down and teach those classes you're doing in July and August. Remember those acts of vandalism we had last week? Well it's starting again. We could use your help to find the perpetrator."

"Okay—what do you need?"

"I'm going to send you a list of people," I said. "I need to find out which of them have some kind of connection to Calvin Whiffletree and the Jazz Hands Art Academy."

"Who and what?"

I spelled the names, and gave him the Web site address.

"And while you're at it, could you also see if any of them have anything to do with Smith Enterprises—that developer who's been pressuring Cordelia to sell Biscuit Mountain to him?"

"I'm on it," he said. "At least I will be once you send me the list."

"Hanging up now so I can send it."

I dropped back into my blacksmithing studio, unlocked the cabinet in which I'd secured my laptop, fired it up, and sent Kevin copies of this week's and last week's student and faculty lists, along with a staff roster. Then I locked up my laptop again and checked my watch. I might have enough time to eat lunch in the dining room after all. Though I waited for Kevin to confirm that he'd gotten my e-mail.

Which didn't take long.

"Seriously?" his e-mail read. "I thought you said a *list* of people, not the whole freaking phone book."

I felt a twinge of guilt—yes, there were dozens of names

on the list. But that was why we needed his help in the first place. I'd send a suitably soothing and grateful e-mail later.

I headed down the hall toward the door that led into the great room, once more checking the studios on either side. And I spied a potential problem in Edward Prine's art studio.

Chapter 3

I stood in the open doorway of Prine's studio, assessing the situation. Grandfather was standing in the middle of the room, head tilted to one side, hands clasped behind his back, studying one of the paintings with a scowl on his face. And Prine was standing nearby, though his pretense of being totally focused on his partially finished canvas was wearing a little thin. Had Grandfather said something insulting already? Or was Prine merely vexed that his lair had lured in not an attractive woman but an outspoken old curmudgeon? In either case, the room seethed with tension, and I suspected they were on the verge of a heated confrontation.

Well, at least it wasn't another attack by the vandal, although I wasn't sure a heated confrontation between Prine and Grandfather was much of an improvement. At least the vandal operated quietly.

"Meg to the rescue," I muttered as I stepped into the room. Though I wasn't sure who needed rescuing from whom.

"Afternoon." I nodded to Prine, and then turned to Grandfather. "I think we can still make it to the dining room in time to grab some lunch. Let's go."

I took him by the arm and tugged gently. He dug in his heels.

"Ridiculous," he said.

I could see Prine scowling.

"There's roast chicken and mashed potatoes—" I began.

"This is all wrong." Grandfather was staring at one of Prine's paintings. I had only seen the back of the canvas when I was walking over, so I braced myself to turn around so I could see what Grandfather was frowning at. Though I could probably guess. He was probably inspecting one of Prine's erotic paintings—although he shouldn't have had the chance. Cordelia had laid down the law to Prine about not festooning the studio with what she called his "bare-naked ladies and pinup queens."

"I don't object to nudes," she told me afterward. "Or scantily clad women. But some of our students don't have my broadminded approach, and besides, that man could make a fully clad portrait of Mamie Eisenhower look smutty and suggestive."

And it suddenly occurred to me where our vandal might have stolen the tacky lingerie—if Prine himself wasn't the vandal. I made a mental note to discuss this with Cordelia.

But to my surprise, the painting that had incurred Grandfather's disapproval was one of Prine's inoffensive ones. In fact, it was really rather attractive: a three-by-four-foot canvas showing a larger-than-life gray-and-white seagull. The bird stood on a white railing in front of a grayish-blue sky. His feet were planted on the railing, his feathers ruffled in the breeze, and he stared moodily into the distance. Of course, I was anthropomorphizing with that moody part. Or maybe Prine was. You got the definite impression that the gull was contemplating the meaning of life, or the secret of the universe, or something equally profound, although any real gull staring into the distance like that would probably just be keeping his eye open for a likely bit of garbage to float by.

"Ridiculous," Grandfather repeated. "You've got this all wrong." He turned to Prine. "There's no such gull."

"Nonsense," Prine said.

"You'll never find a gull with those markings on his wings and those on his tail." Grandfather tapped the offending bits of the painted bird.

"Don't touch my canvas," Prine said.

"And then topping it off with a bill that color and shape—ridiculous. You've conflated at least two completely different species of gulls—possibly three."

"I saw that very gull," Prine said. "And painted it—"

"From life?" Grandfather sounded scornful.

"From photos."

"Photos of two or three different species of gull," Grandfather said. "That's what comes of doing your research on the Internet."

"From half a dozen photos I took myself of the same damned gull."

"Hmph." Grandfather was shaking his head, and looking at the painting as if Prine had slaughtered the gull, and a few hundred of his cousins, instead of merely painting him with less than perfect accuracy. "Waste of canvas, if you ask me."

"Well, no one did, you old coot!" Prine roared.

"Let's go up to lunch and you can tell me all about it." I grabbed Grandfather's arm and attempted to steer him toward the door.

"Old coot! I could beat you in arm wrestling any day, you degenerate twerp!" Grandfather shouted.

"Shut up, both of you!" I snapped. "I won't have behavior like this in front of the students."

"No students here," Prine said.

"There will be any minute if the two of you don't pipe down. You!" I pointed to Prine. "What do you care what he thinks? He's not an art critic. And you!" I whirled back to face Grandfather. "Stop picking on your fellow instructors and come have some lunch."

I half-coaxed, half-nagged Grandfather down the hall and breathed a sigh of relief when the door that separated the great room from the studio wing slammed shut behind us.

Even as I hurried Grandfather toward the dining room, I couldn't help looking around with pleasure. The great room was one of my favorite parts of Cordelia's newly renovated craft center.

In its heyday, the rambling building had been a well-regarded art pottery factory. Unfortunately its heyday had been around the 1880s. The Biscuit Mountain Art Pottery had gone bankrupt during the Depression and Cordelia's family, the Lees—no relation to the more famous and wealthy Virginia Lees—had sold it. By the time I first saw Biscuit Mountain, nearly a century later, it had been abandoned for several years and was on the verge of falling apart. Cordelia had bought the property, renovated the building and grounds at great expense, and hoped to recoup her investment by running craft classes.

Luckily for us, when the Lee family had built the factory, they'd had the money to do it well and the taste to want even a factory to be aesthetically pleasing. A graceful and inviting porch ran along the front of the building, and when you entered, you found yourself in the great room—one of the rooms carved out of what had once been the enormous high-ceilinged main factory floor. The dining room, library, and several other public rooms also filled the central block. At the back of the great room a wide terrace gave a sweeping view of the Blue Ridge. Downstairs were the kitchens and staff bedrooms which, because the land sloped down so steeply, were as full of light as the main floor, with almost as good a view. Upstairs a series of echoing storerooms had been converted to small but elegant and comfortable bed-rooms for the instructors and students.

To the left of the main building was a wing that had also once been an enormous factory workroom, this one con-verted into a small but well-designed theater and two roomy rehearsal rooms. This week, Michael was teaching a children's theater camp in one rehearsal room while in the other a veteran hoofer taught a class she called An Introduction to Dance for Musical Theater.

To the right of the main building was the wing contain-ing the nine studios. The rooms there had actually started life as studios, in which artists had once done all the hand painting that made Biscuit Mountain pottery famous, so Cordelia hadn't needed to do much remodeling there.

Above the theater and the studios were more guest rooms, but since there were not nearly enough rooms for the stu-dents, we'd set up a rustic campground in a field that bordered the front drive and compiled a list of nearby bed-and-breakfasts and Riverton residents willing to rent rooms to our students. We'd even set up Cordelia's enormous Victorian house on the outskirts of town as a temporary bed-and-breakfast, with Cousin Mary Margaret acting as chatelaine. But even the students staying in town tended to hang around the great room and the terrace when not in class, and al-most everyone soon figured out that Marty, Cordelia's cook, was so good that the meal plan was well worth signing up for. Cordelia offered pro-rated meal plans to the skeptics who didn't believe her brochure's promise of delicious gour-met feasts. By the end of last week's classes, nearly everyone at the center had signed up.

Thank goodness for the food, I thought as I steered Grandfather across the great room and into the dining room. Grandfather's quarrel with Prine would have been a great deal harder to avert without the prospect of one of Marty's meals to tempt him.

As soon as we entered, Caroline Willner spotted us and waved us over to her table.

"What's got you all riled up?" she asked Grandfather.

"The miserable degenerate of an artist," he said.

Hmm. Perhaps this was not the first time Grandfather had inspected Prine's studio.

"He's not worth blowing a gasket over." Caroline steered him to a seat. "Meg, go up to the buffet and get him a plate."

"He's completely unsound on seagulls," Grandfather was saying.

"Well, what do you expect?" she retorted. "He's an artist, not a naturalist. I bet you'd be completely unsound on Pointillism, gouache, and the proper use of cadmium yellow."

"Nonsense," Grandfather said. But he sounded more mellow than usual. Caroline's good influence no doubt, or perhaps the prospect of the plate I'd be fetching.

But just as I was turning to head for the buffet and follow Caroline's orders, I heard Grandfather hiss in a stage whisper.

"Damnation! What's *she* doing here?"

He was frowning thunderously and pointing across the dining room. Caroline and I both craned our necks to see who had upset him.

Grandfather was pointing to a small clump of gray- or blue-haired matrons, clad in pastel tracksuits or skirt-and-sweater sets, who were seated together, picking at chicken-salad or tuna-salad lunches while eyeing the desserts with which they probably planned to undermine their healthy main meal choices. They all looked fairly typical of our student body, which skewed heavily toward women, many of them retirees or at least empty nesters.

"She who?" Caroline asked.

"That Venable woman," Grandfather snarled. "There—on the end. In the purple."

"Ah." Caroline nodded as if that answered her question. It didn't answer mine. The woman at the end of the table was clad in a lavender tracksuit and had a pair of lavender-framed reading glasses dangling from a purple cord around her neck. She looked like someone's twinkly-eyed grandmother.

"What's a Venable woman?" I asked.

"A menace," Grandfather muttered. "A blot on the face of the earth."

"A lady bird-watcher," Caroline said. "Of whom your grandfather does not approve."

"I wouldn't call her that," Grandfather said.

"Not a lady, then?" I asked.

"Not a *real* bird-watcher," he said. "What the hell is she doing here?"

"Presumably taking a class," I said. "Probably the jewelry-making class—I don't recognize everyone at her table, but the ones I do are all from the jewelry class."

Grandfather snorted and pointedly turned his back on Mrs. Venable.

I decided it was not the time to ask why he disliked her so intensely. Perhaps she was unsound on the issue of Wilson's Snipe, a subject about which Grandfather had recently insisted on lecturing me at great length. I could no longer remember what it was about the particular snipe that had divided the birding world into separate and warring factions. But I came away more convinced than ever that birders were capable of the most passionate feuds over things we mere mortals couldn't begin to understand. I'd ask Caroline about Mrs. Venable later. For now, probably wise to see if a good meal would mellow Grandfather's temper.

I went through the buffet once to fill a plate for him. Caroline looked relieved when I delivered it, and both of us were relieved when Grandfather left off sulking over the presence of Mrs. Venable and tucked into his meal with gusto.

And then I went through again for my own lunch, though I decided to take mine in one of the carryout boxes we kept for people who wanted to eat in their rooms or studios. I'd been doing that all too often lately, because if I didn't, something invariably interrupted me before I could wolf my food down. The students who'd invited me to lunch were just leaving, so instead of mingling with them I joined a table where Amanda was sitting with my cousin Rose Noire.

"Just the person I was looking for!" Rose Noire exclaimed. "Meg, I have a Plan."

Yes, I was usually just the person Rose Noire looked for when she came up with plans, in spite of the fact that at least half the time I shot them down as impossible, impractical, or just plain cuckoo.

"I've been thinking about how we can prevent any more problems like the ones you had last week," she added.

"Too late—we've already had one suspicious incident." I explained about the lingerie display, and managed to get in a few bites of salad while they exclaimed over it.

"This makes my plan all the more vital!" Her tone seemed to imply that had we turned to her for assistance last week, most of the nastiness could have been averted. "I'm going to arrange a cleansing ceremony! My students can help me make the preparations."

"It's actually more or less on topic," I said, seeing Amanda's puzzled look.

"I'm teaching the practical and spiritual uses of herbs," Rose Noire explained. "And this is absolutely on topic!"

"Just don't get anyone upset by mentioning this latest incident. Or last week's, for that matter. Some of them were here last week for other classes—if they choose to gossip, there's nothing we can do, but let's not stir things up unnecessarily."

"Of course," Rose Noire said. "I'll merely explain that the cleansing will dispel any negative energy that might be lingering from past events, and help prevent any future unpleasantness. And if we use the right combination of herbs, it will also boost people's creativity. It's really one of the most useful, general-purpose things you can do with herbs."

"Apart from putting them in food," I said. "I'm rather partial to that use myself."

"And I'd already planned to take them walking in the woods this afternoon to gather native herbs," Rose Noire went on. "We can keep our eyes out for ones we can use in the cleansing. I must run! So much to do!"

She dashed out—though not without taking her tray up to the service hatch to drop off the dirty dishes on her way out. She might be a free spirit, but she was a very tidy and law-abiding one. She also paused to stick her head in the service door—probably to see if Marty was there so she could thank him for the excellent meal. Was it just my imagination, or had Marty begun spending more time here in the dining room since Rose Noire's arrival? Was he about to join Rose Noire's small but dedicated troop of admirers?

"That reminds me." Amanda held up a copy of our summer schedule. "Interestingly diverse selection of classes you've pulled together here. Goes a bit beyond the usual craft offerings."

"Yes," I said. "We were going to have nothing but traditional craft classes, but my grandmother had some trouble recruiting participants until I got involved."

"That's understandable," she said. "No one knew her or had any idea if she was sane and reliable. They know you."

"And figured my brand of insanity was one they shared, or at least could tolerate." I was actually pleased at the praise. "Once I got involved, we managed to reach critical mass, with enough craft instructors to make it worthwhile. But in the meantime, every family member who has teaching experience or aspirations volunteered to put on a class, and since we had enough space to house them all, we decided to go for it."

"I see your cousin is also doing yoga and mindfulness meditation in the evenings." Amanda was studying the schedule. "And your mother is doing flower arrangement and principles of interior design next month. This Kevin McReady who's teaching the computer class for kids in August—another relative?"

"One of my nephews," I said. "You've met Eric—Kevin's one of his older brothers. If you think that's diverse, you should see the full schedule. Come July we'll be having a whole track of classes that law enforcement officers can take to fulfill their in-service training requirements, and believe me, getting approval for all that from the Department of Criminal Justice Services was no picnic. Kevin will be teaching a couple of classes for police officers on stuff like using online resources in an investigation and proper handling of cyber evidence. Dad's teaching several sessions of CPR and first aid for first responders. My cousin Horace is coming up to teach some forensic classes."

"A pity you didn't start the in-service classes a little sooner," Amanda said. "I bet your vandal would think twice about doing anything if the place was crawling with off-duty cops."

"Cordelia and I have already noted that for the future," I said. "Assuming we survive this summer, in future we hope to have the place crawling with cops at all times. Quite apart from the security benefits, it looks as if those in-service classes could be quite a nice profit center. And Caroline Willner—have you met her yet?—is going to help me talk my grandmother into installing a state-of-the-art high-tech security system."

"Good. But in the meantime, how about a low-tech system?"

I just had taken a bite of chicken, but gestured for her to continue while I chewed.

"My church was having a problem with vandalism a while back," she explained. "We were pretty sure it was a couple of wild teenagers, possibly from our own congregation. So we recruited a bunch of sweet little old grannies to sit and knit in the most vulnerable places. Not only did that protect the rooms they were guarding, but eventually they spotted the troublemakers trying to sneak away after spray painting some rude words on the men's room wall. We almost had to rescue the juvenile delinquents from the grannies—there are few things more terrible than the righteous wrath of an upright Baptist church lady."

"It's a thought." In fact, if I hadn't been eating, I'd have jotted it into my notebook. "Mother could probably recruit any number of volunteer security guards from our family if we could find a place to house them. Thanks."

"You're welcome." She pushed back her empty plate and frowned at it. "I am going to gain ten pounds this week; I just know it. I'm not sure whether to thank or curse your grandmother for hiring such a good cook."

"Glad you're enjoying the food," I said. "Hearing compliments like that almost makes up for the hassle of dealing with our cook."

"A lot of cooks are temperamental."

"Temperamental is a polite way of putting it. Marty's like a cross between a drill sergeant and a wolverine. We already had to replace two junior kitchen staffers who were terrified of him, and then he almost resigned in a temper tantrum over compost."

"Is he for or against?" Amanda sounded puzzled.

"For—as are Cordelia and I. Which is why we set up a perfectly lovely garbage, recycling, and compost center half a mile downhill from here—far enough from the main building that the guests couldn't smell anything and weren't apt to be troubled if any raccoons or bears came scavenging. Marty begrudged the time it took his kitchen lackeys to haul the compostable trash down there—he had them flinging it in a ravine behind the building."

"Oh, my." Amanda shook her head in sympathy as we got up and headed back toward our studios.

"By the second day, we started searching the crawl space under the terrace to see if anything had died under there." We were crossing the great room, and I lowered my voice to make sure none of the students who might be nearby overheard me. "And since by that time we'd already started seeing the first acts of vandalism, we thought the smell was another in the series. Then the third or fourth day we deduced from the number of birds and animals swarming all over the hillside that there was something untoward happening on the slopes below us and figured out it was Marty instead of the saboteur."

"Unless, of course, he was the saboteur," Amanda suggested. "Did you consider that?"

"We're still considering it," I said. "There's no evidence pointing to him, but there's nothing that definitely clears him, either. Well, except for the fact that he seems to begrudge spending even a few minutes on anything not related to food. Anyway, we had to hire several workers to help us pick up all the rotting garbage—not an expense we had planned on—and harsh words were exchanged in the kitchen."

"From the sound of it, I should enjoy his cooking while it lasts, then." Amanda sighed and patted her stomach. "Because even with you to keep the peace, I have a hard time imagining Ms. Cordelia putting up with that kind of nonsense for long. Well, here's my studio."

I peeked in, just for a second. I had to admit that the fiber arts studio was a lot more festive-looking than mine, and I was very proud of the way we'd arranged it to support a wide variety of classes. Just inside the door were several rows of sewing machines, with the half dozen looms beyond them in the main body of the studio. The walls were covered with cloth hangings and racks of brightly colored cloth and thread. Dangling overhead on a pulley system were several spinning wheels and quilting arms that weren't in use this week. The sewing machines could also be hoisted on high when not in use, and we even had a plan that I hoped we wouldn't have to execute this summer for rolling the looms into storage if we needed the space they occupied.

Then I glanced at my watch and realized that I needed to hurry back to my own studio before the students showed up and began beating down the doors.

Only two of them were waiting, thank goodness, which would make it easier to ensure that I was the first one in the room—the better to deal with anything our vandal might have done while I was gone. I unlocked the door and flung it open—and realized that I was holding my breath until I could see what was inside.

Chapter 4

Fortunately the studio was just as I'd left it. I strolled up and down the neat row of anvils and forges, making sure. The students were so busy chatting that they probably didn't notice my brief flurry of anxiety.

The afternoon passed slowly—but not quite as slowly as the morning. Shortly after class resumed, we lost Victor the Klutz—at least for the rest of the afternoon. For reasons he never satisfactorily explained, he felt it necessary to pick up one of my anvils, and proceeded to drop it on his left hand. Fortunately he did it early enough in the afternoon session that Dad was still at the craft center rather than wandering the woods with the photo class. Performing first aid on Victor and then escorting him down to the county hospital greatly enlivened Dad's afternoon. And although I felt a little guilty about it, I had to admit that Victor's absence made for a serene and productive class.

At six o'clock my students all hurried off to clean up before dinner. I battened down the studio and then sat down and opened my phone to see if any voice mails, texts, or e-mails had come in while I'd been teaching. I smiled over a couple of texts from Michael with pictures of what the boys had been doing. I sighed upon reading the e-mail from next week's jewelry-making teacher, asking if the meals included vegetarian options. I sent a quick reply: "Briefly, yes. Can send more details when I'm at my computer." Apart from the fact that I'd already answered the same question for her at least twice, did people really even need to ask anymore? Were there really that many places that ignored the growing numbers of committed vegetarians? Probably, but Biscuit Mountain wasn't one of them. Later today I'd reassure her that not only did we have vegetarian options, we had a cook who was passionate about ensuring that the vegetarian options were at least as delectable as the carnivorous ones. But I didn't feel like tapping that out with my thumbs.

Then I realized I had an e-mail from Kevin.

"I decided to start with the faculty," it began. "Nine of the twelve names you gave me have some past association with the Jazz Hands Craft Academy. Details follow."

Nine out of twelve? Holy cow! Maybe Cordelia wasn't just being paranoid. Though I calmed down a little when I read through the details. Still—my grandmother needed to hear about this.

I locked up my studio and hurried upstairs. I found her getting ready to leave her desk.

"Got a minute?" I asked, stepping inside.

"For you, always." She sat back down.

I shut the door and took one of her guest chairs.

"I asked your great-grandson Kevin to do some research for me," I began. "Apparently, of the twelve craftspeople on the faculty last week or this, nine of them have some past association with Jazz Hands."

"Nine? Holy sh—I mean good grief."

"Forwarding Kevin's e-mail to your computer," I said. "Let's print it out and study it."

A few minutes later we were both peering down at printouts of Kevin's e-mail.

"This is bad." Cordelia was shaking her head in apparent dismay.

"Not necessarily," I said. "Two of these people took classes at Jazz Hands, twelve years ago in one case, ten years ago in the other. From what I remember of their résumés, that would be early in their careers. And you'll notice that they didn't go back for any refresher courses."

"True," she said. "And for that matter, it was early in Jazz Hands's history as well. I think twelve years ago would have been their first year of operation."

"The other seven taught there, but only one of them recently."

"Edward Prine." She grimaced as she said the name. "I knew there was something I disliked about that man."

"There's much to dislike about him," I said. "But I wouldn't necessarily hold Jazz Hands against him. I mean, would you have hired him if you'd known what a jerk he was? Maybe until you came along, they were the only ones who would hire him to teach. Of the others, Gillian the potter taught there in two consecutive years, but she hasn't done so in four years. The rest all taught classes for one session during the first three years Jazz Hands was in existence. Doesn't sound as if they're Jazz Hands stalwarts. More like maybe they felt the same way about the place as you did."

"Maybe." Her words came out through a tightly clenched jaw. "Or maybe I invited the Trojan horse in the door."

"Let me talk to some of them." I tucked my copy of the list into my tote. "I'll start with Amanda—I've known her longer than Jazz Hands has been in existence."

"Good," she said. "Keep me posted. While Kevin's checking people out, can he do a few more? Well, a lot more, I guess if—"

"I also gave him a list of this week's and last week's students, plus our staff," I said. "He's going to check them out, too, but yeah, there are a lot of them. It will take time."

"Remind me to do something nice for that boy when he gets down here—assuming we keep our prankster from destroying the place before he comes."

She sounded worried. My stomach tightened briefly. How badly would failure of the craft center hurt her? I couldn't figure out a diplomatic way to ask, so I pushed down the worry and gave what I hoped would look like a reassuring smile.

"Whatever Kevin finds, we'll deal with it. Don't forget, the entire Langslow/Hollingsworth clan has your back."

She smiled at that, though it wasn't exactly a carefree smile.

I hurried back upstairs to Amanda's studio. She was still talking to a couple of her students. I waited till she finished with them, then stepped into the studio and shut the door.

"May I pick your brains for a minute?" I asked.

"I hardly have any left," she said. "And I'm still not sure half of my students know their warp from their weft. But what brains I have left are at your disposal."

"What do you know about the Jazz Hands Art Academy?"

"Those miserable crooks!" she exclaimed. "If you ask me, they're part of the reason your grandmother had so much trouble recruiting craft teachers for this summer."

"Why?" I asked. "Were they bad-mouthing her?"

"No—actually, if they had, it would have sent craftspeople flocking to her. They suckered me into teaching there one summer—this would be, oh, maybe nine or ten years ago. Only job I ever had that lost me money. My own fault, really, for not reading the fine print in the contract. They pay you by the student, so I figured if I did a little marketing for myself, I'd make out like a bandit. What I didn't realize—because, stupid me, I didn't read the fine print in the contract—is that if the student drops out, they dock your pay, even if the student dropped out for something that wasn't your fault—like the fact that Jazz Hands had only one working loom for a dozen students and no air conditioning in a Charlottesville summer. And they docked our pay for what they called a materials fee—at marked-up prices; I could have filled a dump truck with fiber for what they charged me for the materials fee. Complete crooks. I never went back, and from what I've heard, hardly anyone ever does. So when your grandmother started contacting people about teaching here—well, no one knew her, and too many of us had been burned by those Jazz Hand jerks, so it wasn't till you came on board and reached out to people that we figured out it might be legit. Why are you asking about them, anyway?"

"They have it in for Cordelia and Biscuit Mountain," I said. "They keep threatening her with legal action for supposedly stealing the idea of having a craft class center."

"Yeah, that sounds like them. What's-his-face, the owner—"

"Calvin Whiffletree," I put in.

"Yes, that's him. He was always was a litigious son-of-a-biscuit-eater."

"Cordelia's wondering if he might be behind the vandalism," I added.

"Wouldn't put it past him."

"So if you notice someone here, faculty or student, that you know is associated with Jazz Hands—"

"I'll let you know," she said. "Though I have to say, I haven't been anywhere near them since that summer I taught there, and neither has anyone else I know. So I might not know who's been hanging with them lately. Apart from Eddie Prine, of course. He's been teaching there for years, which should tell you all you need to know about them."

"Eddie?" I repeated. "You're on friendly terms with him?"

"Not hardly," she said. "But I do know how he hates being called Eddie. Try it sometime if you want to see him go ballistic."

"I'll keep it in mind." I had to smile at the suggestion. "But I'm more likely to want to calm him down."

"Purrs like a kitten if you call him a genius. So if you think you can pull that off with a straight face. . . ."

"Probably beyond my powers," I said.

"Just out of curiosity, did your vandal do anything to him?"

"Splashed his studio with red paint. Ruined a bunch of paintings. He was pretty philosophical about it until he realized a painting he'd just started was one of the casualties."

"Yeah, that sounds like his style." She shook her head ruefully.

"So what are your plans for the evening?"

"I plan on taking a long, hot soaking bath. Rose Noire gave me some of the herbal bath stuff her class was making today. And then I plan to make a pig of myself at dinner, after which I'm undecided between movie night, bridge, or your cousin's yoga class."

"All good options."

"From what I've seen so far, word of mouth should make it no problem getting faculty for next year. You definitely know how to treat people here. Good studio spaces, nice amenities. Assuming you can solve this vandalism thing, of course. I'm off for that bath. Laters."

"Laters," I replied.

Assuming we could solve the vandalism thing. Easier said than done.

I headed for the dining hall.

On my way, I ran into Rose Noire.

"I had a fabulous idea this afternoon," she said. "And you were busy with your class, so I just decided to go for it."

"Go for what?" I was mentally bracing myself.

"Horace!" she exclaimed.

"What do you mean, going for Horace?" I asked. Horace Hollingsworth—my second cousin and Rose Noire's fifth cousin once or twice removed—had a long-standing crush on Rose Noire, who either didn't reciprocate his interest or perhaps hadn't quite noticed it yet. Rose Noire was the reason Horace had given up his job as a crime scene technician for the York County Sheriff's Department in favor of being a mere deputy and part-time criminalist in Caerphilly. Odds were Horace would do just about anything if Rose Noire coaxed him into it, so I needed to make sure her latest idea was a sensible one. Sensible and Rose Noire did not often travel together.

"I've asked him to come up to help your grandmother find the person who's doing all these unpleasant things," she said. "He has some vacation coming anyway, and Chief Burke said okay. He hopes to be here in time for supper."

"That's actually a really good idea," I said.

"You don't have to sound so surprised."

"I'm just surprised Dad didn't think of it," I said. "He'll be very pleased. You know how much he enjoys working a crime scene with Horace, though thank goodness they don't often get the chance."

"Yes," she said. "And this is almost as good as a murder."

"Better, if you ask me. We don't want any dead bodies blighting Biscuit Mountain's reputation."

"But without a body there's really not much medical stuff for your father to do," Rose Noire pointed out.

"He can use his vast knowledge of criminal psychology to probe the culprit's motivation and predict what he'll do next." Of course, Dad's knowledge of criminal psychology had been largely acquired from mystery books rather than through observation of actual criminals, but still, with any luck his favorite authors would have gotten most of the details right.

"Ooh, yes—he'll like that. I'll go and tell him!" She hurried off with remarkable speed, considering that she was wearing a long, trailing, gauzy flowered dress that looked as if it came straight out of one of Arthur Rackham's fairy paintings.

I followed more slowly, checking my phone for e-mails and messages as I walked. Dad reported by text that Victor the Klutz had a broken hand and would be withdrawing from the blacksmithing class. However, since he did happen to have his camera with him, Dad had convinced him to transfer to the nature photography class, so luckily there would be no need to refund his tuition.

"Awesome," I muttered. Had even Dad picked up on Cordelia's anxiety about keeping up enrollment?

Michael and the boys were waiting for me at one of the long tables.

"Mommy! I'm going to be Peter Pan!" Jamie called when he saw me.

"Big deal," his twin Josh said. "I'm going to be Captain Hook."

As usual, each boy wanted to be the first to tell me all about his day, and Michael and I might have had trouble keeping peace if Grandfather hadn't arrived.

"Guess what I found in the woods today," he announced.

Chapter 5

In one of the murder mysteries Dad read by the dozens, the answer, of course, would be a body. Fortunately the boys read a different sort of book.

"Bears?" Jamie guessed.

"Pirates?" Josh ventured.

"I was about to guess that," Jamie protested. "What about a crocodile?"

Clearly Peter Pan and Captain Hook were having their effect.

"A family of weasels!" Grandfather exclaimed. "Caroline, show them the pictures."

Caroline pulled out her digital camera and began clicking through it to find the pictures she had taken of the weasels, while Grandfather regaled the boys with facts about weasels, such as their remarkably varied diet.

"Mice, rats, moles, shrews, voles, chipmunks, rabbits, squirrels, and even bats," he recited.

"Curious," Michael said. "My appetite's not what it was a few minutes ago."

"Small birds, of course, and their eggs," Grandfather went on. "Lizards, frogs, fish, earthworms, and insects generally."

"Do they eat them raw?" Jamie asked.

"Of course, raw," Grandfather said. "And they enjoy lapping up the blood of their prey."

"Perhaps just a small salad," Michael murmured.

Just then I saw Edward Prine enter. He paused in the archway and appeared to be scanning the room.

"If he's trying to make a dramatic entrance, he picked the wrong time," Michael said to me in an undertone.

"Yeah." I kept my voice equally quiet. "We're the only ones watching—everyone else is too absorbed in their food."

But when Prine spotted us he began striding across the room toward us.

Or, more likely, toward Grandfather.

"Uh-oh," I muttered.

I pushed back my chair in case I had to intervene, and I noticed Michael was doing the same.

Prine arrived at our table and loomed up behind Josh and Jamie, who were sitting opposite Grandfather.

"Here!" Prine flung something down on the table in front of Grandfather. Several sheets of eight-and-a-half-by-eleven paper. "Don't tell me my paintings are all wrong! Take a look at those!"

Grandfather rather deliberately averted his eyes from the papers and continued his nature lesson.

"So what survival advantage do you think the weasel's varied diet gives him?" he asked.

But the boys had picked up the sheets of paper.

"Seagull," they exclaimed, nearly in unison. Dad and Great-great, as they called Grandfather, frequently organized little competitions with bird identification flash cards—a game the boys might not have enjoyed nearly as much if their successes weren't so often rewarded with chocolate.

"Weasels!" Grandfather repeated. "Do you know what animals are closely related to the weasel?"

Since this sounded like the sort of question that might eventually lead to the consumption of chocolate, the boys abandoned Prine's papers and returned to competing for Grandfather's attention.

"Fine. See if I care." Prine stomped over to the cafeteria line and grabbed a tray. I kept an eye on him, and was relieved to see that he was having the servers put his food into a couple of carryout boxes. I wasn't the only person to breathe a sigh of relief when he picked up his boxes and stormed out.

Grandfather studiously ignored Prine's papers during the rest of the meal, but I noticed that when he got up from the table, he casually picked up the papers, folded them, and stuffed them into one of the pockets in his khaki sportsman's vest, being careful not even to glance at them. Though he did glare briefly in the direction of Mrs. Venable. Who appeared to be paying absolutely no attention to him. A little odd, since years of appearing before TV cameras on various nature shows had made Grandfather a first-class ham. People tended to watch him, in no small part because even when he was doing something utterly mundane, like delivering his tray to the service hatch, he managed to give the impression that he was about to pull off a stunt that would make Moses and the Red Sea look small time. I suspected that Mrs. Venable was merely pretending to be oblivious to him, and I wondered why.

Ah, well. She was on the list of people Kevin was checking out. And if he didn't find much about her, I'd send him back to take a closer look.

But later. I was ready to stop thinking about the vandal for a while. I'd spent the meal listening to weasel lore with one ear while studying my fellow instructors—I was trying not to think of them as suspects. Five of the nine who had some association with Jazz Hands were here this week. Of course one of the five was Amanda, who was such an old friend that I didn't really consider her a suspect. And while it was easy to suspect Prine of any kind of unpleasantness, the vandal had displayed a certain degree of ingenuity and inventiveness that I wasn't sure Prine possessed.

But I had an even harder time imagining any of the other teachers doing anything so nasty.

Peggy Tanaka, our jewelry maker, a slender, bubbly Japanese American woman in her twenties, was sitting with Rose Noire, and from the look of it they were discovering all kinds of common interests and becoming each other's newest best friends. While I wasn't sure I believed in Rose Noire's talk of auras, premonitions, and flashes of intuition—and sometimes winced at the mystical or New Age phrases in which she cloaked her pronouncements—I knew her to be a fairly keen judge of character. Peggy was low on my personal suspect list.

Dante Marino, our woodworker, was the center of a lively group that, from the words I could overhear, was having an intense discussion of dadoes, miters, and rabbets, whatever they were. If I watched Dante's gestures long enough I might actually figure it out. Although it was only the first day of this week's class, the woodworking students had already grasped the importance of moving breakable or spillable things far away from Dante's elegant and ever-active hands. Hard to imagine him as our sneak vandal, either. If Dante didn't like something, he told you about it. Maybe even took a swing at you, if you were a guy. But sneaking around—distinctly out of character.

And then there was Gillian, our potter, always so cool and self-contained. I suddenly realized that if it were merely a case of figuring out who had the brains, boldness, and subtlety to carry out the vandalism campaign, Gillian would be top of my list. But I'd seen her expression of disapproval and distaste when we'd found the damage in the papermaking studio, not to mention her quiet anger when her students' pots were ruined. Both had seemed quite genuine. So either Gillian wasn't the culprit or she should be helping Michael teach the acting class. And since Rose Noire seemed to have taken to her almost as much as Peggy, my money was on her innocence.

In addition to the three Jazz Hands veterans, there was also Valerian, our leather worker—who hadn't come up in Kevin's research on Jazz Hands, but the Virginia craft scene was a small world. He could have known them. Valerian was, in Cordelia's words, an odd duck—a brilliant craftsman, an excellent if low-key teacher, but with so bland and colorless a personality that he tended to disappear altogether in social situations. In Dad's eyes, of course, this would make him the prime suspect. But Dad had read hundreds—possibly thousands—of mystery books whose authors were constantly trying to make their bloodthirsty killers blend into the woodwork until the next-to-last page. In real life, I doubted that Valerian's passive and phlegmatic exterior hid anything but more of the same. I'd keep my eyes on him anyway, if only so I could reassure Dad that, yes, I wasn't overlooking the quiet one.

Perhaps my problem was that I was reluctant to suspect any of my fellow craftspeople of wrongdoing. I found myself hoping that it was one of the students instead. I studied them, particularly the familiar faces who had also taken classes last week. A couple of them saw me looking and waved. I put on my most cheerful face and waved back. Perhaps the dining hall wasn't the best place to ruminate over my suspicions.

One student did stand out in my mind—the Slacker. Whose actual name was Joe something. He was sitting at the

same table as Valerian. Probably a good move if he was looking for peace and quiet. Valerian not only didn't talk much,
he tended to dampen conversation around him. Not in a
negative way—the one time I could remember sitting at the
same table as Valerian I'd found it curiously easy to fall into
a comfortable silence, concentrating on Marty's food, even
pointing rather than speaking when I'd wanted the salt and
pepper. From the mellow look on the Slacker's face, he felt
the same way. Though, unlike Valerian, who ate with his eyes
half closed, the Slacker was constantly studying everyone
around him, waiting expectantly for his fellow beings to en-
tertain him. Maybe I should be calling him the Voyeur instead of the Slacker.

And why was he here, anyway? After the way he'd hopped
from pottery to papermaking to watercolors last week, I'd
fully expected him to cancel for this week, and yet here he
was, back again, drifting around the center with a vague
smile on his face, seemingly perfectly content no matter what
was going on. He answered genially when anyone addressed
him but seemed equally happy if everyone left him alone. According to his teachers from last week he occupied the first
third of each session by slowly and methodically setting up
his work space, filled the last third with cleaning up after
himself, and in between spent more time appreciating his
fellow students' work than performing any of his own. Did
all that make him suspicious? Or was I only suspicious of him
because I couldn't imagine spending more than a week with
busy, creative people while doing next to nothing myself.

"Maybe he just likes hanging out with creative people," I
reminded myself as I watched him saunter out of the dining
room onto the terrace with a wineglass in his hand and park
himself in one of the Adirondack chairs as if planning to
spend the rest of the evening there, people-watching.

Although my suspicion of him rose when someone else came and took the chair next to him—Mrs. Venable, the bird-watcher whose presence had so irked Grandfather.

I glanced around, spotted Caroline, and beckoned to her. She strolled over.

"What's up?" she asked.

"I don't know." I gestured unobtrusively toward Mrs. Venable. "What's her story?"

"Irma Venable." Caroline sighed and shook her head. "Not your grandfather's favorite birder."

"Well, I gathered that. What's he got against her—did she fail to genuflect when he entered the latest Audubon Society meeting?"

"She's not a *responsible* bird-watcher." Caroline frowned as she said it.

"Let me guess—she inflates her life list with birds she hasn't really seen?"

"I'm sure she does." Caroline waved dismissively. "Your grandfather would only laugh at that. But she's also careless of the welfare of the birds. Indifferent to it. That maddens him."

"Doesn't keep her feeders filled and her birdbath free of ice?" I asked. "Because I have a confession to make—I'm pretty bad at stuff like that myself."

"I'm sure your grandfather will be delighted to hear that you actually have feeders and a birdbath nowadays. No, the problem with Irma is that she's in it for the glory. Having the longest life list. Being the first to report a rare bird or an interesting vagrant."

That sounded to me like just about every hardcore birder I'd ever met. I didn't say it aloud, but Caroline could read my face.

"Okay, here's an example. A few years ago we went up to

New England to film a segment on the piping plover. It's threatened or endangered—I can't remember which—though conservation efforts are helping bring it back. One of your grandfather's contacts told him that a small colony of them, just a few pairs, had begun nesting in an area where they hadn't been seen for decades. Your grandfather scoped the site out and decided it wasn't safe to film just yet—there was a danger that all the lights and noise and human traffic would upset the parent birds and distract them from sitting on their nests and then caring for the young as they hatched. We decided to wait a few days, maybe a week or two—however long it took till all the eggs had hatched and the chicks were a few days old. And if you think it's fun, hanging around with your grandfather when he's bored and waiting for something, think again."

"You deserve a medal," I said. "A whole bunch of medals. What does this have to do with Mrs. Venable?"

"She found out about the plovers. She was probably keeping track of your grandfather's whereabouts in the hopes that he'd lead her to something interesting. Next thing we know, she's posted a selfie of herself with her head right up against one of the plovers' nests—you just don't do that with wild birds! And then she shared the location with a whole bunch of so-called birders as clueless as she is. By the time we got out there again the next day, the whole area was trampled, and something had eaten most of the eggs. Could have been a raccoon, attracted by all the activity. Or a dog that came with one of the gawkers. Either way, a promising new breeding ground was destroyed. Completely irresponsible. And you know the most maddening thing of all?"

I shook my head and raised an inquisitive eyebrow.

"She convinced everyone that she'd found the plovers first, all by herself. Faked evidence to prove it."

"Faked it how?"

"She pushed back the date on her digital camera so it looked as if she'd taken her pictures the day before your grandfather and I got there. Started bragging all over the birding lists about how she'd succeeded in finding the plovers before the great Dr. Blake."

"I'm starting to see why Grandfather dislikes her."

"Baptiste was able to disprove her claims—he took one of her pictures of the shoreline and blew it up big enough that you could read the hull number on a Navy ship that was still hundreds of miles away in Norfolk on the day she claimed to have taken her pictures. But that didn't settle things—some people claimed Baptiste had faked the ship to make her look bad, and others that Mrs. Venable probably didn't realize her camera was set wrong and made an honest mistake. There are still people sniping back and forth at each other in some of the forums."

"Who knew the birding world was such a contentious place?" I said. "Remind me not to let those two bird feeders of mine escalate into a full-scale addiction."

"Indeed." Caroline stared at Ms. Venable for a few more moments. Then she shook her head. "Don't turn your back on her. She may look like a mild-mannered, slightly ditsy granny, but she's really a snake in the grass."

She strolled off. I studied Ms. Venable and the Slacker for a little while longer. I couldn't hear them, but based on the body language and facial expressions, Mrs. Venable was trying to get some information from the Slacker—information he either didn't know or had no intention of sharing. He was starting to look a little harassed. She was starting to look a little irritated. Good.

I planned to keep my eye on her. I couldn't figure out how engineering our vandalism wave could possibly advance her quest for birding glory, but she was a known liar and an enemy to Grandfather. What if she thought she could annoy him back attacking the center? Of course, that would mean she'd have had to lurk around here last week, before the start of the class she was taking. I made a mental note to warn Cordelia about her, and find out when she'd registered. If she'd done so right after Grandfather's class was announced, more proof of Caroline's theory. Then again, if she'd registered at the last minute, it could mean that she'd lurked last week and decided that this week it would be easier to spy on him at closer range. Suspicious either way.

As the dinner period ended, students and faculty went off in various directions. Cordelia had laid in a large supply of kid-friendly movies, so Michael and Eric took the boys and the rest of their classmates to the theater for a showing of that 1960 Disney classic, *Swiss Family Robinson*. Two bridge tables formed on the terrace, with light provided by large strings of white paper lanterns overhead and the Slacker standing by as kibitzer-in-chief. Grandfather and Baptiste, his photographer, set off on their usual evening nature walk, accompanied by the entire photography class plus anyone else whose idea of fun included stumbling along in the dark in Grandfather's wake. Rose Noire's two-hour class on relaxation and meditation was popular, though I suspected more relaxation than meditation was happening—whenever I passed the open archway that led to the library turned yoga room, I could hear several gentle snores rising over the soothing bell and flute music.

I didn't join in any of the organized—or disorganized— fun. Instead, I indulged in something I knew would make me feel better—tackling many of the smaller or more urgent to-do items in my notebook. Though I didn't plan to tell anyone what I was up to—except, perhaps, for Cordelia, whom

I suspected was doing the same thing. And I carried around one of Dad's Agatha Christie paperbacks in my pocket, so if anyone took me to task for not relaxing, I could pull it out and explain that I was just doing this one little thing before getting back to my reading.

I thoroughly inspected the theater and the drama and dance studios, not just checking for undiscovered vandalism but getting a feeling for what they were supposed to look like this week, the better to spot anything that might be amiss later. I even took a few photos of each room with my phone.

When Dad arrived back, I made much of poor Victor, who was sporting a rather large cast, and reassured him that Grandfather and Baptiste were delighted that he'd be joining the nature photography class. And then I ordered him and Dad both to their rooms with a promise that I'd send up a tray with dinner. Dad looked as done in as his patient, possibly as a result of spending the entire afternoon with Victor. Although apparently Victor shared Dad's passion for crime fiction—at least I hoped he did, since by the sound of it, they had spent most of their wait in the ER discussing Agatha Christie.

About the time I finished with them, Horace arrived, and I got him settled in the last vacant staff room.

"Are any of the crime scenes intact?" he asked.

"Sorry, no," I said. "We've basically been trying to clean them up before anyone knew there was a problem. But Cordelia has some of the evidence. And we took pictures. You can tackle it first thing in the morning. Have you eaten? I can send up a tray."

I went down to the kitchen to arrange for all the trays I'd offered. Marty had already gone to bed, which was a relief—he always seemed to glare at anyone invading his kitchen as if he suspected them of contaminating his spotless counters.

But his two assistants jumped to assemble the trays and assured me they'd deliver them right away. I suspect they were glad to take a break from peeling potatoes for the morning's hash browns. While I was there—and since Marty wasn't—I inspected the ravine behind the main building, to make sure he hadn't reverted to flinging garbage back there. I went back to my studio and checked my e-mail to find that Kevin had sent a preliminary rundown of the students who had some connection with Jazz Hands—only a dozen of them, thank goodness. I annotated the list to show what class they were in, forwarded it to Cordelia, and tucked a printed copy in my notebook beside the list of faculty with Jazz Hands connections.

And finally I made my rounds of all the studios. Most of the doors were locked—at least my nagging was having some effect. I inspected them all, even the locked ones. For one thing, we had no way of telling if the vandal had a key, and for another, I wanted to check the windows. Sure enough, several carefully locked studios had open windows. And no one but me was making effective use of the lockable storage cabinets we'd installed along one wall of each studio for supplies. Of course we'd also installed lots of display spaces. Shelves for pottery and iron. Hooks and hanging wires for art. Rods for quilts. Our vision was that when not actually in class, the students would wander through each other's studios. We imagined potters and fiber artists inspiring each other . . . art class students sketching Rose Noire's herbs . . . multimedia collaborations . . . students becoming inspired to stay on another week to try a new medium. If—no, when—we caught the vandal, I'd be hard pressed not to strangle him for the damage he'd done to that vision.

Edward Prine, of course, had left both doors and windows wide open. He hadn't bothered locking up last week, either, and then had made an enormous fuss when he found his studio splashed with the red paint. I slammed his windows closed and muttered a few words that I usually tried not to use when the boys were around. As usual, his studio looked as if it had been ransacked by particularly thorough and vindictive burglars, but that was the way it always looked. Next year I hoped we could find a tidier painter. I locked up and left him a stern note, reminding him to lock up in the future. Not that he'd pay any attention.

The other teacher who'd left her studio unlocked was Peggy, who was in her first week here. I left a note for her, too, but a kinder one, and added an item in my notebook to explain more carefully why locking up was required, and to remind everyone about the windows.

By the time the movie was over, I had crossed a dozen items off my to-do list and was reasonably sure all the studios were secure, which left me in a better mood to enjoy what had become Biscuit Mountain's evening ritual. Michael had two dozen children in his class—about a third of them here with parents who were also taking classes, while the rest stayed in the campground under the watchful eyes of several counselors. Every night at around nine we brought all the children to the terrace, served hot chocolate, and allowed everyone to make s'mores on the half dozen fire pits that dotted the area. Josh and Jamie, now in their second week at Biscuit Mountain, considered themselves master s'more makers, and were giving lessons to some of the newcomers. All of the parents—and for that matter, nearly all of the adults staying here—joined in the fun. Sometimes we had singalongs or told ghost stories, but many nights, like tonight, we just gathered, talked quietly, and decompressed from the busy day. Eventually the parents would lead their children away, the counselors would shepherd their charges down to their tents, and even the unencumbered adults usually turned in early to recharge for the day ahead—and to make sure they got up in good time for Marty's excellent breakfast.

As I sipped my hot chocolate, I could feel the tension gradually leaving my system. In spite of the efforts of the vandal—or vandals, if Cordelia was right—Biscuit Mountain was basically a good place. A safe place. A place full of people who cared enough about some craft or art to spend a week of their lives learning it. Or, in the case of my fellow instructors, to spend much of their lives practicing and teaching it. After the first few incidents I'd been a little nervous about whether the center was a safe place for the boys to stay, but Michael had convinced me I was overreacting. The boys would never be out of either his sight or Eric's, and anyway, the targets were Cordelia and the center, not the boys. And if we took the boys away, we'd have to go with them, leaving my grandmother that much less protected.

Here around the fire pit my confidence returned. I'd talk Cordelia into installing the security cameras. With their help, we'd catch whoever was trying to hurt the center. Cordelia wouldn't lose her investment—wouldn't have to sell to the developer or anyone else. And Biscuit Mountain would return to being the safe, serene place it was supposed to be.

By eleven, the boys and Eric had retired to the caravan and Michael and I were in our tent. We talked quietly, catching up on each other's day, and eavesdropped on Eric as he settled the boys in for the night.

For a little while we heard residual giggles from the direction of the caravan, or occasionally the telltale sounds of minor combat being rapidly squelched. I reminded myself that Eric was a wonderful babysitter—calm, patient, with enough sense of humor to put up with the boys' antics and enough common sense and authority to shut them down when they started to go too far. Still, I knew I'd find it hard to sleep until the faint sounds from the caravan died out.

"Right about now I'm regretting that we gave up the hotel room," Michael murmured.

"Missing that nice comfy mattress?" I whispered back. "And the ceiling fan? Or is it having a bathroom a few steps away you regret?"

"Actually I'm mainly regretting the lock on the door that would keep people from barging in. Kind of limits what we can do with an otherwise quiet, romantic, kid-free evening."

"I think it's getting pretty quiet out there. Late enough that we could take our chances and live dangerously. After all, if anyone wants to find us—"

"Meg!" came a shout from somewhere outside. "Michael! Where the blazes are you?"

"If anyone wants to find us, they'll just wander around bellowing our names," Michael said, with a sigh. "Like that."

Chapter 6

"Meg!" came another bellow

"It's Grandfather," I said. "We should see what's wrong."

"And if nothing's wrong, we can shush him before he wakes the boys."

I crawled out of the tent, stood up, and tried to figure out from which direction the sound had come.

"I am not going owling again tonight." Michael stood up beside me and turned on his giant flashlight. "I don't care what kind of rare mountain owls he's found this time."

"Meg! Michael!"

"Shut up," someone shouted from the direction of the camping area. "Some of us are trying to sleep out here."

I switched on my own flashlight and stumbled in the direction of Grandfather's voice. I found him standing beside the main driveway, halfway between us and the campground. He was just taking a deep breath in preparation for yelling again when I reached him.

"Meg—"

"Shh!" I hissed at him. "You're waking everyone up."

"I had to find you." His voice was overloud, as usual.

"Shh!" "Shut up!" "Quiet out there!" various people shouted from their tents.

"Let's go inside." I grabbed his arm and steered him toward the front porch. "We'll wake fewer people there."

We strode into the great room with Michael trailing behind us.

"Now what's so important that you're running around bellowing your head off at . . . whatever very late hour it is right now?"

"A little before midnight," Michael put in.

"I need to find that wretched painter."

"His name's Edward Prine," I said.

"Well, I know that," Grandfather said. "He's not in his studio. I got his cell phone number from the faculty roster, and I've been calling it, but he's not answering."

"It's nearly midnight," I said. "He probably turned his phone off so he could get some sleep. Even if he hasn't, considering how rude you were to him all day today, I wouldn't be surprised if he's ignoring your calls."

"But this is important!"

"Class starts again at eight a.m., you know. For both of you. For that matter, you should be able to catch him at breakfast."

"This can't wait till morning! It could be an emergency! I have to talk to him!"

"About what?"

"This!" He thrust several folded sheets of paper at me. I opened them up and found I was holding three pictures of a gull. Not particularly good shots—one was fuzzy, and one was crooked, and the third, though the best of the lot, wouldn't have passed muster for a minute with Baptiste, who regularly did photo shoots for *Nature* and *National Geographic*.

"You're having a gull emergency?" I asked.

"That's not just any gull," Grandfather said. "They're Ord's gulls."

"Who is Ord, and why does he get to have gulls?" I asked.

"I thought it was against the law to own wild animals unless you're a certified wildlife rehabilitator."

"They don't belong to him." Grandfather's exasperation was making him louder, so I held my finger to my lips in a shushing motion. "They're named after him," he went on in an infinitesimally softer tone. "George Ord. Early naturalist. Bitter enemy of Audubon. Supporter of Audubon's rival, Alexander Wilson—after Wilson's death, Ord finished the last couple of volumes of his *American Ornithology*. He also—"

"Okay, important bird guy, and the namesake of the gull in these pictures, and I assume these are the papers Prine dumped on the table at dinnertime. The ones he thinks prove he didn't conflate two different gulls in his paintings. What's so important that you need to talk to Prine about them in the middle of the night?"

"Ord's gull was thought to have gone extinct decades ago," he said. "But unless these photos are some kind of clever fake, he's got pictures of them. I need to find out where these were taken. Given the fact that no one has seen an Ord's gull since the 1920s, the only reasonable explanation is that a small pocket of them survived here, in this isolated part of the Appalachians—perhaps near a mountain lake. They'll need to be protected! And he's the only one who knows where they might be."

Should I ask if it was even feasible to have gulls living here in the foothills of the Blue Ridge? Probably not, unless I wanted a long lecture about the breeding and nesting habits of every species of gull on the planet.

"Okay," I said aloud. "We'll find Prine and make him take you to the gulls—in the morning. If they weren't extinct yesterday, it's unlikely that they'll disappear in the next few hours."

From the expression on his face, I suspected he was about to argue with me.

"And may I point out that if you'd looked at these pictures when Prine first gave them to you, maybe we could have found your gulls already. But no, you had to pretend to ignore them, just to spite him. Prine just might be the only person here almost as stubborn as you—what if all this calling and yelling to find him makes him mad and he refuses to tell you where he took these photos?"

"How could he?" Grandfather asked. "This is an important scientific issue!"

"And Prine's a painter, not a scientist. He doesn't give a hoot whether or not Ord's gull is extinct; he only cares that it makes a pretty picture. If he ran across that new species of slug you discovered a couple of years ago, do you think he'd have painted a picture of it, or just stomped on it?"

"Barbarian!" Grandfather shuddered. "Yes, that sounds just like him."

"So I'll tackle him about this," I said. "Let me keep the photos. First thing in the morning I'll hunt him down."

"All right. But don't let him give you the runaround."

With that, Grandfather stomped upstairs.

"He's going to wake everyone on his hallway," Michael muttered.

"At least they won't mistake him for a burglar," I said.

"Let's get back to the tent—morning will come all too soon."

"You go," I said. "And make sure Grandfather didn't give the boys nightmares. I'm going to check something first."

I did another quick pass through the studio wing, making sure all the doors were still shut. And after I'd rattled the doorknob of Prine's studio, I knocked.

"Mr. Prine?" I called. "Are you in there?"

No answer. If I'd had my master key, I'd have checked inside, but it was back in the tent, in my tote bag, so I put my ear to the door. I didn't hear anyone moving around. I knocked again.

"Mr. Prine?"

No answer. I had a hard time imagining Prine crouching in his studio, waiting for me to leave. If someone knocked and he didn't feel like answering, he'd just bellow "Go away!" So I gave up and went back to the tent.

Chapter 7

Considering that I'd probably been one of the last people at Biscuit Mountain to fall asleep, it seemed particularly unfair that I was also one of the first to wake up. It wasn't even six o'clock when the first rays of sunshine found their way through the tent's ventilation window. Only a few of them, and they were softly filtered by the mosquito netting, but they were definitely there. I could have gotten up and closed the flap that normally kept out the early morning sun, but I was already awake.

I lay quietly for a little while, listening for sounds of human activity, but apart from Michael's gentle, not-quite-snores, nothing competed with the racket the birds were making. Somehow the sounds of humans waking up would have been more soothing in my present mood.

"I give up," I muttered. I grabbed my toiletry bag and some clean clothes and left the tent.

Eric and the boys were still asleep in the caravan. I saw no signs of life out in the main campgrounds. Of course, what you got on Biscuit Mountain was camping lite, with indoor plumbing and catered meals, so anyone who woke up early wouldn't have to bother with camp stoves for their morning coffee—they could head for the main building as I was doing.

Coffee first or shower? I debated as strolled up the path.

But when I arrived at the great room, I realized that both would need to wait—I wouldn't enjoy either until I'd checked all the rooms for vandalism.

Glancing down the hall, I could see that the door to Prine's studio was open. Which didn't necessarily mean the vandal had struck there. Prine was an insomniac and given to painting at odd hours. He could have gone in to paint after I'd locked up, or come down early. It occurred to me— not for the first time—that if I were the vandal, I might try to convince people I was an insomniac who liked to paint in the middle of the night, which would make Prine our prime suspect in the vandalism.

I started with the nearest studio—Valerian's leatherworking studio. It was still locked, but I opened and inspected it anyway, because for all we knew the vandal could have acquired a key. Everything looked much the same as it had when I'd checked at bedtime. No sign of trouble in Gillian's pottery studio, or in Amanda's fiber arts room.

Maybe this will be my lucky day, I thought, as I locked the door to Amanda's studio and headed for the open door to Prine's. Maybe I'll find him there already so busily painting that he doesn't snarl at me when I walk in. Or staring moodily at his canvas and lost to the world. And if I start talking to him, maybe, instead of bellowing at me or hitting on me, he'll be delighted to tell me all about his gull pictures. Even if he was his usual unpleasant self, I hoped he was in there, because if the vandal had targeted his studio, I'd be in for a difficult morning, even without the added challenge of getting him to reveal the whereabouts of the Ord's gull.

I paused just outside the studio to put a calm, pleasant look on my face. Then I threw my shoulders back, mentally braced myself, and strode in.

At first I thought that the vandal had struck again, and the same way, with red paint. Odd, since so far all the pranks had been unique—but of all the craftspeople affected, Prine had been the angriest—maybe the vandal wanted an instant re-play of Prine's volcanic rage when he'd discovered the paint all over his studio and his ruined canvas.

But a step or two later I realized that there wasn't as much red paint, and it wasn't bright red—more of a dark reddish brown.

Then I spotted the feet.

I closed my eyes and took a couple of the deep, calming breaths Rose Noire always recommended at times of stress. Then I opened them again and resolved to be calm and practical.

The feet belonged to Edward Prine, who was lying half on his side in the middle of the room, surrounded by over-turned easels. A knife handle protruded from his back. And I didn't have to get much closer to tell that he was probably dead. His eyes were open and unfocused.

Still, while pulling out my cell phone and dialing 911, I crossed what I now realized was a blood-spattered stretch of floor to check him for a pulse. I didn't find one, and his skin was cold.

"This is nine-one-one," a voice on my phone said. "What is your emergency?"

"I'd like to report a murder." As I spoke, I took a few steps away from Prine's body. And then a few more, so I could stand in the doorway and head off anyone who might have decided to get in a little early morning painting. Getting far-ther from the body was an added benefit.

I told the 911 dispatcher my name, my location. No, I didn't think I was in any danger. Yes, I was pretty sure the victim was dead.

"I can get a doctor to come in and double check," I said.

"Hold the phone for a moment," the dispatcher said. "Chief Heedles would like to speak to you."

And then, almost immediately, a familiar voice was on the line.

"Meg, are you sure you're okay?"

"I'm fine." A few minutes ago that would have been a lie, but it helped to have something practical to do—calling 911 and guarding the scene. Still, I felt better hearing her voice. Chief Mo Heedles and I had met a few years earlier, when I'd come to town with Grandfather and some of his allies to locate a flock of feral emus and ended up finding my long-lost Grandmother Cordelia.

"You're sure?"

"Hey, I'm a doctor's daughter," I said. "I can handle a little blood." Of course, this was more than a little. I focused back on the phone.

"There's blood, then? Are you sure he's dead?"

"Pretty sure, but if you like I can get Dad in to second-guess me."

"Probably a good idea," she said. "And you can tell your dad that if he likes, he can stay to assist our local medical examiner." In other words, I should remind him that this isn't his case. "Do you have an identification on the deceased?"

"Edward Prine," I said. "A painter who's teaching here at the craft center."

"Is he famous?" she asked. "Can't say I've ever heard of him, but I'm a Philistine when it comes to art—am I going to have to worry about crowd control on top of a murder investigation?"

I found myself taking a few more steps away from Prine before I answered. Silly, because he couldn't hear me, but then if he were alive, the answer I was about to make would wound him.

"No," I said quietly. "He's not famous. If he were a famous painter, he wouldn't be teaching here."

"So I'll still get reporters, but only the ones who want to cover a juicy murder, not *People* and *The Washington Post*."

Was it my imagination or did she sound a little disappointed?

"Well, cheer up," I said. "Grandfather's here. Reporters know he's always good for an outrageous quote."

"He's not involved, is he?"

"Not as far as I know," I said. "I suppose he'll be one of your suspects, of course; I'm sure all of us up here will. Maybe Grandfather more than most, because he had a couple of arguments with Prine yesterday. But actually, he would have had a very strong reason for wanting to keep Prine alive. I'll fill you in when you get here."

"On my way."

I ended the call and looked at the time. Good grief, not even six thirty. I hated to wake up Dad so early. But better me than the sirens that would soon be arriving.

He didn't pick up until the fourth ring.

"Meg? What's the emergency? Should I bring my medical bag? It's not one of the boys, is it?"

"The boys are fine and still asleep," I said. "You should definitely bring your bag—we have a dead body in one of the craft studios. Edward Prine," I added before he could ask. "And in case you were wondering, yes, I think it's murder. Chief Heedles is already on her way."

"Oh, dear. Yes, I'll be right there."

I took a good look around, and just for good measure, I took a bunch of shots of Prine and his surroundings, using the camera in my phone. Not that I was nosy or anything, but what if something happened to disturb the crime scene in the time it took for the first Riverton police officer to get here? Of course, anyone who wanted to disturb it would have to get past me first, but I was taking no chances. And keeping busy helped.

Then I dialed Cordelia.

"Sorry to wake you," I said.

"Don't be sorry." She sounded pretty awake already. "I assume you're up and calling me because the vandal has struck again. How bad is it?"

"It's not vandalism this time," I said. "It's murder."

She didn't say anything for a few moments, and I could picture her, closing her eyes and flinching as if from a physical blow.

"Edward Prine," I said, because I knew that would be her next question. "I'm guarding the door to his studio. Dad's on his way here. Can you get someone to make sure Prine's bedroom is locked and stand guard there? And we'll need to head off the painting students—in fact, I'm not sure how much of the studio wing Chief Heedles will cordon off and for how long. Head off all the students."

"So we'll need to come up with a way to have classes go on as normally as possible in some other space," she said. "You handle the police—I'll work with the teachers to come up with a plan. I suppose it's crass of me to think about that at a time like this."

"Not really," I said. "We have dozens of people who have to be fed and kept safe and entertained, or at least out of the police's way." And a business to keep afloat. Neither of us said it, but I suspect we were both thinking it. "We have a lot to do."

"So I guess we'd better get cracking."

She hung up. Not for the first time, I was struck by how

seamlessly we worked together. It was like having another me who could take on half of the tasks in my notebook-that-tells-me-when-to-breathe. I wondered if she felt the same way.

I'd ponder that another time. I had more calls to make.

Michael answered his phone with a yawn.

"Even the boys have only just begun to stir," he said. "I assume you're up keeping your grandfather and the seagull painter from coming to blows."

"Actually, I'm guarding a crime scene. Someone killed Edward Prine last night, and I'm hoping no one jumps to the conclusion that it's Grandfather."

A short pause.

"You're sure?" he asked.

"Am I sure it wasn't Grandfather?" I said. "Obviously I can't prove that he didn't sneak back downstairs after we left, to confront Prine again, but yeah, I'm sure it's not him. I can't see Grandfather stabbing anyone in the back."

"I meant were you sure Prine is dead," he said. "But yeah, you're right about your grandfather. Whacking someone over the head with his cane, or any conveniently handy blunt object, maybe, if he lost his temper. But I can't imagine your grandfather stabbing anyone in the back. He'd meet the enemy head-on."

"Let's hope Chief Heedles shares our point of view," I said. "Meanwhile, we have a lot to do, and since I'm the one who found the body, I'll probably be tied up with the police for a while."

"What can I do to help out?"

"Keep the boys away from all this," I said. "Keep your class going so everything's as normal as possible."

"Speaking of classes, do you have a plan for who's going to take over Prine's class?"

"I haven't even thought that far," I said.

"Then let me take care of it," he said. "After all, the show must go on. And I probably already know someone who can fill in."

"Good," I said. "Look, I just told you to keep the boys away from all this—do we need to rethink whether it's safe having them here?"

A short silence.

"Let's see how it goes," he said. "If the victim had been some poor inoffensive soul without an enemy in the world, I'd worry more. But Prine—well, it's not as if he's short on enemies. It will probably turn out to be someone who had it in for Prine and isn't a danger to the boys—or any of the kids."

"Okay," I said. "And speaking of Prine's enemies, can you find Grandfather and make sure— Damn. Never mind, here he comes. Just what I need."

"I'll send Caroline down to help you deal with him," he said. "And before you even ask, I won't let the boys out of my sight."

"Where is the rascal?" Grandfather was striding down the hall toward me.

"Stop right there!" I barked. To my surprise—and, I suspect, his—he followed my orders and stopped short.

"What's wrong?" he asked.

"The good news is that I've found Prine."

"Well, I assumed you could," he said. "Where are my gulls?"

"The bad news is that we'll have to find your gulls on our own."

"If he won't tell us where he took that picture—" he began.

"He can't tell us where he took that picture," I said. "He's dead."

"Oh." He frowned slightly. "A pity. He wasn't as clueless a painter as I originally thought."

Coming from Grandfather, that was almost fulsome praise.

"And now I suppose I'll never find my gulls," he went on, reverting to his usual curmudgeonly self.

"Your gulls aren't exactly the top priority here," I said. "We're talking about a human life."

"And I'm talking about an entire species."

"A species that seems to have survived just fine on its own for the last century without any help from you and your fellow naturalists. But I think I know how we can find your gulls—just cool your jets for a while and cooperate with Chief Heedles when she gets here."

"Chief Heedles?" he repeated. "What do we need her for?"

"Because Prine didn't just die," I said. "He was murdered. And for all I know you're going to be one of her chief suspects, so try behaving yourself for the time being."

"Nonsense! Why would I want to kill the blighter? He had my gulls."

I could hear a siren in the distance.

"You had several noisy quarrels with Prine yesterday," I said. "And you were running around late last night, banging on his door and calling him and generally making a ruckus in your attempts to find him. Yes, you're a suspect."

"Well, if she thinks I wanted to kill him, she's a fool. If I'd known he was in danger, I'd have tried to protect him."

He lifted his chin and stuck out his chest, and for a moment the idea of a man in his nineties protecting a burly artist half his age from a knife-wielding killer didn't seem the least bit silly.

To my relief, the door at the far end of the hallway opened and Caroline came trotting in. Her short, round form was disheveled, as if she'd thrown on her clothes while still half asleep. But she was awake enough now. And I was relieved to see her, because the siren was rapidly getting closer.

"Monty, you old fool," she called out. "What are you doing here bothering Meg when she has a murder on her hands?"

"How was I supposed to know we'd had a murder?" he said. "And what kind of dangerous place is Cordelia running here, anyway? Teachers getting knocked off right and left—I should probably get myself some bodyguards."

"We can talk about that later." Caroline linked her arm in his and began tugging him back toward the great room. "Let's have breakfast, and then we can figure out what to do about today's classes."

"What to do about them? We teach them. Unless someone knocked off Baptiste, too."

"Baptiste's fine." Caroline clearly had more patience than I did at the moment. "But when the police get here, they could declare the whole studio wing off limits for who knows how long. We need to have a plan."

"We'll take them on a nature walk," Grandfather said. "Maybe they can find my blasted gulls."

They disappeared into the great room.

I breathed a sigh of relief. I didn't want Grandfather underfoot, complaining about Prine's failure to disclose the whereabouts of the Ord's gulls, while Chief Heedles made her first inspection of the crime scene.

Chapter 8

The sirens were right outside, and I took a few steps into Prine's studio so I could see out his windows. One police car had parked right in front of the building and turned off its siren, although the lights were still flashing. The other car pulled up right behind it and followed suit. Blissful, siren-less silence ensued. A tall uniformed officer stepped out of the first car and turned to scan the crowd that was gathering at the edge of the campground. Chief Heedles stepped out of the second car and looked up at the main building.

Every time I saw Mo Heedles I found myself thinking that she'd missed her calling by not going into undercover work. She was of average height and weight, with features so regular that they somehow didn't stick in your mind when you left her presence. But she was a capable chief of police and a good friend of Cordelia's.

I stepped back out into the hallway and waited. In a couple of minutes, she was striding down the corridor toward me, followed by the young officer.

"And here I was hoping your vandal had gone home so I could stop traipsing up here every day."

"You're exaggerating," I said. "We didn't even call you about it until Thursday last week, so you've only traipsed three or four times."

"Around here, that's a crime wave." She nodded at the doorway. "In there?"

"In there," I echoed.

She took a few steps into the room and took a long, slow, level look around. Then she stepped back out.

"Get an ETA on Keech," she told the officer. He nodded and walked down the hallway a ways.

"I have one officer with some crime scene training," she said to me. "When she gets here, we'll do what we can on the room. I've already put in a call to Richmond for additional resources, but apparently they're having a crime wave of their own down there."

"Don't take this as interfering, but remember my cousin Horace? He's also had some crime scene training."

"A lot more than Officer Keech," the chief said. "But since she's who I have available and your cousin's an hour's drive away in Caerphilly, Officer Keech will have to do for the time being."

"Horace happens to be here," I said. "Rose Noire talked him into taking some time off and coming up to help us catch the vandal. He arrived late last night. I'm sure if you cleared it with his boss, he'd be happy to help out with the murder as well."

"Thanks—that's a good idea. Meanwhile—isn't our victim the same guy whose studio was splashed with red paint last week?"

"Yes," I said. "Edward Prine."

"You found him?"

I nodded.

"Any particular reason you were here at this hour of the morning?" she asked. "It would have been barely light when you found him."

"Insomnia," I said. "Of the waking-up-early-and-not-able-to-get-back-to-sleep variety. So I thought I'd get started checking to see if the vandal had struck again. I've been doing it every morning, since Thursday of last week, though not usually this early."

"I thought you were going to tell the crafters to lock up after themselves?"

"We *are* telling them—repeatedly, because getting creative people to do anything practical is practically the textbook definition of herding cats," I said. "And because I know some of them will still ignore the instructions, I go around every night after dinner and check all the studios. I did it around eight p.m. last night. Closed and locked any unlocked windows, locked all the doors again, and saw no signs of vandalism. And then I did a mini patrol around midnight—I hadn't brought my keys so I didn't go inside any of the studios, but they were all still locked."

"When did you last see the deceased?" she asked.

"At dinner." I explained, as succinctly as I could, about Grandfather's quarrel with Prine over the authenticity of his gull painting, Prine's triumphant delivery of the photos he thought would prove his case, and Grandfather's belated discovery that the photos proved the survival of the Ord's gull. "Which is why you're going to hear that Grandfather was running around yelling and waking people up last night around midnight. He wanted Prine to tell him where the photos were taken so he could locate the gull."

"In other words, your grandfather's going to be one of my suspects." She was smiling slightly. I had no idea if that was a good sign or a bad one.

"Yes, he's going to be one of your suspects," I said. "Which is ironic, because he just might be the only person here even a little upset by Prine's death. Not that he's any fonder of the man than the rest of us, but with Prine gone, he's going to have a much harder time finding those gulls."

Just then the door from the great room flew open. Dad trotted in, followed by a tall, slender black woman in a Riverton PD uniform. Dad was carrying his black medical bag, and the officer was carrying a similar satchel, so I deduced that she was Officer Keech of the forensic training.

"And now you'd probably like me to get out of your way," I said. "I'm sure I stepped in some of the blood—shall I leave my shoes here for Horace?"

"Please. And don't go far." Her focus had already shifted to Dad and Officer Keech.

"I'll be in the great room," I said. "Or possibly the dining room, if Marty's got breakfast going."

To my relief, breakfast was in progress, and considering the early hour, an unusual number of people were partaking of it. Normally the last half hour before classes began was the busiest time for breakfast. But here it was, barely 7:00 A.M., and the crowd was overflowing into the adjoining game room and onto the terrace.

Though from the way they kept staring at the door I'd just come through, I suspected rubbernecking was at least as much of a draw as the food.

Amanda and Caroline sat at the table closest to the door, and when they spotted me, they waved me over.

"You can help us guard the doors," Caroline said as I sat down at their table. "Chief Heedles's orders—if anyone tries to go into the studio wing, we repel them."

"So just what is going on?" Amanda asked. "Rumor has it that someone finally bashed Annoying Eddie's head in."

"Rumor only has it partly correct," I said. "He wasn't bashed—he was stabbed. In the back."

"Wasn't that a tactical mistake on the part of the killer?" Amanda mused. "I mean, bashing someone's head in, you could always plead self-defense or heat of the moment or some such thing. But stabbing someone in the back—hard to pass that off as anything but homicide."

"A very good point," I said. "Should I feel compelled to add to this week's body count—which seems much less likely with Eddie no longer around—I will be careful to tackle my victim face-to-face."

"I gather you didn't like him," Caroline said. "And I'm noticing a distinct lack of distress on the part of the folk hereabouts. No one's popping champagne or setting off fireworks or anything, and everyone's doing their best to look somber and thoughtful, but . . ."

She let her voice trail off and shook her head.

"He was a first-class jerk," Amanda said. "I'm sure somewhere he has family and friends who will mourn him, but I don't think he's won many friends around here."

"No, you won't see sorrow dimming anyone's appetite," I said. "So I think I'll make my way through the buffet line before they run out of bacon, if they haven't already."

I grabbed a tray and got in line behind a couple of women I recognized as students from Prine's painting class. We wished each other good morning, and they went back to a conversation they'd been having in low tones. When I realized they were talking about Prine, I pulled out my phone and studied its screen, to make it less obvious that I was eavesdropping.

"Anyway, she said if they can't get a substitute or we're not satisfied with the quality of instruction by the substitute, she'll give us a refund. On the tuition, of course. Not the room and board."

"The room and board would be worth it even if the class was totally useless."

"Yeah—and if you ask me, anyone she gets would be an improvement on him. It's not that I haven't learned anything—I have. But I've been getting a little tired of his snotty, superior attitude."

"No, he's not a people person. And you were here last week, too—and you came back for more?"

"Well, I did learn a lot, and I've got a pretty thick skin. I did have a talk with Cordelia, and we agreed that if I got to the point that I was about to strangle Prine, she'd switch me into any other class of my choice. I still might do that if I don't like the replacement. I hear good things about the nature photography class—"

By this time, we'd all filled our trays. The painting students headed for a table near the terrace. I headed back to Caroline and Amanda's table. My grandmother had joined them.

"Just the person I needed to talk to," Cordelia said as I sat down. "The chief's going to give us back the lower floor at eight, and the rest of it as soon as she can—but we need to come up with a plan for the other six classes."

"Grandfather's photography class is easy." I found it was a relief to have something practical to focus on. "He and Baptiste can just take them on a photo expedition all day, instead of only in the afternoon."

"And Rose Noire has offered to take her class on an all-day herb-gathering trip." Cordelia was making a chart. "So someone can use her studio. I'm thinking what's-his-face—the leather worker. Julian?"

"Valerian," I said. "Yes, his equipment's the most portable."

"If it's okay with you, I'd like to take my crew out on the terrace and teach them about hand looms and maybe even do a little spinning," Amanda said. "So as long as there's no rain in the forecast—"

"The forecast is for partly sunny but dry, and the terrace is all yours," Cordelia said. "Meg, that will leave you and Gillian's pottery class and the painting students to share the barn, for this morning at least. Assuming you can figure out some way to teach without all your equipment."

"I've got my portable forge in the van," I said. "The one I used for that open air demonstration. And a couple of anvils. I can have them work on their hammer technique."

"I'll go make sure Gillian can figure out something to do with her potters," Cordelia said.

"And we'll need a replacement for Prine," I asked. "Michael had some ideas."

"Yes, he already recruited a colleague of his from the college—actually, he bribed her with an offer that she could enroll her nine-year-old daughter in the kids' theater class."

"Do you mean Frankie?" I asked. "That would be great."

"If Frankie's real name is Francesca Zambrano, then yes," Cordelia said. "I take it you approve."

"She's awesome, as the boys would say."

"Then we're lucky that she originally planned to take the whole summer off to paint and finds that she can't get a thing done with a nine-year-old underfoot." Cordelia sounded amused. "Apparently this is as much of a godsend for her as it is for us."

"Excellent," I said. "Though let's not mention that in front of Chief Heedles, shall we? Because I can almost see the need for childcare as a motive for murder, so I'm sure she'd be all over it."

"Right." Cordelia smiled at the thought. "Oh, good. Here's Horace. Chief Heedles needs all the help she can get."

Horace ambled over to our table. His stocky figure was clad in blue jeans and a gray t-shirt with I LOVE HERBS! printed on it. He was holding a carryout box and a travel mug and nibbling a slice of bacon.

"This is a prank, right?" He held up his phone.

The screen showed a text from Cordelia, telling him "Report to the studio wing ASAP to help chief with murder investigation."

"No," Cordelia said. "I meant it. What are you doing still standing here?"

"Really?" His eyes bugged, and he took a big gulp from the mug. "Rose Noire said you wanted me to help investigate the vandalism. She didn't tell me anything about a murder."

"We didn't have a murder when you arrived last night," I said. "We only found him an hour ago."

"Aha!" Horace's face brightened, and then fell again. "It's not anyone we know, is it?"

That was the peril of police work in small towns. Most of the culprits and victims tended to be friends, relatives, or at least people you nodded to when you passed them on the street. And a fair number of Horace's friends and relatives had migrated up to Riverton for the summer to teach or help with the craft classes.

"No one you'd know," I said. "And quite frankly, no one whose demise is going to cause general consternation."

"Good," Horace looked relieved. "I don't mean good about the murder but—oh, you know. So where is the studio wing?"

"That door." Caroline pointed.

"I know the murder is more important, but don't forget about my vandal," Cordelia said.

"Isn't it probably the same person?" Amanda asked.

"Possibly the same person," Horace said. "But we have to keep our minds open."

Just then the door opened and the tall young Riverton police officer strode out. He smiled when he saw Cordelia.

"The chief's ready for you, ma'am," he said.

Cordelia followed him out, with Horace tagging along behind.

Chapter 9

We all watched until Cordelia had disappeared. Then we looked at each other. I took another deep, calming breath. Amanda and Caroline seemed to be doing the same thing.

"I guess that means I get to organize the class locations." I stood and picked up my tray to take it to the service hatch.

"I can help you till it's time to take off on the nature photography hike," Caroline said as she followed my example.

"I'll go haul my stuff onto the terrace," Amanda said, as she brought up the rear.

When we got to the service hatch we found Marty standing on the other side, peering out into the dining room. He frowned as we set our trays down.

"What's wrong?" he asked.

"Nothing," Caroline said. "Breakfast was fabulous."

"The highlight of my morning," Amanda said.

"Yeah, right," he said. "I mean, why are there cops crawling all over the place?"

"Someone killed Edward Prine last night." I didn't see any reason to mince words with Marty.

"That loudmouth painter?" Marty asked.

"That's him."

"Hmph." Marty nodded, turned on his heel, and disappeared through the door that led to the back stairs.

"I suppose a token exclamation of 'how terrible' would be

too much to ask," Caroline said as we headed toward the studio wing.

"Cordelia didn't hire Marty for his social graces," I reminded her.

By shortly after eight we had installed Valerian, the leather-worker, in Rose Noire's studio. He seemed to find his temporary quarters slightly unsettling. Rose Noire had gone a little overboard in decorating her studio. Dozens of crystals and suncatchers hung in the enormous windows, whose sills were crammed with pots full of herbs and flowers. The walls were bedecked with at least a dozen inspirational sayings, hand calligraphied in flowing cursive, encrusted with glitter, and festooned with flowers and curlicues painted in pastel shades of blue, green, pink, and lavender. Bunches of fragrant drying herbs, tied with pastel ribbons, hung from the ceiling. The ambiance was utterly feminine and New Age, and in his tattered jeans, work boots, and faded denim shirt, Valerian looked distinctly out of place.

"She does know I use real leather, right?" he asked. "As in, deer and cows died so we could have this class."

"I don't think she's focused on that," I told him. "If it occurs to her to be upset about it, I will explain that you only use deer and cows of advanced years that have died happy, peaceful, natural deaths."

He looked as if he wasn't sure whether or not I was kidding. I wasn't entirely sure myself. So I just left him to unpack his dead animal skins on the tables where Rose Noire's students had been making potpourri and sachets on Monday. She could always do an herbal cleansing of some sort if Valerian's intrusion disturbed her.

Rose Noire's herb-gathering students and Grandfather's nature photography students set off en masse in the official Biscuit Mountain bus, aiming to find a promising trail high atop one of the nearby mountains. The understanding was that they'd amble along together until one group or the other found something worth lingering over. I suspected Grandfather would be steering his group in the direction of what he referred to as a "promising mountain lake." Since he couldn't yet find out where Prine had taken the gull photos, he'd decided to operate on the theory that perhaps the painter had taken them somewhere near Biscuit Mountain. He'd been spilling maple syrup and strawberry jam on several local maps all during breakfast, trying to figure out the most likely locations.

"Don't let him go chasing gulls at the expense of giving the class a good outing," I told Caroline.

"I'll do what I can." She gritted her teeth, so I deduced that she did not expect this to be an easy task. But she was the only one who could do it—well, apart from me, and possibly Cordelia, and we'd be back here, doing our jobs for the day and keeping an eye on Chief Heedles's investigation.

The Slacker hung around the great room all morning, watching the police officers come and go. I was half-expecting him to pass up the herb class's expedition for the day in favor of kibitzing on the investigation. But when the driver bellowed "last call," he scuttled out to the bus.

Although the last to board were Victor, sporting his impressively large cast, and Rose Noire, who was fussing over him with what looked to be several vials of essential oils and an earthenware mug of some steaming liquid. A healing herbal tea, no doubt. Given how vile-tasting most of Rose Noire's herbal teas were, I hoped he found an opportunity to pour it out while she wasn't looking, the way most sensible people did. I waved good-bye to the bus with genuine relief, knowing several people who might quickly try Chief Heedles's patience were out of the way for the time being.

By shortly after eight, the barn was humming with activity. Actually, banging more than humming, at least at my end of the barn, since I was using cold iron to give my students practice in hammering techniques. Gillian's pottery students were at the far end, working on hand shaping. And in the middle, a grad student, sent up as a kind of advance guard by Frankie, the new painting instructor, was teaching the art students how to make their own canvases. They were contributing their fair share of the noise, nailing one-by-two wood slats into rectangular frames, stretching sheets of canvas over them, and then nailing the canvas into place.

I found it interesting to watch how Gillian adapted to our makeshift classroom. Her own work tended to be large-scale—among her most popular pieces were enormous planters, three or four feet in diameter and almost as tall—large enough to hold small fruit trees. I wondered if she hired teams of bodybuilders to haul them into her kiln, and for that matter, where she'd found a kiln large enough to fire them. But today she had her students working on a very modest scale. Their pots weren't quite Barbie doll-sized, but awfully close. Did she always do this with beginning students? Or did she have only a limited supply of clay not barricaded behind the yellow crime scene tape.

"Think you can hold out for the rest of the day?" Cordelia asked me when she stopped by a little before ten.

"We're doing fine. But ask the potters. This is pretty tough on them. Not sure how well they're going to survive today, and what if this goes on for the rest of the week?"

"Shouldn't have to," she said. "Mo Heedles has set up her interrogation room in Fabian's studio. That's a good sign."

"Fabian?" I echoed. "We don't have a Fabian."

"Leather guy."

"Valerian."

"Valerian. Valerian. Why can't I get that man's name into my head? It would help if he wasn't quite so nondescript. Do you suppose that makes him a good suspect? Being the sort of nondescript character nobody remembers?"

"Only in those mystery books that I suspect Dad has been sharing with you," I said. "Why is it a good sign that Chief Heedles is interviewing people in Valerian's studio?"

"She wouldn't be doing that if Horace and Lesley Keech hadn't cleared it. If she's okay with dragging dozens of suspects into it, she shouldn't give me a hard time about releasing it tonight so we can go back to having classes in their usual spots tomorrow."

"Except for the painters, I suspect," I said. "Odds are she'll want to keep the actual crime scene intact for a little longer."

"They can work out here," she said. "Mo wanted me to warn you that she'd be interviewing the students one by one. Starting with the painters. Here comes Lesley Keech now to collar one of them."

Officer Keech's tall form appeared in the doorway. She probably wasn't any taller than my five foot ten, but she was much skinnier than me, which made her seem taller. Or maybe it was the uniform. She consulted a sheet of paper she was carrying and studied the three ongoing classes. Then she strode over to the painters, cut one student out of the herd, and escorted her out of the barn.

The chief had worked her way through the painters and started on the potters by the time we broke for lunch.

"Don't we get to be interrogated?" one of my students asked as we packed up for the break.

"I'm sure you will," I said. "Obviously the chief wanted to start with the painters, since they knew Mr. Prine best, and I expect they're doing the potters next because their studio is right across from his. I'm going to check with the chief and see if I can find out when she expects to get to our group."

They hurried off in a much better mood. Of course, now I had to find a way to talk to the chief, who was probably a bit too busy to bother with me. Maybe I should start by checking in with Cordelia.

But when I arrived in the great room, I saw the chief standing just outside the door to the studio wing.

"Ah, Meg," she said when she saw me. "I was looking for Cordelia."

"So was I," I said. "I expect she's either in her office or the dining room."

"Actually, for my purposes you'll do just as well. Can you come and talk with me for a few minutes?"

I didn't wait to be asked twice. I followed Chief Heedles into the studio wing, and then into Valerian's leatherworking studio. The chief had claimed one of the long work tables as her desk. She sat behind it, motioned to me to take one of the stools on the other side, and pulled out her notebook.

"So what can I do for you?" I asked.

"This vandalism you've been having." The chief pulled out her notebook. "I want to make sure I know about all of the problems you had last week."

"You think they could have something to do with Prine's murder?"

"No idea," she said. "But just in case they do—review the list of incidents for me."

"Okay." I pulled out my own notebook and flipped it open to the page where I kept my list. "Monday morning we had the slugs in the clay in the pottery studio." The chief shuddered at that, from which I deduced she had some experience with touching slugs. "Tuesday morning we found the rain damage to some of the student watercolors. Wednesday morning we found all the student pottery ruined because someone messed with the thermometer on the kiln. Thursday someone scattered ball bearings all over the dance studio floor."

"And since that was not only mischievous and destructive but dangerous, that was the point when you called me," the chief said, nodding. She seemed to be ticking off items in her notebook. That was one of the reassuring things about police officers, from my point of view. They usually came wielding notebooks. I could relate to someone with a notebook, or at least a well-organized to-do list.

"Friday was the double event—red paint all over Prine's studio, and the soy sauce and ketchup splashed on Baptiste's prints. Finally, Saturday, my nephew Eric checked the sound system one last time before the kids' dance recital began and caught the fact that someone had altered the playlist so instead of 'The Dance of the Sugar Plum Fairy' the six-year-olds would have made their entrance to George Carlin's 'Seven Words You Can Never Say on Television.' "

"Yikes." She looked up from her notebook. "You never mentioned that one."

"Well, it was a close call rather than anything really destructive," I said. "And we were pretty crazed Saturday and Sunday, what with helping all the first week's students pack up and check out and then having to clean everything up before this new batch arrived, so I guess I forgot. And we were hoping whoever was doing it was one of the outgoing bunch, rather than someone who was staying on for more classes this week."

The chief nodded, and made a few more notes.

"By the way," I said. "As part of our effort to figure out who's behind the vandalism, I put together a list of everyone who was here last week as well as this—students, faculty, and staff. No idea if last week's residents are of any interest for the murder investigation—"

"This isn't exactly Fort Knox," she said. "If someone who was here last week had something against Prine, there's no reason they couldn't sneak back to knock him off when we wouldn't suspect them as much. So yes, I'd like to see that list."

"I'll send it to you." I scribbled a reminder to myself. "I also asked one of my computer-savvy nephews to do some research for me—to figure out which of them had any kind of connection with Jazz Hands, that rival craft center that's been harassing my grandmother."

"The one she suspects is behind the vandalism?"

I nodded.

"I'd be interested in that information, too," she said. "Did Prine have any enemies here?"

"He had nothing but." I didn't see any reason to sugarcoat my opinion of Prine. "By the end of last week, if we'd asked the faculty and students to vote on who was the most likely to get bumped off and have his killer acquitted on grounds of justifiable homicide, Prine would have won by a landslide."

"So just about everyone here is a suspect—except possibly your grandmother—I doubt if she'd have done something like this, given how big a problem it's going to be, losing one of her faculty in the middle of a class week."

She was smiling slightly when she said it—for her it was probably the equivalent of a broad grin—so I was pretty sure she didn't really suspect Cordelia.

"Actually, you should probably keep her on your suspect list," I said. "Because if she wanted to knock him off, she'd have known that between my contacts on the craft fair circuit and Michael's friends in the college, we could come up with a substitute for Prine if we really tried. In fact, one of Michael's colleagues is already on her way to wrangle the art students for the rest of the week."

"Don't believe in making my life easier, do you? Okay, Cordelia stays on the suspect list. Although I expect that, unlike your dad, she won't enjoy being a suspect. So that's the complete list of incidents last week?"

"That we know of," I said. "We didn't make a big fuss about the incidents, at least not with the students—just tried to remind them that there are a lot of people walking in and out of the center all day, and they should keep their valuables secure. That kind of thing. So if something minor happened and the victim thought it was accidental or maybe knew someone they thought might be responsible, it's always possible that they just didn't report it."

"Possible. Unlikely, though. Something comes along to spoil my peaceful craft vacation in the mountains, I'm going to report it. They seem to have hit a fair cross-section of the crafts, too."

"Yes," I said. "Whoever's doing this wanted to spread the joy around. Every class didn't get hit, but he—or she—was working on it. And no studio got hit twice."

"Except the art studio, I assume." She was studying her list. "The red paint, and then you mentioned watercolors. Wouldn't that also be in Prine's studio?"

"Oh, no," I said. "Prine doesn't—didn't—do watercolor. He considered it a lesser, inferior medium, suitable only for women and weaklings who aren't up to bold, virile, courageous media like oil and acrylic. That's pretty close to a direct quote, by the way. We had two art studios last week, Prine's and one downstairs where a very well-respected watercolor artist taught her class. Given how monumentally rude Prine was to her, I dearly hope she's alibied for last night."

"She'll be on your lists, I assume," the chief said. "No incidents this week, then?"

"One, yesterday morning." I described the lingerie exhibit Michael had dismantled before the children entered their work room. "Of course it was more in the nature of a prank than actual vandalism," I added. "But then so was substituting George Carlin for Tchaikovsky."

"Interesting." Her frown seemed to suggest that the chief found this week's prank even more distasteful than I did. Or did she see some more sinister meaning in it?

"What did you do with the lingerie?" she asked.

"My grandmother has it."

"Where?"

"I haven't seen it myself. Probably in her office."

"I need to see it."

So I called Cordelia's cell phone—she was in the dining room, as I expected—and the chief and I met her in her office. The chief watched impassively as Cordelia opened a locked file cabinet drawer and pulled out a small armload of peculiar garments. Yes, there was the leopard-print corset with the froth of pink marabou feathers . . . a scrap of filmy red fabric that you could probably roll up and stuff into a lipstick tube . . . and enough black vinyl and leather, with or without chains, to outfit a coven of dominatrices

"More strip joint than Victoria's Secret." The chief's grimace told us what she thought of our collection. "Mind if I take possession of this collection for the time being?"

"Be my guest." Cordelia emptied the last two reams out of a copier paper box and swept the outré lingerie into it. "As part of your investigation of the vandalism? Or are you thinking that the murder could be related?"

"Too soon to tell." The chief picked up the box. "But after seeing this . . . come and take a look at something."

Chapter 10

We followed her back to Prine's studio, and she lifted up the yellow crime scene tape for us to enter.

"Horace and Lesley Keech have gone over this room pretty thoroughly," she said as she led us through the studio. "We want to keep it more or less intact for a little longer, to see if we can get some additional forensic muscle on it—there's a blood spatter expert down in Richmond that Horace is hoping we can get in here, though I'm not entirely sure if he thinks she can learn more than he has or if he just wants to commune with a kindred spirit about viscosity, angle of impact, and points of convergence. But in the meantime—have you seen some of the paintings Mr. Prine keeps locked up in here?" She stopped beside one of the large built-in storage cabinets along the side wall and reached into her pocket to pull out a key ring that I recognized as Cordelia's spare set.

"If it's the paintings I'm thinking of, I'm probably the one who made him lock them up," Cordelia said as the chief unlocked the cabinet doors. "I have nothing against nudes as a general rule, but something about that man's nudes made me want to run away and take a long, hot, soaking bath. Is there some reason you want us to look at them?"

"It wasn't the nudes I wanted to ask you about." She surveyed the contents of the cabinet, which was six feet tall, three feet deep and nearly as wide, fitted inside with four sections in which you could store paintings on their sides, so all we could see was the end where the canvas wrapped around the frames. The chief flipped through the paintings and pulled out one.

"Recognize this?" she asked.

It was a buxom blond woman wearing the leopard-print and marabou corset, along with fishnet stockings and six-inch Plexiglas heels. The corset covered a lot less skin than I'd have expected, and to call the expression on the woman's face suggestive was like calling King Kong tall.

"I recognize the garment," Cordelia said. "As for the model, I haven't had the pleasure."

"What about this one?" The chief pulled out another painting, this one featuring a brunette woman wearing several small wisps of red lace.

"Fascinating," Cordelia said. "I don't think I've ever seen a grown woman wearing a Barbie outfit before."

"And this?" The chief pulled out a painting of a redhead wearing a complicated tangle of leather straps and silver buckles that somehow failed to cover any areas that even bikinis were usually designed to protect.

"If you're asking if these appear to be the same garments with which our vandal decorated the children's work room, then yes." Cordelia's face wore a disapproving look. "I can definitely recognize them."

"Not just the garments." I pointed to the face of the woman wearing the bondage gear. "Look—that's Misty."

Cordelia peered more closely at the painting.

"You could be right," she said. "I don't think I ever saw her with quite that expression on her face."

"You didn't see her drooling over Michael last week." I tried to keep my tone calm, but my annoyance at Misty's blatant flirtation with my husband probably leaked through. "Fortunately, he's very good at fending off unwanted advances from fans, thanks to his years on *Porfiria, Queen of the Jungle.*"

"His years on what?"

"*Porfiria, Queen of the Jungle,*" I said. "A syndicated TV show on which Michael had a part for a couple of years. A while ago—pre-kids—but it's still quite a cult favorite in some circles. You must not watch much late-night cable TV."

"Only the cooking channels. Who is this Misty person?"

"A student from last week's interpretive dance class," Cordelia said. "Not enrolled in anything this week, thank goodness."

"I wondered what she found to do with herself after Michael succeeded in discouraging her," I said. "Maybe now we know."

"Let's see if you recognize any of the other women in these paintings." The chief turned back to the cabinet.

"I am definitely going to need that bath," Cordelia said.

We looked at twenty-three paintings, all either nudes or women clad in lingerie or fetish gear, but Cordelia didn't recognize any more of the models and I only knew one—a slender blond potter who hadn't been here last week and wasn't here this week.

"Although come to think of it, she used to be quite an item with Phil," I said. "Phil Santiago, a jewelry-maker who taught here last week."

"His contact information will be on that list you're going to forward me?" Chief Heedles asked.

"Along with everybody else's. Speaking of which . . ." I pulled out my phone and sent my lists to the chief, along with the information Kevin had sent so far. And then I e-mailed Kevin and asked him to share any future information with the chief. As I was tapping away, the chief gestured to the paintings now stacked against the walls.

"You said you made Prine lock these paintings up," the chief said. "Were they all out on display?"

"Not all." Cordelia pursed her lips slightly at the memory. "Only three of them. That was enough."

"Which three?"

"One of these two—don't ask me which." She indicated two nudes of remarkably similar women, both blond and in the same come-hither pose. "And that one." She pointed to the painting of the blond potter whose boyfriend had been at the center last week. "And this." Misty.

"Interesting." The chief pointed to the blond potter. "He actually had this displayed in his studio while her former . . . significant other was a teacher here?"

"Not for very long," Cordelia said. "The faculty all arrived Sunday morning or even Saturday night, and worked with us to make sure their studios were set up the way they wanted them before the students arrived Sunday afternoon. I spotted the nudes and pinups when I was inspecting all the studios to make sure they were all ready for the orientation tour. Had to threaten to fire him on the spot if he didn't take them down. I'm not easily shocked myself, but these craft classes attract a lot of retired people—I offer an AARP discount. I didn't want to give any of the grannies a coronary."

I had to suppress a smile, and I could see that the chief was fighting to do the same. Cordelia was in her eighties, a decade or two older than most of the grannies whose frail sensibilities she was worrying about.

"But do you know if Phil saw it?" the chief asked.

"No idea." Cordelia shrugged.

"He could have," I said. "A lot of us know each other from craft fairs or other craft class venues, so while we were setting up our studios there was a lot of visiting back and forth and catching up. Of course, I don't remember Prine joining into the visiting or being visited. He was not well liked. Still, some of the folks could have made a brief visit, just to be polite."

"You're thinking one of Prine's paintings could have been the motive for his murder?" Cordelia asked.

"No idea," Chief Heedles said. "The man had no shortage of enemies, apparently, but there is something about the paintings. Along with a rather suggestive bit of bloodstain evidence Horace found."

She pointed to an area where we could see a little orange evidence cone with the number seven on it sitting on the floor beside some reddish brown stains. We moved closer to peer at the stains.

"That's not blood spatter," Cordelia said, after a few moments. "Looks more as if someone dragged something through a small spot of blood."

"Something about the width of one of those canvases," I added.

"Very good," the chief said. "Of course, we don't know that whatever was dragged came from that locked cabinet. There were five overturned easels on the floor, and only two canvases. Could have been a painting from one of three empty easels."

"But the drag mark is pretty directly in the path you'd follow if you were taking a canvas from the cabinet to the door," I pointed out.

"Which could mean that somewhere in this building there's a painting with a smear of Mr. Prine's blood in the corner. I'm asking Judge Klein for a warrant to search the entire premises. As soon as he gets back to me—"

"Jake Klein's slow as molasses," Cordelia said. "Why wait

for him? I already told you that you have my permission to search from attic to cellar."

"And we're already searching the public areas, since we have your permission," the chief said. "But I'd rather wait for the guest spaces until I have that warrant, in case anyone gets huffy and calls in a lawyer to argue that he has a reasonable expectation of privacy in his pup tent."

"So I assume you'll want to keep this studio sealed for a while," Cordelia said. "Any chance we can get the rest of the studios back anytime soon?"

"I'll be releasing them in a few minutes," she said. "So you can have your classes in the usual locations in the morning. Except for this one, of course. Oh, and that includes the one I'm using as my office so I'd appreciate it if you could find me another spot."

"How about a nice, empty storage room right down the hall from my office," Cordelia said. "No view, but plenty of space."

"That should work."

"While we're talking logistics, any idea when you'll want to interview my blacksmithing students?" I asked. "They're feeling a little left out."

"Shortly after the lunch break is over." The chief chuckled slightly. "Reassure them that they'll get their turn in the hot seat. And speaking of lunch—"

"Let's get you to the dining hall before all the good stuff runs out," Cordelia said.

So the chief accompanied us to the dining room. There was already an unofficial police table, with Horace and Dad and Officer Keech all eating with more speed and less attention than Marty's food deserved. I hoped they were using their indoors voices—the tables near them were chock-full of people who didn't seem to be talking as much as usual.

I could almost imagine the would-be eavesdroppers' ears swiveling the way a horse's ears would, so eager did they look to catch every word. At least they weren't staring—well, except for the Slacker, who'd actually turned his chair around and was gazing with a look of placid contentment on his face, as if watching an entertainment Cordelia had arranged especially for his enjoyment. I glanced over to see if the chief had noticed him, but she was already on her way to the buffet.

I saw Grandfather and Caroline sitting at the other end of the room and went over to see them.

"How did this morning's expedition go?" I asked.

"Disastrous!" Grandfather snarled.

Chapter 11

"Disastrous?" I echoed. "What happened?"

"He's exaggerating," Caroline said. "As usual."

"It was a complete failure," Grandfather muttered.

"We saw deer, foxes, woodchucks, several kinds of woodpeckers, rabbits, weasels, otters, and I forget what else," Caroline said. "So from the students' point of view, it was a grand success. Even Baptiste was impressed. But just because we didn't find his silly gulls, your grandfather is moping."

"If I get my hands on the wretch who killed that Prine fellow," Grandfather muttered. "My only clue to the whereabouts of those gulls, gone forever. Our only chance is to search his belongings to see if we can find out where he spotted them, but that stupid police chief doesn't seem to recognize the urgency."

"She's got her priorities. She's trying to solve a murder."

"Mixed up priorities, if you ask me," Grandfather said. "Prine's dead; finding his killer won't bring him back—but time could be of the essence in finding the gulls."

"Just hold your horses for a day or two about your gulls," I said. "I've been thinking about the gull problem during my class, and I'm pretty sure I know how we can find out where those photos were taken, but you have to be patient."

"I don't believe you." Grandfather actually pouted, and the petulant look on his face gave me a clue to what he'd have looked like as a toddler. "You're just telling me that to shut me up."

"No, I'm not." Well, only partly. But it occurred to me that perhaps I'd have a better chance of getting him to behave if I explained my plan. I reached into my tote and pulled out the sheets of paper with the gull photos on them. "Here, look at these."

"I was wondering where the devil those had gotten to." He tried to snatch the papers out of my hand, but I pulled them back out of his reach. "Hey! Those are mine."

"I could argue that actually they're Prine's," I said. "But let's forget about who owns them for the time being. I'm keeping them. I need them to find your gulls."

"How?"

"As you can see, these aren't printed on photo paper—just regular printer/copier paper." I handed him the worst photo so he could see for himself.

"That's true." Grandfather frowned at the photo. "Of course, he's not exactly a brilliant photographer. I wouldn't have wasted photo paper on these. In fact, if not for the subject matter, I wouldn't consider them worth wasting any paper on."

"But the fact that they're on printer/copier paper means Prine printed them from a computer," I pointed out. "Probably his own computer, which means there's a good chance it contains the original digital photos."

"How does that help us?" he asked. "Original or copy, they're still lousy photos. And I assume he was showing us his best shots."

"He might have other photos that don't show the gulls as well but do include more of the surroundings," I explained. "That would give us a clue to where they were taken."

"Now that's a useful idea."

"And unless he's a lot more paranoid than most people, the photos' locations may be embedded in the digital files," I went on. "A lot of mobile phones and an increasing number of digital cameras tag your pictures with location coordinates. And from the look of these, I think it's very likely he took them with his phone."

"How can you possibly tell?"

"See that little pink thing in the top left corner of this photo?" I pointed to the photo he was holding.

"Yes." Grandfather squinted and peered at the photo over his glasses, then shook his head. "No idea what that is."

"Looks to me like a finger," I said. "Happens a lot when you're taking photos with a phone. Though it's also something particularly inept photographers can do with a small camera." I knew this from experience—at least twenty percent of the pictures Dad had ever taken of our family had those telltale pink sausage shapes lurking in one upper corner or the other, as if we'd been shadowed all our lives by small, furtive, camera-shy blimps.

"So once you get the digital files of photos, you can read the location?" Grandfather was beginning to sound less despondent.

"No, actually I would have no idea how to read the location," I admitted. "But once I get the photos, I can get one of Rob's techies to do it for me. Assuming location's embedded in the file. "

"And if it isn't?"

Actually, I hadn't thought that far ahead. But I'm good at thinking on my feet.

"Well, we'll at least have the time and date when the photos were taken. That can help us figure out where Prine was when he took them. If he took them last week, the gulls are probably somewhere near Biscuit Mountain. If he took them some other time—well, maybe we hire Stanley to trace his recent whereabouts." Grandfather rather liked Stanley, who had overcome his previously low opinion of private investigators.

"He's a busy man," Grandfather said. "Maybe I should call him now to see if we can get on his schedule."

"I already did, and he's promised to come up to Riverton as soon as he finishes his latest case." Actually, Cordelia had called him, but I knew Grandfather would react better if he thought it had been my idea. And the original plan had been to have him investigate the vandalism, but if it would keep Grandfather out of our hair, maybe Cordelia would let him take on the case of the missing gulls at the same time.

"Hmph." Grandfather was still frowning slightly. "Not exactly foolproof, this plan of yours."

"Well, what was your plan?" I countered. "Hold a séance and torture Prine's ghost till he coughs up the location of the gulls?"

"Don't be silly." He stood, hitched up his cargo pants slightly, then threw back his shoulders in what I'd come to recognize as his preparation for action stance. He assumed the same pose at least once in every one of his *Animals in Peril* documentaries—usually just before doing something foolhardy and dangerous that would look dramatic on camera and might even help whatever mistreated animal or endangered species he was trying to rescue that week. "Well, what are we waiting for? Let's go get the rascal's computer."

"Sit," I said. "We're not going to get Prine's computer now."

"Why not? No time like the present."

"If you seriously think Chief Heedles is going to give two murder suspects access to the victim's laptop, you've got more loose screws than I thought."

"We have to steal it, then."

"Absolutely not! Don't you even think of it!"

He looked sulky again.

"Remember," I said. "The police are our friends."

He snorted.

"Some of them are even our relatives."

"Oh, I see. Horace is going to steal the laptop."

"No one is going to steal the laptop," I said through clenched teeth. "We don't need the laptop. We only need someone to get us copies of the photos, or maybe just to tell us the location coordinates. I'll speak to Horace about that. But in the meantime, play it cool. Don't try to steal the computer. Don't whine to the chief about photos in the computer. Just let me handle it."

Grandfather stared at me, frowning, for a few moments. Then he nodded briskly.

"Good." He sat down and picked up his fork again. "See that you do."

I exchanged a look with Caroline. She nodded as if to say that she'd do her best to keep him from badgering the chief or attempting to steal Prine's computer.

I headed for the buffet line. Normally I fretted when the people ahead of me took forever picking out what they wanted to eat. Today I didn't mind—I was studying the denizens of the dining room. Although my motive wasn't to pick out likely murder suspects—I wanted to find a table where I could eat in relative peace and quiet. Still, I found myself assessing them with murder in mind. Remembering the negative encounters all too many of them had had with Prine.

I ended up sitting with Amanda. As murder suspects went, she seemed one of the least likely around. She'd probably want to talk about the murder, but then so would everyone else in the room. With the possible exception of Grandfather, and I was tired of talking about gulls.

"So have the police interviewed you yet?" Amanda asked as I sat down.

"Several times," I said. "I found the body, remember. Have they interviewed you?"

"Briefly," she said. "And if you ask me, this Chief Heedles is barking up the wrong tree."

"How so?"

"She kept asking about Jazz Hands," Amanda said. "What did I know about them, how was Prine connected to them. And yeah, maybe Calvin Whiffletree and the rest of the Jazz Hands people are jerks, and maybe they're behind the vandalism, but are they going to kill someone over your grandmother supposedly copying their idea? Sue her, maybe, but commit murder—I don't think so. And in the unlikely event they did want to kill anyone, why Prine?"

"Maybe because he deserted them for us?"

"If I were them, I'd give you guys a medal for taking him off their hands. No, I don't see them as killers. What's more, your chief seems to have a peculiar fixation on those sleazy paintings of Eddie's. Not that I want to ignore the possibility that some jealous husband did him in, but I think there's another motive that she's completely overlooking."

She paused dramatically.

"And that motive is . . . ?" I asked.

"Money."

"Money?" I repeated.

She nodded.

"Could you be a bit more specific?" I asked. "Does Prine have money? Owe someone money? Are those sleazy paintings more valuable than they look?"

"He cost a lot of people a lot of money a few years back,"

Amanda said. "He was one of the people who went in for that Dock Street Craft Collective thing down in Richmond. You heard about that? Bunch of craftspeople trying to cut out the middleman and set up their own shop."

"I vaguely remember someone asking me if I was interested," I said. "But my life was pretty crazy then—can't remember why, since it would have been before the boys were born, but for whatever reason I didn't even have the breathing space to check it out."

"Planning your wedding, maybe?" she suggested.

"We eloped, remember?" I said. "Cuts down amazingly on the amount of planning required. But getting back to the Dock Street thing—another reason I didn't think much about it was that I couldn't figure out why they were going in for a shop instead of trying to sell online. A lot less overhead with that. So how is the collective a possible motive for killing Prine?"

"The now-defunct collective," she said. "A lot of people lost a lot of money on that project. And a lot of them blame Eddie."

"Were you one of them?"

"No—lucky for me," she said. "I'd already moved to North Carolina, and I figured I'd be too far away to look out for my own interests. But ask Gillian—she can give you chapter and verse."

I looked around for Gillian, but she wasn't in the dining hall—or the adjoining library, or out on the terrace where the looms and spindles lay waiting for Amanda's afternoon session. Not surprising—I'd figured out last week that mingling with the students—or, indeed, with anyone—was never going to be Gillian's strong suit. Her idea of a fabulous meal in good company was a watercress sandwich, a cup of green tea, and a book of poetry. But we'd be teaching together in the barn all afternoon. Surely I could find a chance to talk to her.

I went back into the dining room. Most of the diners were gone, or finishing up their dessert. The exception was at Chief Heedles's table. She, Horace, Dad, and Officer Keech had finished their meals but were still hunched over the table, deep in conversation.

I decided this might be the perfect time to begin my attempts to find Grandfather's gulls. I strolled over to the chief's table. They fell silent and looked up when I came near.

"Sorry to barge in," I said. "But I have a question for the chief."

"We should be going anyway," Horace said.

He, Dad, and Officer Keech stood, carried their trays to the service hatch, and hurried off, resuming their conversation when they were out of earshot. Victor the Klutz, who had been sitting nearby, straining as if to hear their conversation, looked back and forth between them and the chief. Just as they were about to disappear, he jumped up and followed them out. Evidently he thought he had a better chance of eavesdropping on them than on the chief and me.

The chief pointed to a seat and waited, as if inviting me to ask my question without promising an answer.

"Prine had a computer with him, didn't he?" I took the offered seat. "Assuming he did, have you taken it into custody yet?"

"We found a laptop in his room that we assume is his," the chief said. "And a small portable printer. We've taken them into evidence."

"So the laptop's safely off the premises?"

"It's down at my station." She sounded slightly alarmed. "Is it dangerous in any way?"

"Not that I know of," I said. "I just wanted to make sure it was safely out of Grandfather's reach." I explained about the pictures of the gull that Prine had presumably printed from his computer, and Grandfather's resulting interest in the computer. "So if there's any way you can give us a clue about where the gull photos were taken, we'd all very much appreciate it. Though I understand that maybe you can't, or even if you can, the murder has to come first."

The chief studied me in silence for a few moments.

"I am second to none in admiration for the fine work your Grandfather does for the environment," she said finally. "I'll consult the town attorney to make sure there's no legal impediment to sharing this information, and if she approves doing so, I will."

"Thanks." I was turning to go when the chief spoke again.

"Is it possible that this missing gull could have something to do with the murder?" she asked.

"I can't imagine how it could," I said. "Why would anyone kill Prine over a bunch of gulls?"

"Your grandfather seems to think there's a connection."

"Well, he would." I shook my head. "He probably thinks some bloodthirsty rival ornithologist forced Prine to divulge the location of the long-lost Ord's gull and then killed him to keep him from sharing the information with Grandfather."

"More or less," the chief said. "It seemed a little over the top to me, but then so does a lot of what birders get up to. Is there a rival ornithologist nearby?"

"Not that I know of." Then a thought struck me. "Although there is a rival bird-watcher. Or at least a bird-watcher Grandfather doesn't approve of. A Mrs. Venable. She's ostensibly here to take the jewelry-making class."

"Ostensibly? You think she could be here because of the gulls?"

"I'm sure Grandfather thinks so."

"Do you?"

"I don't know her well enough to guess," I said. "But Caroline Willner thinks she's here because of Grandfather."

"Because of him? Or the gulls?"

"Because of him. Mrs. Venable knows that most of the time, when Grandfather goes someplace, there's a nature angle of some sort. Caroline suspects she found out Grandfather was teaching here this month and registered for a class so she'd have an innocent reason to come to Biscuit Mountain and snoop around. That way, if Grandfather's here to film some rare bird, she can rack up another entry on her life list, or at least brag that she spotted it before Grandfather did." I related the piping plover incident.

"And as it turns out, there may be a rare bird," the chief said. "Proving the wisdom of her strategy. But it's odd that your grandfather didn't mention this Mrs. Venable to me."

"He was probably trying to be subtle," I said. "Not something he does very often, so he's not very good at it."

The chief smiled slightly at that. But the smile faded, and I could see she was thinking. I watched her and waited.

"Also odd for him to be teaching here, if you ask me," she said. "You said yourself that if Prine were a famous painter he wouldn't be teaching at Biscuit Mountain. So why is the world-famous Dr. Blake teaching here instead of rescuing lions in Africa or breaking up dogfighting rings or whatever else he's always doing on television."

"To help Cordelia," I said. "Oh, he won't admit it—if you back him into a corner, he'll claim I twisted his arm to do it. Or maybe that Caroline did. But that's not what happened. When he heard she was starting the center, he started fretting about whether she was being impractical and extravagant.

And when he heard she was having trouble getting crafts-people to teach here, he came up with the idea of him and Baptiste teaching wildlife photography. Wouldn't take no for an answer."

"That was nice of him." The chief looked surprised. *Nice* wasn't a word you normally associated with Grandfather.

"Of course, ever since he got here he's been more curmud-geonly than ever." I sighed and shook my head. "As if he has to prove he hasn't gone soft."

"And unless I miss my guess, Ms. Cordelia has been giv-ing it back to him with interest."

"Definitely. She hates being indebted to anyone, but espe-cially to him. But at least if you asked her point blank, she'd admit the debt. Not only is he teaching the classes, he publicized them on his Web site and in the newsletters he sends out to every bird-watcher, animal lover, and environ-mentalist on the planet. A few days after that newsletter went out, his classes were filled, with a waiting list, and registra-tion picked up on all the rest of the classes."

"That answers another of my questions," the chief said. "How this Mrs. Venable found out your grandfather was here."

"She'd have had plenty of opportunities to find out. And who knows? Maybe she doubted that he was just teaching a class in a brand-new craft center in the middle of nowhere. No offense," I added, hastily. "But that's how Riverton prob-ably looks to someone from any kind of a city."

"We prefer to think of ourselves as remote and unspoiled." Her mouth was quirked in a smile, so I deduced that I hadn't offended her too badly. "So even though Mrs. Venable was wrong in her suspicions—your grandfather was only here to teach his class—the fortuitous discovered of the long-lost gulls seemed to confirm her suspicions."

"Yes," I said. "But I still have a hard time believing anyone would kill someone over a bird. In fact, I just came up with another more plausible suspicion."

"And that is?"

"I'm sure not everyone who gets Grandfather's newsletters is really a supporter," I said. "If I were one of the people he tends to target—greedy developers, animal exploiters, people who are up to something that threatens the environment— I'd probably subscribe under a pseudonym just so I could keep an eye on what he's doing."

"Because just as Mrs. Venable assumes his presence here might lead to a rare bird, his other enemies might assume he's here to do something that would threaten their interests."

"Exactly."

"You're not exactly making my life easier," the chief observed. "So in addition to checking out Mrs. Venable, I will need to find out if there's anyone in the area whose nefarious commercial schemes Dr. Blake threatens."

"Sorry," I said. "But yeah—what if wherever the gulls are living is some place targeted for development by someone who knows exactly what a pain in the neck Dr. J. Montgomery Blake can be if he finds an endangered species right in the middle of their planned factory or golf resort?"

"You think that's likely?" Chief Heedles asked.

"Likely? No. I think Cordelia and the center are the more likely targets. But possible? Yes. I suppose it's possible that once the killer figures out that knocking off Prine won't protect the secret of the gulls' location, he'll go after Grandfather. At least he will if Grandfather doesn't shut up about his determination to find the long-lost Ord's gull, and fat chance of that."

"Given all that, it wouldn't be a bad idea to keep a close eye on him for the time being."

"We always do," I said.

But she had a point. I looked around for Caroline, who'd made looking after Grandfather almost a part-time job.

Chapter 12

Caroline wasn't in the dining hall, but I did spot Baptiste, the photographer who was teaching the actual photography part of Grandfather's class. He was sitting at a corner table sipping an after-lunch coffee with his nose in a beige Gallimard paperback with the title *Des chauve-souris, des singes, et des hommes*. Bats, apes, and men—yes, that sounded like Grandfather's cup of tea, and presumably Baptiste's as well.

"*Bonjour*," I said as I reached his table. My French vocabulary is limited, but I like to air it occasionally.

"*Bonjour*," he replied. "And a very good morning it has been. Your admirable cook knows how to make a proper cup of coffee."

I noted, enviously, that his English carried only a trace of a French accent. Had he switched our conversation out of French as a courtesy to me, or because he found it painful to hear me butchering his native tongue?

"I gather you'll be out in the field again this afternoon," I said aloud. "Could you keep a close eye on my grandfather?"

"I always do," he said, echoing what I'd said to the chief. "Is there any particular danger today?"

"Could be." I explained the conversation I'd just had with the chief. "Of course, we don't know that the murder has anything to do with Grandfather—"

"But the estimable Dr. Blake has a gift for making enemies," Baptiste said. "Only among those who are also the enemies of our good earth, but still—he does not know the meaning of caution. I will be vigilant."

I felt reassured. Baptiste's mild manner, his round caramel face, his wire-rimmed glasses, and his rather formal way of speaking gave him an academic air, but he was tall, broad-shouldered, and had survived a childhood in one of Haiti's most dangerous *communes*. He was eminently capable of defending Grandfather against whatever two- or four-legged enemies they might encounter.

"And to think I passed up a chance to photograph the blue wildebeest in its native habitat to teach this course," he added.

"I'm sorry," I said. "Were you really looking forward to the wildebeest?"

"The wildebeest, yes." Baptiste laughed as he tipped his cup to get the last few drops of his coffee and rose from his seat. "The political unrest in its habitat, not so much, so when the good doctor promised me a quiet month in the country teaching a class, I leaped at the opportunity. *Enfin,* it will be much more quiet without the insufferable Monsieur Prine to annoy everyone."

"You didn't like him?"

"No one liked him." Baptiste shrugged. "But I would not have thought anyone's dislike was so great that they would feel obliged to kill him. He kept trying to commence a quarrel with me—saying that photography was merely a trade, not an art. I refused to rise to his bait. I have heard that sentiment often before, though seldom with such bellicose persistence. I confess, I asked your grandmother how much longer Prine would be here, and was relieved to hear that he would depart at the end of this week. I could contain my annoyance for a few more days. Evidently, someone could not. So yes, I will keep my eyes on your grandfather. And may *le bon Dieu* help anyone who tries to harm him." He glanced at his watch and his eyebrows rose. "Your pardon—I must go and gather our students."

He nodded at me, picked up the camera bag that was never more than a few feet from his side, and strode toward the door.

I dashed through the buffet line again—just the dessert end, because I decided that, given everything that was going on, the comfort value of one of Marty's brownies was worth the calories. Then I headed for the barn. I still had almost half an hour before the afternoon session started, but the odds were that on the way I'd run into someone who wanted to talk to me.

Or someone I wanted to talk to. I found Gillian sitting in one of the white Adirondack chairs on the front porch, sipping lemonade and talking with some of her students. I hovered around the edges of the group for a few minutes. They were discussing raku, which I knew to be a kind of pottery, and the differences between traditional Japanese and modern Western techniques of making it. I understood about one word in ten.

I was just about to slip away when Gillian glanced up at me, smiled, and sat back in her chair in a way that suggested the conversation was over.

"But let's continue this discussion later," she said. "You only have twenty minutes until the afternoon session starts—and I want to talk to Meg for a few minutes before then."

The students dispersed, and I sat down at the now-vacant Adirondack chair next to hers.

"So what did you want to talk to me about?" I asked.

"Actually, I deduced that you wanted to talk to me, so I thought I'd clear the way for you."

She smiled. She had a curiously cool and self-contained

smile, a smile that managed to suggest that while she kept the world at a distance, she'd let you in a little closer, just for the moment. Or maybe that she just wanted you to think that way.

"Tell me about the Dock Street Craft Collective," I said.

She nodded as if she'd been expecting the question.

"You think it could have something to do with Edward's murder?"

"You don't?" I countered.

"I have no idea," she said. "I suppose it could. It was a long time ago. Nine years? Maybe ten. A long time, at any rate. But some of the people who were involved are probably still furious with him. And it is rather curious that of those ten people, you had four here this week."

"Who besides you and Prine?"

"Dante and Peggy." Our woodworker and our jewelry artist. "It's Dante I'd be worried about. He lost more than any of us. And he has that Italian temper."

"Just what happened, anyway?"

She sighed, checked her watch, then leaned back in her chair and closed her eyes for a few seconds as if gathering her thoughts.

"You know the general idea behind the collective, I suppose," she began, opening her eyes again. "A lot of us were looking for a way to have a more settled lifestyle. You can make a living on the craft fair circuit—maybe even a good living—but unless your spouse or partner travels with you, it's hell on family life. That's what ruined my marriage—my ex got tired of my never being around on weekends."

"I hear you," I said.

"So you start thinking it would be nice just to stay home in the studio and sell your work through a bunch of craft shops," she went on. "But when you try to get into the shops, you find out what an uphill battle that is. There are so many of us and so few shops, and even when you get in, they take a big cut of the sales price—after all, they have to make a living, too. So we came up with the idea of starting our own shop. Not a new idea, but we actually went ahead and did it."

"A lot of craftspeople think about doing that," I said. "Most never get beyond the pipe dream stage."

"Lucky them." She took a sip of her lemonade. "We found a nice warehouse in the Shockoe Bottom district of Richmond and fixed it up to be our shop. Dante took out the lease, and the rest of us chipped in for the building supplies and fixtures. A couple of people didn't have much cash, but they contributed significantly with elbow grease. In retrospect, we should have done it differently."

"My first step would be to set up a limited liability corporation," I said. "Take out the lease under that. And hire a lawyer to get everyone's rights and responsibilities clearly stated to make sure every eventuality was covered."

"Wish you'd been involved," she said. "That's just what our lawyer said we should have done—the lawyer we should have hired up front, rather than when things started going wrong. But no. We all agreed to keep it uncomplicated. Informal. Friendly. We'd settle everything by consensus." She shook her head. "I bet you're thinking to yourself 'what idiots'—right?"

"You're craftspeople," I said. "Not lawyers or accountants."

"You're not a lawyer or an accountant, but you'd have seen that we needed them," Gillian went on. "We definitely should have had someone like you involved. Someone practical and businesslike. None of us were, although most of us thought we were. The people who put in more money thought they should have more say and the people who'd contributed a great deal of their time thought that should count for more than money. We spent way too much time arguing over every little thing. Couldn't get anything done. Well, to make a long story short, Edward got fed up and wanted out. Wanted his money back, and unfortunately he was the one who'd had the most money to put in. We didn't have the money to give back, so he hired a lawyer, and we had to hire one, and it all got ugly. Thank God it's all in the rearview mirror."

"You sound rather philosophical about the whole thing," I said.

"I consider that I learned a valuable lesson," she said. "Paid dearly for it, but I've moved on. And I wasn't one of the ones who blamed Edward for everything. The collective would have gone belly-up sooner or later. I see that now. He didn't cause the failure. He made it happen a lot sooner than it would have otherwise. Maybe that was a good thing. If he hadn't pulled out when he did, and demanded his money back, we'd probably have kept trying to make a go of it. Pouring every penny we could raise into it, throwing good money after bad, year after year."

"So you're grateful to Prine for giving the collective a quick, painless death."

"There was nothing quick or painless about it." Just for a moment I could hear the edge in her voice. "And I'm not grateful. I hate that he was the one smart enough to cut the cord and get out. I wish I'd been smart enough—and ruthless enough—to do the same. But if you're wondering if I'm still angry enough to kill him—no. I don't blame him for being the first to see the writing on the wall. Especially since he tried very hard to talk me into leaving at the same time he did. I blame myself for not listening to him."

"What about the others?"

"Who knows?" She shook her head and then stared into the distance for a few moments. "Dante lost more than any of us," she said finally. "He had to declare bankruptcy, and the stress broke up his marriage. I think most of us have re-covered, financially at least, but he's still trying to claw his way back. But even so—I can't believe that Dante did it. Not his style—stabbing someone in the back like a sneak. If Dante had killed him, it would have been at the tail end of a very noisy argument that escalated into violence."

I agreed with her. And I couldn't help thinking that if Gil-lian had decided Prine had to die, stabbing him in the back might be just the way she'd do it. After all, he was nearly a head taller than she was, and probably a lot stronger. I could see her coolly assessing the situation and deciding that a knife in the back was the rational, sensible approach to the problem.

If she decided he should die. But she'd need a good rea-son, and I couldn't think of one.

"I suspect you think I should tell your police chief all this," she said.

"Yes," I said. "Before someone else does. Have you talked to her yet?"

"Not yet." She shook her head. "I gather I'm on her agenda for this afternoon, when she finishes with my students." She closed her eyes for a moment, pressed her forefingers to her temples, and took a long, slow, deep breath. Then she opened her eyes and gave me the small, tight smile again.

"I suppose you wish you'd found some different teachers," she said. "Ones who wouldn't drag old feuds into your lovely new center."

"A different painter, anyway. I was wishing that long be-fore Prine was killed—my grandmother hired him before I got involved. And nothing he's done since arriving has made me any fonder of him."

"You know what the real irony is?" she asked. "About the Dock Street project, I mean?"

I shook my head.

"We started a bricks-and-mortar craft shop right about the time that selling crafts online really took off. You ever been to Etsy.com?"

"I've sold a few things there."

"If we'd been smart, we'd have started a Web site like that instead of renting a big white elephant of a warehouse," Gillian said. "Online is where it's at these days. For that matter, it was already where it was at when we set up the wretched collective. We were idiots."

"Online sales are easier for some craftspeople than others," I said. "A lot easier—and cheaper—to ship earrings or belts than andirons. And some of those huge planters of yours would cost the earth to ship."

"Yes," she said. "But I've found anyone willing to pay what one of my big pots is worth doesn't quibble about the shipping costs."

She glanced at her watch.

"Yes," I said. "Time we were in class."

We strolled down to the barn together in what I suppose you could call companionable silence. I had a lot to think about and nothing else in particular to say, so it was rather pleasant to feel that Gillian didn't much care whether or not I made small talk.

Though when we got to the barn, I did let her go in ahead of me. I walked a few paces away from the door, pulled out my phone, and called my nephew Kevin again.

Chapter 13

"You didn't tell me you were having a murder," Kevin said by way of a greeting.

"Sorry. It wasn't a planned part of the festivities, and it hadn't happened the last time I talked to you, and this is the first chance I've had all day to call you."

"I had to find out from *Eric*." Clearly his younger brother had gotten maximum mileage out of knowing about the murder before Kevin. "And before you ask, yes, I sent that stuff to the police chief."

"Excellent," I said. "I have no doubt that she is very grateful. You might want to remind her how helpful you've been when one of her officers stops you for speeding, which they're very likely to do if your driving habits haven't changed since the last time you gave me a ride. Would you like to increase her and my sense of indebtedness to you?"

"If I don't, you'll sic Gran on me, won't you? So what now?"

"The Dock Street Craft Collective," I said. "Located in the Shockoe Bottom district of Richmond, Virginia. Founded about ten years ago, now bankrupt. The murder victim was a member, and it's possible his killer was, too. Let me know anything you can find out about it, including who was involved. There should be at least some legal trails out there."

"I'm on it," he said. "Anything else?"

"I'll let you know if there is."

"Yeah, I'm sure you will." He hung up.

I pocketed my phone and went in to start my afternoon class.

Frankie, our new painting teacher, had already arrived.

"We need to catch up later!" She gave me a fierce hug. "But for now, I'm dragging my class away. Come on, everyone! We will paint *en plein air*, like the Impressionists!"

Maybe she really was a fan of open air painting. Or maybe she had already heard about the perils of trying to paint in a barn full of blacksmiths. I couldn't blame her. Gillian's potters continued doggedly patting and shaping their little pots, but out of the corner of my eye I spotted a couple of them passing around an aspirin bottle.

Probably not a good idea to ask them to share, since my class was the source of the headache-inducing noise. I almost dug into my tote to see if I had any. It wasn't so much the hammering—although I'd already figured out, the first day of class last week, that listening to other, less proficient people hammering wasn't as restful as the steady rhythm of my own working. No, it wasn't the amateur hammering that was getting to me but the stress of watching as first the rest of the potters and then my own students were led off for their interviews with Chief Heedles.

"Chill," I muttered to myself.

At six, the bell rang to notify us that the class session was over. But unlike grade school or high school, there was no mass stampede to vacate the room. The students tended to linger, talking with each other and with the instructors or maybe just working a few minutes longer on their projects. I tried not to be too impatient about having to wait around until they all left so I could lock up.

I ran into Amanda in the great room, and we strolled toward the dining room together.

"Any more . . . incidents?" she asked in a low voice.

"Not that I've heard," I said. "And I think I'd have heard."

"That's good, then."

I nodded.

"You think there's any significance to the timing?" she asked.

"Significance to what timing?"

"Prine bites the dust, and suddenly no more vandalism."

"Could be," I said. "Then again, it could be more a case of the place is suddenly swarming with cops and the culprit decides to lie low for the time being. Give it a few days before we declare ourselves vandal-free."

"I guess only time will tell." She paused and frowned slightly, as if thinking. "Didn't you tell me that he was one of the ones the vandal targeted?"

"Prine? Yes," I said. "Pretty spectacularly. Red paint splashed all over his studio."

"Cordelia's studio that he was teaching in. Nasty cleanup job for you people—but did he actually lose any paintings?"

"He had to scrap the one he was working on," I said. "I don't think anything else of his was lying around."

"One unfinished painting—a pretty small sacrifice in return for looking like one of the victims instead of a suspect. And maybe a painting that wasn't going very well, one that he was going to scrap anyway." She shook her head. "I hate to speak ill of the dead, but I think maybe the killer took care of your vandalism problem."

"Leaving us with a murder problem," I said. "It's not an improvement."

"There's something else, but I'm not sure if I should mention it."

I waited for a few moments, but she didn't seem inclined to continue.

"You're not going to tell me, then?" I said finally. "Just taunt me with the fact that you know something I don't?"

"I'm feeling guilty about telling you," she said. "Maybe I ought to tell the chief, but if it has nothing to do with the murder or the vandalism, I'll feel like a heel for having invaded someone's privacy."

"Whereas if it turns out whatever you're hesitating to tell me has something to do with one or both, you will be the heroine of the hour. So why not tell me and I'll help you decide if you should tell the chief?"

"Fair enough," she said. "You think the chief would want to hear about someone sneaking out at night?"

"Definitely. Who did you see sneaking out?"

"I didn't see anyone." She frowned. "It's all gossip. One of the ladies in my class is rooming with a lady who's taking Rose Noire's herb class. According to the herb student, one of *her* classmates—a woman named Jenni something—has been seen sneaking out of the center after campfire the last few nights to meet someone. The whole class is abuzz with it."

"The chief will want to hear about that," I said. "The last few nights? She's a returning student, then?"

"Yes—and either whoever she's been meeting is also back this week or she's found a replacement for him awfully quick."

"How do they know she's sneaking out to meet anyone?" I asked. "I can think of a lot of other reasons to sneak around." Like committing acts of vandalism—though since all of those had taken place inside the center, someone sneaking out wasn't necessarily going to be high on my suspect list.

"The roommate followed her one night and spotted her slipping out a side door and meeting someone. Male, relatively tall—she couldn't get a good look at him before they disappeared into the gardens. So it definitely could be exactly what they think it is—a rendezvous."

"Or maybe we've got a team of vandals—one male and one female."

"And if they're perfectly innocent?"

"Then maybe while rendezvousing they saw something that would help the chief solve one or both of our crimes."

"Been a while since you had an illicit rendezvous, hasn't it?" she said. "If you think they'd be noticing much going on around them."

"Maybe they wouldn't notice anything during the rendezvous, but what about on their way there and back?" I said. "If they're sneaking, they'd keep a pretty wary eye open to make sure they're not seen. And why would they be sneaking, anyway? It's not as if we have a curfew or rules about fraternizing with the opposite sex."

"I gather the lady in the case is married," Amanda said.

"Okay, that explains the sneaking," I said. "But it doesn't prove she's not the vandal. Tell the chief."

"I will." Amanda paused at the foot of the stairs. "I'm going to change for dinner. My, that sounded impressive, didn't it? Don't expect to see me in a ball gown—I'm going to shower and put on something really comfortable so I can go straight from dinner to Rose Noire's class."

"Enjoy." I watched her climb the stairs, trying not to mind that she was heading off to relax after dumping yet another mystery on my plate.

Chapter 14

As I crossed the great room, nodding and waving to people as I passed, I pondered Amanda's new information. It wouldn't be all that hard to figure out who the lovelorn Jenni was meeting. Enrollment at Biscuit Mountain, this week and last, was about 85 percent female. Even if you added in the staff and faculty, not that many candidates. And if you eliminated those who hadn't been here last week, even fewer. I pulled out my notebook and made a note to compile a list and get it to the chief. Of course it was always possible that Jenni and her lover were innocent of all the crimes that had happened here and hadn't seen a single thing that would be useful to the chief. But maybe—just maybe—this would be the clue that cracked the case. Or cases. At least one of the cases.

"The chief's problem, not mine," I reminded myself as I opened the door to the dining room.

When I walked in, Jamie ran over to give me a hug and tell me a few highlights of his day. Then he ran back to the table where the rest of the children's theater class were all happily eating together. Josh, when he spotted me, contented himself with a smile and a wave.

I waved back to him, and to Michael, who was riding herd on the table. The kids appeared to be having a raucous good time and Michael and the counselors were there to keep it from getting out of hand, so when I had gone through the line I looked around for some grown-ups to eat with.

I considered and abandoned the notion of joining Rose Noire, Peggy, and Gillian. I could see that Marty was delivering some special vegetarian tidbit to them, his burly figure oddly graceful as he offered the platter to each in turn. Marty certainly wasn't a vegetarian, but he did seem to take a special pleasure in making sure our vegetarians were sumptuously fed. The fact that our three faculty vegetarians were all easy on the eyes probably didn't hurt. But I was in a carnivorous mood and my tray showed it. I didn't think I'd be good company for them tonight. I smiled and passed by.

At another nearby table, Dad sat across from Victor the Klutz, and the two of them were talking with great enthusiasm. What could the two possibly have in common? I sidled a little closer so I could eavesdrop.

"No, no," Dad was saying. "It's much too early to start thinking about serial killers. I know the mystery books are full of them, but in real life they account for no more than one percent of all homicides."

"But what if it is?" Victor said. "And we could catch him? Wouldn't that be cool?"

I sidled away again before they could notice me and invite me to join them. Either Victor shared Dad's fascination with crime, both real and fictional, or perhaps during their trip to the ER together Dad had infected Victor with his obsession. Either way, not a table I wanted to join.

And I didn't think I was in the mood to eat with Grandfather, who was morosely shoveling food into his face. Clearly the afternoon's hike had produced no gulls to gladden his heart. Caroline and Baptiste and several of the students were sitting at his table, watching him anxiously. Baptiste had a stack of battered old books at his elbow. He was eating with one hand and holding a book open in the other.

"But why limit ourselves to searching for mountain lakes?"

I overheard him say as I walked by their table. "Not all gulls nest near water. The grey gull, for example—*Leucophaeus modestus.* It breeds in the Atacama Desert, in northern Chile. Not merely a desert, but one of the most dry deserts in the world. And science did not discover their breeding grounds until the seventies. None of our sources give any information about the breeding grounds of Ord's gull." He gestured to the stack of books. "So why do we assume it must be a lake?"

"You're just trying to cheer me up," Grandfather said. "It's not working."

"I am not trying to cheer you up," Baptiste said. "I am pointing out that the few locations we have already explored do not even begin to exhaust the possibilities for discovering the gulls. Courage!"

"Don't give up!" Caroline thumped him on the back with an enthusiasm that would have proved equally useful if he'd been choking. "If finding Ord's gull was an easy job, they wouldn't have given it to you."

Which didn't make sense—no one had given Grandfather the job of finding the gulls—he'd taken it on himself, in spite of the probability that the gulls had survived just fine without him for decades. But he perked up a little and scowled in my direction.

"It might be different if some people pitched in a little," he remarked.

"I'm doing what I can." I turned to continue my search for a more restful table. I saw that Cordelia was approaching us, so I waited to see what she wanted.

"Meg," she said. "Can you—"

"Where's Horace, anyway?" Grandfather snapped. "Shouldn't he be doing something? Tell him I want to talk to him."

"Horace is busy." Cordelia whirled to face him and put her hands on her hips. "The blood spatter expert from the state crime lab in Richmond arrived and Horace is showing her the crime scene. What do you need with Horace anyway?"

"I want to know what's taking him so long," Grandfather snapped. "When is he going to get me my photos?"

"Your photos?" Cordelia looked to me for an explanation.

"Prine's photos," I explained. "The ones of the gulls."

"I should go talk to him." Grandfather started to stand up.

"No, you really shouldn't." I gently shoved him back down into his seat.

"What foolishness," Cordelia said. "You don't need to badger Horace to get you those photos."

"We don't need the actual photos." Grandfather's condescending tone made me want to whack him, so I could only imagine how it affected Cordelia. "We just need to know where he took them."

"Well, I happen to know where he took them," she said. "I was there at the time. Got a few photos of my own—a lot better than Prine's. He may have been a decent painter, but he was a rotten photographer."

"You have pictures of the Ord's gull?" Grandfather didn't sound pleased. In fact, he sounded seriously annoyed.

"Is that what it's called?" Cordelia said. "I knew it wasn't any of the commoner gulls—been meaning to look it up in my birding book, but things have been a mite busy between starting up our first session of classes and chasing the vandal."

"You probably won't find it in your birding book," Grandfather said. "Because it's thought to have been extinct for nearly a century. I need to see your pictures!"

"Or maybe you could just ask her politely to tell you where she took her pictures," I suggested. "Because maybe if we know where she took the pictures, you and Baptiste could take your class there tomorrow and take some even nicer pictures of your own."

But Cordelia had already pulled out her phone and was clicking buttons on it.

"Here." She thrust her phone at Grandfather's face, so close that he had to pull his head back to see it. "Here's your gull."

As Grandfather studied the picture, his scowl grew deeper.

"This Ord's gull is dead!" he exclaimed finally.

"Dead as a doornail," Cordelia agreed. "It was just as dead in Prine's picture—we took them at the same time. It was lying out there on the terrace one morning last week."

"On the terrace?" Grandfather echoed. "That terrace?"

"That terrace."

"Damn." Grandfather shook his head and sighed. "It's looking more and more as if this was a vagrant. That's a bird that's found very far outside its normal breeding, wintering, or migrating range." He had switched to his lecture hall voice. "Also known as an accidental. And of course—"

"I know what a vagrant is," Cordelia said. "I've watched a bird or two in my time. And this was no vagrant. Vagrants are almost always solo birds, right? Or at most two or three. Well, we had whole flocks of those gulls swarming all over the terrace last week. Messy as all get-out and you couldn't eat out there for them dive-bombing your table."

Grandfather scrambled to his feet and was striding toward the doors that led to the terrace.

"You won't find them there now," Cordelia called after him.

"Why not?" He whirled and stormed back toward her. "Those gulls are an endangered species! What did you to do them?"

"I didn't do a thing to them," Cordelia said. "I just got rid of the garbage that was attracting them."

"Garbage?"

"The garbage," I groaned. "Of course."

"It was Marty's fault." Cordelia glanced over to see if Marty was nearby, but apparently he'd gone back to the kitchen to whip up a few more soy and tofu delicacies for Rose Noire's table. "He's a great cook, but just a little annoying on the subject of composting and recycling. He—"

"There's nothing annoying about composting and recycling," Grandfather bellowed. "We need to do everything we can to conserve our natural resources! If everyone—"

"Stow it," Cordelia snapped. "I know how important recycling and composting are. You're talking to the woman who singlehandedly browbeat the town of Riverton into starting a recycling program when most Virginia towns were still dumping tons of reusable resources into landfills! When I say Marty was annoying on the subject of composting and recycling, I mean that he seemed to think it was perfectly fine to throw all the food scraps and waste paper down the ravine behind the main building so they could rot naturally."

"That's ridiculous," Grandfather said. "A health hazard."

"And annoying," Cordelia repeated. "Especially since I spent good money to build a very nice recycling and composting area far enough from the main building that any minor odor problems wouldn't bother us up here."

"A properly managed compost pile shouldn't have any odor." Grandfather had found another of his pet topics.

"Yes," Cordelia said. "But look who I've got to help me manage it. People who think it's perfectly fine to throw garbage down a ravine. We started noticing the smell on Monday, and by Tuesday it was so bad we thought it was something the vandal had done. Meg was the one who finally figured out what the problem was."

"I just followed my nose," I said with a shrug.

"And I had to hire some workmen to clear out all that rotten garbage," Cordelia went on. "And the smellier things got, the more of those gulls we saw, cruising up and down the ravine, circling over the terrace, pooping on the guests. One stupid gull kept dropping clam shells on the terrace."

"That's a very natural behavior for gulls," Grandfather said. "And a sign of their high intelligence. They do it to crack the shell open so they can eat the clam."

"I know that, you old fool," Cordelia said. "But this stupid gull wasn't dropping clams—just empty shells. We'd already steamed the clams and eaten them. Maybe there's a Darwinian reason your silly Ord's gulls are extinct everywhere but here."

"Well, if they showed up that quickly after you started throwing garbage, they must be living nearby," Grandfather said. "If we could get them to show up here again, we could catch a few, put some little GPS trackers on them, and follow them back to their main habitat. So let's throw out some garbage down the ravine again and see what happens."

"No," Cordelia said.

"But—"

"Absolutely not."

"But I need to find my gulls."

"And you can't find them here," she said. "The vandal's already doing his best to drive people away—he doesn't need your help. I'm lucky the health department didn't close us down after last week's fiasco. Find someplace else to strew your garbage."

"Where?" He was doing the sulky toddler face again.

"There must be thousands of acres of woods and meadows out there that aren't within smelling distance of my craft center," Cordelia indicated the surrounding mountains with a sweeping gesture. "Exert yourself a little. If you bring your own truck, I'd be happy to supply the garbage—just don't dump any of it on my property."

Grandfather stormed out. Onto the terrace, as if he didn't want to take her word for it that the gulls were gone.

Cordelia sighed and closed her eyes. Counting to ten, no doubt. When she opened them again, she saw me looking at her.

"Yes, I know," she said. "I shouldn't rile him up like that. But he has such an amazing gift for getting my goat."

I nodded.

"And I know he only does it because he cares so much about wild creatures and the environment. But I just wish he'd develop a little common sense. And I really can't have him bringing the health department down on me. Talk to Caroline. Maybe the two of you can make sure he doesn't get up to anything."

She marched out—in the opposite direction from Grandfather, toward her office.

"That's a pretty tall order," I muttered. But I knew what she meant.

Chapter 15

I was still standing there, fretting, when I heard a strangled sound behind me. Either someone was in need of the Heimlich maneuver or someone had overheard my grandparents' latest sparring match and was trying to suppress a fit of laughter. I turned to see Chief Heedles, sitting nearby, chin resting in her hand in a way that let her partially cover her mouth. She seemed to be fighting a smile.

I went over to her table.

"May I join you?" I asked.

She gestured to the place opposite her. I set down my tray, containing the food I hoped hadn't gone stone cold while I was trying to referee Grandfather and Cordelia's latest encounter, and fell into my chair rather than sitting in it.

"If you're just being polite and would rather be rid of me, there's an easy way to do it." I cut a bit of Smithfield ham off the slice on my plate. "Just start talking about gulls."

"If it's any consolation, the town attorney sees no problem with sharing the location of Prine's photos, when Horace has time to do that." She dipped a spoon into her chocolate mousse and maneuvered it to get just the right proportion of whipped cream to chocolate. "So if Prine did succeed in tracking the you-know-what to its nest, we should be able to tell Dr. Blake where it is very soon."

"Thanks," I said. "Although frankly I'd be astonished if Prine went any farther than the terrace in search of the gulls.

As far as I can see, the whole time he was here he barely left his studio except to eat and sleep."

"I think he would surprise you," she said. "His phone records have come in. Can you think of any legitimate reason for Mr. Prine to be calling the Jazz Hands Art Academy?"

"Maybe he was teaching there later this summer?"

"No, apparently after his two weeks here he was planning to paint in Tuscany. A village called Monteriggioni." She rolled out the syllables with relish in an authentic-sounding accent. "So you'd think he'd have no reason to talk to his former employers at Jazz Hands. Certainly not twenty times over the last three weeks."

"Unless he was the vandal." I found my hands instinctively closing into fists. "The miserable jerk."

"Or at least *a* vandal," she said. "Cordelia's theory that there could be more than one isn't crazy, really. Keep this under your hat—but if you do think of any legitimate reason for Mr. Prine to have made all those calls, I'd like to hear about it."

Since my mouth was full of green beans, I only nodded, but I made it an enthusiastic nod.

"One more thing while I have you," she went on. "How well do you know this Deshommes fellow?"

"Well enough that I don't suspect him," I said. "Of any of what's been going on here."

She nodded and kept looking at me. I realized that of course she didn't see Baptiste as I did. To her he was just another unfamiliar face. Still, why was she asking about him in particular? I was sure it didn't matter to her that Baptiste was black. But then, who knew about the swarm of outsiders who might be descending on Riverton to help with the case, report on it, or just gawk at its progress? However enlightened the chief might be, we were in a very rural county in a southern state. Maybe she wanted to know as much as possible about Baptiste so she could keep him safe.

"I've known him almost as long as I've known my grandfather," I went on. "He can earn top dollar for his photos anywhere he likes—I've lost count of the times he's been in *National Geographic*. But he seems to like traveling with Grandfather, and thank God for that, because I've also lost count of how many times Baptiste has saved Grandfather's life. He can play the diplomat when needed—which it often is, since Grandfather doesn't have a tactful bone in his body. And he's jumped in between Grandfather and any number of dangers—wild animals, angry mobs, armed poachers—you name it."

"But as with your grandfather, I find myself wondering why he's here."

"Because Grandfather's here," I said. "He's very loyal to Grandfather."

"Loyal enough to take action if he thought Dr. Blake was in danger?"

"Yes, but also smart enough to know Edward Prine was no danger to Grandfather."

"Baptiste didn't suffer much damage from the vandal," she said. "Just a few photos splashed with soy sauce. No equipment damage."

"I doubt if he left any equipment where the vandal could find it," I said. "He's done a lot of work in less-than-idyllic parts of the world. Places where if you turn your back on a high-end Nikon for two seconds you can kiss it good-bye. If I ever find that photo bag of his without Baptiste a few feet away, I'll be calling you, because I'll know something has happened to him. And it's not as if any of the other craftspeople suffered much equipment damage. Student projects took the brunt of it with most of the vandal's attacks."

"That's true."

"Do you have some reason to suspect Baptiste?" I asked.

"Not really," she said. "Except that he seems a bit of an outsider here. Most of these people have known each other for a decade or more. They've got a shared history."

"I'd have called it baggage. Yes, Baptiste's a bit of an outsider. He has taught photography before, but mostly at the Smithsonian or the Corcoran. So he never met most of these people before, and unlike them, he didn't walk in preloaded with a reason to hate Prine."

"Yes." She nodded and stood up. "You'll probably be relieved to know that I share your feeling that Baptiste is an unlikely suspect for the murder. But 'I suspect everyone.' Was it Sherlock Holmes who said that?"

"Not that I know of," I said. "I think it was Inspector Clouseau in one of the Pink Panther movies. But an excellent policy, no matter where it comes from."

She smiled and nodded farewell.

I realized I was, for once, glad to see her leave. Because while I'd hinted at it, I didn't really want to discuss in detail the final reason I didn't suspect Baptiste—my gut feeling that the murder had its roots in the relatively small semi-closed world of craftspeople—the murder, and for that matter, the vandalism that preceded it. And I was a part of that world. Normally I saw it as a friendly one, but in the last day or so I seemed to see nothing but its dark side—tensions, feuds, old secrets, jealousies—was one of them the motive for Prine's murder?

"Meg?" Michael was standing by my table. "Everything okay?"

"You mean apart from the murder?" I said. "Just peachy."

"You look like a woman in need of a movie fix," Michael

said. "They're debating between *Mary Poppins* and *101 Dal-matians.* Come cast your vote."

I ended up casting my vote with the majority, for a double feature. To my surprise, I managed to lose myself in the movies and forget about murder and vandalism and seagulls for several hours. Not having the police around helped—although Chief Heedles did leave Officer Keech to sleep on the premises, in the room no longer needed by Edward Prine. But she'd changed into jeans and a University of Virginia t-shirt and morphed into just plain Lesley Keech, so it was easy to forget for minutes on end that we still had a police officer watching everything.

As I held my s'more sticks over the fire pit, I found myself thinking how much easier it would be to solve mysteries if all villains were as easy to spot as Cruella de Vil. And how much easier it would be to catch them if I had Mary Poppins's magical powers.

At least the movies seemed to have restored everyone's good humor—the movies, or for some of the adults, a few bridge games or a couple of hours of Rose Noire's class. In fact, everyone seemed to be making more of an effort than usual to mingle instead of just hanging out with the people they knew from class. Even the Slacker joined in, although about the only concrete thing he actually said was that he was completely incapable of toasting a marshmallow without dropping it or setting it on fire—which caused Josh and Jamie to take pity on him and share a few of their own marshmallows.

I also noticed that Dad seemed to be spending a lot of time conversing with the Slacker. Or perhaps interrogating him. Yes, from the look of it, Dad clearly found him suspicious. Though even Dad in full Sherlock Holmes mode didn't seem to unsettle the Slacker, who never lost his usual bemused expression. Luckily, about the time I decided that someone had to intervene, Josh claimed Dad's attention. Was it just my imagination or was the Slacker settling back in his Adirondack chair with an ever-so-slight sigh of relief?

Eventually the children began singing songs from *Mary Poppins,* which made for a tuneful end to the evening.

The familiar evening ritual worked its usual magic on my mood. Especially since the boys seemed oblivious to the fact that we were watching them like hawks. To them, it probably seemed only normal that their mom, dad, grandfather, great-grandfather, great-grandmother, and assorted cousins would be hovering over them all evening. And they were basking in the attention. And before too long, Chief Heedles would probably catch the killer, and maybe the vandal as well, and things could go back to normal. But even if it took a while, with us watching over them, the boys were safe.

It took a while before the cheerful warbling of "A Spoonful of Sugar" and "Supercalifragilisticexpialidocious" died down in the caravan. And just when we thought the boys had gone to sleep, the soft strains of "Feed the Birds" came to my ears.

"They really do have nice voices, don't they?" I asked.

Michael snored slightly, so I decided to postpone any discussion of the boys' musical talents until the morning. I closed my eyes and let the boys' voices lull me to sleep.

"Let's hope it's a quiet night," I murmured.

Chapter 16

Something woke me up.

I wasn't sure what it was. I had a vague impression of a crashing noise, but couldn't think of anything in the tent that would make such a noise—especially not one loud enough to wake me. Michael was sound asleep and not snoring at all. I felt around the side of my pillow for my phone. Three fifteen. Not a time when you expected to hear noises here at Biscuit Mountain. I grabbed my big flashlight, slipped on my flip-flops and crept out of the tent, but I kept the light off as I made my way quietly over to the caravan. No sound there, and the caravan door was still locked. Spike growled softly when I tried the doorknob, but I shushed him and he went back to sleep without waking the boys.

"I should just go back to bed," I muttered. But by now I was wide awake. Had I imagined the noise that roused me?

I followed the path to the front drive. The campground was dark and quiet. I glanced over at the main building. Also dark and—

Wait. Was I imagining it or had a light just flicked quickly on and off somewhere in the building?

I made my way as quietly as possible up the front drive and went inside.

The great room was dark—a lot darker than outside, where there was at least some moonlight filtering through the scattered clouds. I stood just inside the door, listening and letting my eyes adjust.

I heard the ticking of the huge grandfather clock along the wall that divided the great room from the dining room. The whirring of an air conditioner unit. A creak that could be someone walking upstairs or even a ghost come to haunt us but was more likely just a floorboard making the kind of noises really old floorboards sometimes made when the temperature and humidity got to them.

Then I saw it again—just a quick flicker of light, coming from somewhere behind the building. On the terrace, perhaps. I crept over to one of the long line of French doors that led out onto the terrace and peeked out.

The light flashed again. It wasn't on the terrace but someplace below it.

Like maybe near the kitchen door, on the floor below me. If I wanted to burgle the center, the kitchen door would be where I'd try first. It was on the narrow end of the building, so very few rooms had a view of it.

I crossed the room to the stairwell, and slowly crept down. At the bottom I peered out into the kitchen. I didn't know the layout here as well as I did in most of the rest of the building—Marty didn't welcome trespassers in his domain, so I'd only been here occasionally when I had business. It took a while to study and identify all the unfamiliar silhouetted shapes. The pots hanging from the ceiling. The hulking coffee machine. An industrial-sized knife block.

The light flashed again—outside the kitchen door.

I pulled out my phone and made sure I had it ready to call 911. Then I crept over to the door and slowly eased it open a few inches. I heard a faint rattling, scrabbling sound outside.

I flung the door wide open, stepped outside, and turned on my flashlight.

"Freeze!" I shouted, pointing my flashlight in the direction of the noise.

The beam of light revealed Grandfather, slightly downhill from the doorway, frozen in place, holding a black plastic garbage bag in one hand and a slice of overripe cantaloupe in the other.

"Turn that blamed thing off before someone sees it," he said.

Actually, that sounded like a sensible idea, so I turned the flashlight off. There was enough moonlight at the moment to keep an eye on him.

"What are you doing?" I asked.

"Luring the gulls back. You could help me if you like."

He tossed the cantaloupe into the darkness, reached into the bag, and pulled out a curved section of watermelon rind.

"I'm not going to help you strew garbage down the ravine," I said. "If you ask me nicely, I will help you pick it all up before Cordelia finds out what you've been up to."

"If you pick up my garbage, I may never find my gulls."

"If Cordelia catches you doing this, you won't live to find your gulls. Please tell me why you're out here doing exactly what she told you that she absolutely didn't want you to do? Don't pretend she didn't—I was there. She can call me as a witness that it was justifiable homicide."

"She might be a little overly fussy about things like this." He waved at the garbage at his feet. "But she's a bird lover. I knew she'd come around once we found the gulls."

"You hope," I muttered.

"And she's no fonder of that Venable creature than I am. She has designs on the gulls; I know it. Once we explain that to your grandmother—"

"I'll let you do the explaining," I said. "Look, you may not need the garbage to find your gulls. Chief Heedles is sympathetic. She's going to tell you where Prine took his gull pictures. She's just waiting for Horace to figure it out."

"We already know where Prine took the gull pictures—on the terrace."

"The ones Cordelia saw him take," I said. "You never know. From what I've seen of Prine, he could very well have gotten curious enough to track them back to wherever they're nesting. He could be pretty obsessive—almost fell off the terrace one evening trying to get a good angle on the sunset."

"You're not just saying that to humor me?" He was holding, but not strewing, a handful of potato peels.

Actually I was just saying it to humor him, but now wasn't the time to confess that.

"And even if he only took pictures on the terrace, we can find your gulls," I went on. "I know a couple of places not too far from here where you can spread your garbage. Places that aren't on Cordelia's land, so she won't have any say over what you do there."

He growled slightly.

"Places remote enough to be difficult for an old biddy like Mrs. Venable to find," I went on. "You do realize that if you strew the garbage here, she'll have just as good a chance to spot the gulls as you will. In fact better, because she's here all day in the pottery studio, with those big windows looking over the grounds. But if you strew it somewhere out in the mountains, in a location only a few of us know about, you'll have an advantage over her."

I could see that had an effect.

"So for now, let's just wait until the chief gets back to us, so we can strew the garbage as close as possible to where Prine was taking the rest of his pictures. Or if he only took them here, we strew garbage in a bunch of locations, in all directions. Just not here."

He scowled at me for a few moments. At least as far as I could see in the dim light, he was scowling. Maybe I just assumed the scowl because it was one of his most common expressions.

"All right," he said. "I'll postpone Operation Gull Quest for a few days and see if you come through with the goods."

"Operation Gull Quest?"

"Here." He handed me two black plastic garbage bags, one half empty, the other completely empty.

"Please tell me these were the only bags of garbage you brought."

"Yes," he said. "The stuff gets pretty heavy, and I had to haul it all the way uphill from the composting center. Pretty exhausting. I'm going to bed now. I have to get up early for my class."

"And you think I don't?"

"Don't forget to—"

"Stop or I'll shoot!" came a voice from behind me.

I turned to find Marty standing in the doorway, holding a really large knife. Marty was well over six feet and looked burly and athletic. Especially his arms, which showed the benefits of all those hours of kneading and chopping. He looked a little wild-eyed, so I put some more distance between us.

"Marty, it's okay," I said. "It's me, Meg. And Dr. Blake."

"I said stop or I'll shoot," he repeated.

"You're holding a knife," Grandfather pointed out. "What's this 'stop or I'll shoot' nonsense?"

What did he expect—stop or I'll slice? And did he realize that provoking someone Marty's size—with or without a knife—wasn't exactly the smartest thing to do?

Just then Marty flipped the knife down into the ground in front of him. It landed in a half-rotten cantaloupe at his feet with a satisfactory thunk and remained there, quivering slightly. It hadn't come anywhere near me, but still, seeing him throw it was unnerving.

"What the hell do you think you're doing out here in the middle of the night?" he snarled. "I thought maybe the damned vandals had come back and made the mistake of targeting my kitchen. You're lucky I recognized you." His voice sounded less angry than . . . unnerved. Not surprising, really, if he'd been expecting to encounter a trespasser—and one who could very well also be a murderer.

"Sorry," I said.

He turned on his heel and stalked back into the kitchen. I heard him muttering something as he went. I only caught a few phrases like "idiots" and "waking everyone up in the middle of the night" but I got the gist.

"Well, that was interesting," Grandfather said. "I'm going to bed."

"Let me go in with you," I said. "Make sure everything's okay."

"He just disarmed himself, or didn't you notice?"

"Oh, and are you under the delusion that this is the only knife in the whole kitchen? Plenty more where this came from." I plucked the knife out of the melon. "What if he only threw this one away so he could go back in and get a longer, sharper one? I'm going in with you. He knows me better." I decided not to mention that I could probably defend myself more effectively if Marty was lurking inside. It would only offend Grandfather.

Luckily by the time we went in Marty had disappeared.

"Gone back to bed, I assume," Grandfather said. "Figured out we weren't the vandals."

"Go follow his example while I clean up after you."

He didn't need to be told twice. Should I follow Marty

and give him a piece of my mind? I knew where his room was—at least approximately. I could tackle him—verbally, that is—about his weird and unacceptable behavior. See if it was just the thought of having the vandal target his kitchen that had him so upset. Put him on notice that any more knife throwing would get him in trouble with the police and Cordelia. I thought better of the idea almost immediately. I considered notifying Officer Keech, and vetoed that, too. She'd had a long day, and there was no real emergency. The sensible thing to do was to get out of the kitchen as quickly as possible and save any confrontations for the morning, when no doubt Chief Heedles and her troops would be back in force.

I spent a miserable fifteen minutes or so picking up the rotting garbage Grandfather had scattered around the ravine, somewhat hampered by the fact that I didn't have three hands. After all, there was still a murderer on the loose. I wanted to keep both the knife and the flashlight handy, and neither left much room in my hand for picking up the garbage.

"I give up," I said after the fifth or sixth time I'd tripped or stubbed my toe while hunting down a chunk of garbage. Flip-flops weren't ideal for this kind of work. "I can come back for the rest in the morning."

Maybe there wasn't that much more—maybe Grandfather hadn't completely filled the two garbage bags. Everything I'd picked up so far seemed to be vegetable matter—half-rotten, highly smelly vegetable matter—so I emptied the bags into one of the compost holding bins just outside the kitchen door and went back inside.

I turned on the lights and washed my hands thoroughly. I scrubbed the cantaloupe guts off the knife and returned it to an empty slot in the huge knife block. Then I hit the lights and went back upstairs to the great room, feeling more cheerful with every step I put between me and the kitchen.

When I emerged from the stairwell, the great room was still dark, but I saw a line of light showing under the door that led to the studio wing.

"Now what?" I said it aloud, but softly, in case someone—the vandal?—was on the other side of the door. The smart thing would have been to rouse Officer Keech, but that would take time and effort. I was tired and cranky and wanted to get back to bed.

Okay, and maybe just a little curious. So I snagged a poker from the great room's big fireplace, tiptoed across to the door to the studio wing, and yanked it open.

The first thing I saw was broken pottery. One of Gillian's enormous cobalt blue glazed planters lay in pieces on the floor in the doorway to her studio. I stopped short—there were shards scattered all up and down the corridor, some of them a foot long, and I was wearing flip-flops. I had no desire to lacerate my feet. I could see plenty from my end of the hall.

And then, as I scanned the ceramic debris field, I realized that the base of the pot was still in one big piece. Protruding from it was a body—a body whose head would be resting beneath the planter base.

My heart raced, and I felt a distinctly queasy sensation in my stomach, so I closed my eyes for a few moments and took deep breaths. And then I opened my eyes again and forced myself to focus on practicalities. Should I go fetch Officer Keech? No, calling 911 was a better idea. Dispatch could probably rouse her faster than I could, and I wouldn't have to leave the crime scene unguarded. And after 911 I should call Dad, even though whoever was under the pot was clearly past his help. Having a plan—better still, a to-do list—always helps me, even in the direst crisis. I could feel my pulse slowing and my stomach steadying.

I had already pulled out my phone by the time I noticed that the body had a cast on its arm. A fairly new, clean cast, decorated with get-well messages in a variety of bright colors, including one in lavender from Rose Noire.

Victor the Klutz.

Chapter 17

"And you don't know what woke you?"

Luckily by the time Chief Heedles had arrived I'd recovered from the shock of finding Victor's body—at least, sufficiently recovered that I'd been able to give her the condensed version of my middle-of-the night adventures while escorting her to the door of the studio wing. Then I'd dragged a chair in from the great room and sat just inside the door to make sure no one followed her except Horace and Dad and Officer Keech and eventually the other three Riverton police officers. Michael texted me that he had joined Eric and the boys in the caravan, and that they were fast asleep. I felt better, knowing he was with them, and managed—after a fashion—to shove my anxiety over them aside and focus on what the chief was doing.

And right now she was asking for details I wasn't sure I could provide. Particularly not when I knew that I had only to turn my head to see poor Victor's body, still awaiting the medical examiner. The proximity didn't help my focus.

"Meg?" the chief said.

"What woke me? No idea. I thought I heard a noise. Now I figure maybe it was the pot falling on Victor. At the time I had no idea."

Over my left shoulder I could tell that Horace and Officer Keech were clearly enjoying themselves—not in any inappropriately gleeful manner, of course, but you could see they were getting a lot of professional satisfaction out of processing what I gathered was an interesting crime scene. For the last quarter of an hour they'd been taking turns sketching in Lesley Keech's notebook, trying to figure out precisely how the killer had rigged the pot so it would fall on whomever entered the door. I wasn't sure knowing the precise mechanical details of how the booby trap worked would bring us any closer to finding who'd done it, but I didn't want to rain on their parade. From the chief's carefully patient expression when she checked on their progress, I suspect she felt the same way.

"Do you think whoever killed Prine also killed Victor?" I asked.

"Too early to tell yet. Did any of the acts of vandalism involve similar mechanical contraptions?"

"Not that I could see," I said. "They all seemed distinctly low-tech. Using materials at hand—slugs from the yard, soy sauce from the dining hall. Some of them seemed pretty spur-of-the-moment—opening windows, twisting the dial on a kiln. Not like this. Someone had to do at least a little planning to pull this off, right? Then again, if Horace and Officer Keech hadn't been here, would we really have figured out there was a booby trap? I mean, they're experts, and they're still trying to figure out how it worked. It's possible we might have assumed Victor's death was a terrible accident, and that those little bits of wood and string were just rubbish that happened to be lying around."

"You get a lot of fifty-pound pots falling from the ceilings around here?" the chief asked.

"No, but if we were still focused on the vandalism, maybe we'd have jumped to the conclusion that Victor was the vandal, and had accidentally done himself in while trying to pull off his latest prank."

"It's a thought," she said. "Did you suspect Victor of the vandalism?"

"Yes," I said. "Although no more than at least a dozen other people."

Just then the door popped open. We both turned to see Gillian standing in the open doorway. She had frozen in place upon spotting her broken pot and Victor's apparently headless body.

"Oh," she said in a sort of stunned half whimper. Then her eyes rolled up, and before either of us could jump to catch her, she keeled over backward, hitting her head on the floor with a thud that made both of us wince.

The chief rushed to Gillian's side. I pulled out my cell phone and punched the button to call Dad. "You have a live patient here at the crime scene," I said.

"On my way."

"Odd that he's not here fussing over the body," I remarked to Chief Heedles.

"Not that odd." She was checking Gillian's pulse. "I asked him to stay on the front porch, to lead the medical examiner here as soon as she comes, and in the meantime to report any suspicious behavior on the part of any of the guests."

"You do realize that when there's a murder involved, he's all too ready to see suspicious behavior even when no one's asking him to look for it," I said. "You could be in for a long debriefing with him."

"And maybe he'll bring me something useful, and in the meantime, he's out of my hair," she said. "On the surface these two murders appear quite dissimilar—one carefully planned, the other quite possibly committed on the spur of the moment with a weapon that happened to be available."

"Was Prine in the habit of keeping a kitchen knife in his

studio, then? I can't say that I'd noticed it, but then I was avoiding him as far as I could."

"Turns out it wasn't a kitchen knife but something called a palette knife," she said. "Apparently some painters use them either to mix paint or actually to paint with. I'm not at all sure how that works."

"Ask Frankie," I suggested. "The replacement painting teacher. She could explain it to you—or even demonstrate."

"Good idea—not that I expect it to have any relevance to the murder investigation, but I'm curious. And you never know where you'll find a vital clue."

Something didn't sound right about this scenario.

"Was the palette knife sharp?" I asked.

"Reasonably so." Her face clearly showed that she didn't find this a particularly incisive question. "It would have been extremely difficult to stab Prine in the back with a blunt implement."

"Then you might also want to ask Frankie if palette knives are usually all that sharp," I suggested. "I was under the impression that they had fairly dull edges. You want to mix and spread paint with them, not gouge holes in your canvas or your palette."

The chief, who had been studying Gillian, looked up sharply.

"You're sure of that?"

"Not absolutely. All of the palette knives I've ever seen were dull, but I'm not a painter. Maybe some of them have a use for sharpened palette knives."

She nodded. She focused her eyes back on Gillian, but her attention seemed focused inward. No doubt she was also thinking that if the palette knife had been sharpened beforehand, the two murders might have a lot more in common than we'd thought.

Dad burst in, medical bag in hand, interrupting our ruminations.

"Pulse?" he asked.

"Slow, but steady," the chief said. "About sixty-five. She hit her head going down."

Dad nodded, and began gently examining Gillian's head. I decided it was time to put some distance between me and my former student's body.

"I'll guard the door from the other side." I grabbed my chair and dragged it back into the great room.

I sat down and pulled out my phone to check the time— 4:46. Dawn was still an hour or so away, but it was already getting lighter outside. And inside, thanks to all those French doors leading out onto the terrace.

I heard a rattling noise from the direction of the dining room. Marty, doing some kind of pre-breakfast preparation? More likely one of his kitchen staff. Though if Marty wasn't up already, he would be soon, since breakfast service started at six. Maybe that was why he'd been so cranky with Grandfather and me. We'd probably interrupted his last hour of sleep before the start of another fourteen-hour day. Then again, cranky seemed to be his default mode.

The door behind me opened and Dad walked out, escorting Gillian.

"There you are!" Dad exclaimed. "Gillian's going to be just fine." The degree of cheerfulness in his voice made me suspect that he'd been worried for a while. "But she's still a little shaky. Can you keep an eye on her for a little while?"

I couldn't tell whether she needed watching for purely medical reasons or if he was hinting that the chief wanted to make sure she didn't disappear. Either way, I could watch her.

"Sure," I said.

He escorted her over to one of the deep-cushioned sofas and hovered while she sat down. I took the armchair next to her sofa.

"Can you send the medical examiner in when she arrives?" he said.

"Roger."

Gillian sat with her eyes closed. I debated whether to try to talk to her or just leave her alone. Given the early hour, leaving her alone seemed wise.

Though come to think of it, what was she doing here at such an early hour?

A door opened, and I glanced in to see Marty peering out of the doorway to the dining room.

"What's wrong?" he asked. "Is she okay?"

"She's had a shock."

He disappeared without a word. But just as I was writing him off as an insensitive jerk, he reappeared with a small tray that held a steaming mug of coffee and a flaky croissant on a paper napkin.

"You need this." He shoved the mug into her hands and set the napkin with the croissant on the sofa beside her. "Drink."

She lifted the cup and sipped. Then a small smile lit her face, and she took another, larger sip.

"Just right," she said. "Thanks."

"Make her eat." He frowned at me as if I were to blame for Gillian's state. I decided I'd been wrong about Marty's reasons for cosseting the vegetarians. It wasn't Rose Noire he was besotted with—it was Gillian. I wondered if she'd even noticed. "I have to see to breakfast," Marty went on. "But call me if she needs more."

I nodded, and he disappeared back into the dining room, presumably on his way to the kitchen. Gillian sat holding the coffee cup, and staring into it. She looked as if whatever good the sips of coffee had done was wearing off.

"Don't make me nag you," I said—but gently. "Drink."

"It was meant for me." Her face was ashen, and she gripped the mug with both hands as if it was the only thing keeping her from falling off the edge of a cliff.

"The falling pot?"

"Yes. Since we're locking the studios outside of class hours, I should have been the first one through that door this morning. Why was he there? And in the middle of the night? Who is he, anyway, this Victor Kurtz?"

"Victor Winter," I said.

"I thought someone said his name was Kurtz."

"Most of the other students call him Victor the Klutz," I said. "Some of them may not know his real name. But it's Winter."

"I see." She buried her nose in the mug for a moment. "But it wasn't his klutziness that killed him. Someone set a trap for me, and he was unlucky enough to fall into it instead."

"Why would someone want to kill you?"

"You don't believe me." Her voice was calm on the surface, but with a thin edge of budding hysteria underneath.

"I don't disbelieve you," I said. "But I have no idea who could possibly hate you enough to want to kill you. If you do, tell the chief."

"If I knew, I would." She shook her head wearily. "Some crazed person is trying to kill me and I have no idea why."

"They might not be trying to kill you," I said. "Maybe Victor was the vandal. Maybe he was only trying to cause damage and it backfired on him. What if he tried to pick up that pot to throw it on the floor not realizing how heavy it was, and ended up getting smashed under it?"

"That would be a pretty stupid thing to do," she said.

"He was no rocket scientist."

"That would be good, wouldn't it?" she said slowly. "If Victor was the vandal. It would mean no more vandalism. Though I'm not sure what that would have to do with Edward's murder."

"Possibly everything, if Prine caught him messing with the art studio. Victor could have killed him in the struggle. Or deliberately, to avoid being exposed."

"I like this theory of yours. I hope it's true."

"So do I." I decided it wouldn't make her feel any better if I shared my other theory—that Victor had fallen prey to a booby trap meant for someone else—me. Because Gillian probably wouldn't have been the first one in her classroom this morning. The way things were going, even if I'd gotten back to sleep after catching Grandfather in the act, I'd probably have awakened earlier than almost anyone else. I'd probably have made use of the time by checking out every corner of the main building for signs that the vandal had struck again. And it would have been me lying there in the doorway of Gillian's studio.

But what had Victor been doing prowling through the studio wing in the early morning? Maybe he was the vandal, getting back to his work after lying low all day yesterday because of the police presence. Or maybe he was an innocent but nosy bystander—maybe, like me, he had heard a noise in the night or seen a light and had gone prowling around the studio wing to investigate.

It would help if we knew whether or not the vandal was

also the killer. And whether the same person had committed both murders. Did we have one criminal, or two, or three?

I didn't envy Chief Heedles her job.

"What were you doing here this early?" As soon as the words left my lips I realized that what I'd meant as an innocent question sound like an accusation. I hurried to add something to defuse that impression. "Because if the police woke you up just so they could show you a dead body in your studio, I'm going to speak sternly to them. Better yet, I'll sic my grandmother on them."

"Not their fault." She gave me the ghost of a smile. "The arrival of the police woke me, and then I could see that there were lights on in my studio. I thought it was the vandal again, and I wanted to see how much damage had been done. I didn't expect . . ."

Her voice trailed off, and she took another sip of the coffee.

"Do you suppose your cook knows I like my coffee lightly sweetened?" she asked. "Or did he just assume a little sugar would be good for someone in danger of going into shock?"

"I'm sure he knows," I said. "Just as he knows exactly who the vegetarians are so he doesn't offer them anything they can't eat. And I bet he's got a little mental list of everyone who commits the heinous sin of salting their food before tasting it."

She smiled slightly at that, and sat back on the sofa, closing her eyes.

Rose Noire came tiptoeing in. I decided to turn sentry duty over to her. I pointed to Gillian, then at Rose Noire, and then at my eyes. She nodded, and when I got up, she took my place in the armchair.

I knew I should try to go back to sleep. But I didn't want

to wake Michael and the boys, depriving them of their last hour or so of rest. So I went out on the terrace, lay down in one of the recliners there, and closed my eyes. Even if I couldn't actually fall asleep, I could rest.

Chapter 18

Wednesday

"Meg?"

I was on the hillside below the terrace, picking up cantaloupe rinds and potato peelings, but as fast as I picked them up, the person who had thrown them threw more, and I was starting to be pretty sure it was the vandal doing it. And now he was calling my name so I'd look up and the falling garbage would smack me in the face. I shielded my eyes with my hand and peered up, trying to make out his face, but the garbage kept raining down, and my black plastic garbage bag was nearly full. Forget the garbage, I told myself. Just look up and see—

"Meg?"

I opened my eyes to see Chief Heedles squatting in front of me. I was still on the recliner on the terrace. Not a cantaloupe rind in sight.

"You okay?" she asked. "You were sort of thrashing and muttering."

"I'm fine," I said. "Except that I was on the trail of the vandal, and was just about to get a look at him or her when you woke me up."

"Damn." She smiled slightly. "Wish I'd held off a few minutes so you could tell me."

"Did you need me for anything?"

"No." She shook her head. "Just came out to get some peace and quiet to think. You might want to grab a bite to eat—classes start in twenty minutes."

"Thanks," I said. "By the way, have you talked to Amanda since dinnertime?"

"No. Should I have?"

"Some of the ladies in the herb class are all a-twitter over the fact that one of their number, Jenni something-or-other, is sneaking out nights for a rendezvous with an unknown man."

"Do they know for sure it's a man?" the chief asked. "Or did they just assume it was a man she was meeting?"

"Good point," I said. "One of them supposedly saw her with a shadowy male figure, but she could have been seeing what she expected to see. And I realize that sneaking out to meet someone isn't suspicious in and of itself, but maybe that's not really what they're doing, or even if they're innocent, they could have seen something."

"Understood," the chief said. "Your friend Amanda can point out this Jenni?"

"Or can point to someone who can. And incidentally, since they say Jenni's been sneaking out for several days, I assume both she and whoever she's meeting were here last week as well as this."

"That should narrow it down a bit."

"To one of two male students, five male staff members, and seven male faculty," I said. "Three faculty if you don't count Dad, Grandfather, Baptiste, and Michael, and I don't. Not solely because of their sterling characters, but because Michael's been on munchkin patrol every waking moment and the rest of them have been out with the nighttime nature hikes most evenings."

The chief nodded and strode away.

I heaved myself out of the recliner and stumbled into the dining room. I headed for the buffet line. Not many people left—most of the faculty and students had finished eating and were heading for their studios.

I did spot Gillian sitting by herself in a corner. On a plate in front of her was a muffin—well, more like three-quarters of a muffin. As I watched, she picked a small bit off and carefully lifted it to her mouth. From her expression as she chewed, she might as well have been eating sawdust. Not the way people usually ate Marty's muffins.

As I went through the line and packed a carryout box with my favorites—bacon, toast, scrambled eggs, and a big helping of mixed fruit—I pondered. She still seemed shaken. Had finding a dead body affected her that badly? Not even finding it really—I'd done that. She'd only seen it.

Not inconceivable. But what if it wasn't finding Victor's dead body that had shaken her so? If she'd killed Victor and knew she couldn't appear unaffected, what better way to divert suspicion than to make it look as if she fainted at the mere sight of his dead body?

And then I reminded myself that fainting was probably a normal reaction to seeing a dead body. Gillian hadn't grown up with a father who considered details of an interesting surgery or autopsy suitable dinner table conversation. She might never have seen a dead body before, much less a murdered one—I had, more than once, thanks in part to Dad's fascination with mysteries and his keen desire to involve himself in any real-life ones that happened nearby.

I glanced over at Gillian again. She was hunched over slightly, sipping her tea with her eyes closed, eyelids as pale and fragile as the porcelain cup.

Yeah, come to think of it, Gillian's reaction was utterly normal. Maybe taking a deep yoga breath and then making a to-do list was the weirder reaction, though it was just as normal for me.

And maybe Dad's penchant for fictional mysteries was rubbing off on me just a little too much, I thought, as I turned back to my satisfyingly full carryout box. "Suspect everyone!" might be a very good policy if you're trying to beat Miss Marple to the solution of a manor house mystery, but it wasn't a very comfortable way to live your life.

As I closed up my box, I saw Gillian stand up, pick up her tray, and head for the service hatch. As I watched, Marty bustled out of the kitchen, gently took the tray from her, as if he thought her unable to carry it over to the hatch. She smiled her thanks and quietly left the dining room.

I felt almost guilty for suspecting her, even for a moment. Marty, like Dad and Rose Noire, saw her as in need of support, and here I was constructing scenarios of her killing Victor and then staging a fainting spell. Why? I liked her.

Maybe I was projecting. What would I do if I'd had some very good reason for killing someone, and wanted to make sure no one suspected me? Probably just what I'd been imagining Gillian could have done. But Gillian wasn't me. And the more I considered the idea, the less plausible I found her as a killer. In fact, if I was trying to come up with a list of plausible killers—

Morbid thoughts. I shook them off and picked up my carryout box. When I turned to head for the studios, I almost ran into Cordelia. She was standing in the middle of the dining room, studying another latecomer. Grandfather.

"Morning," I said. "Almost time for class."

"Morning. I've figured out an excellent way to test him."

"Test whom about what?" I asked, though I assumed she meant Grandfather.

"To test your grandfather's motivation." She continued to study him with a rather grim half smile on her face. "Does he really want to rescue the Ord's gulls, or does he just want the glory of rediscovering them?"

"Both, I think."

"We'll see." Her expression wasn't grim, I decided. More like determined and smug.

She strode off toward Grandfather. I decided to tag along, in case someone was needed to play peacemaker.

Grandfather was sitting at his usual table, sipping coffee and glancing over at the buffet line, where Baptiste was juggling two trays with carryout boxes on them—one of them doubtless intended for Grandfather.

"You couldn't leave it alone." Cordelia stopped in front of his table and put her hands on her hips. "You had to go strewing garbage all over my land."

Grandfather scowled up at her. Then he looked past her at me.

"I thought you said you were going to pick all that up," he snapped.

"I've been a little busy," I said. "We had another murder, or hadn't you heard?"

"Don't blame Meg," Cordelia said. "If you're so all-fired eager to get your hands on an Ord's gull, how would a dead one work?"

"A dead gull?" Grandfather frowned. "Dammit, I don't want anyone killing any more of my gulls! If their numbers have gotten low, they could already be suffering from genetic erosion."

"I'm not killing any gulls for you," Cordelia said. "But I

might be able to get you the one that died last week. You could study it and take your own photos."

Baptiste arrived and hovered over Grandfather's shoulder. "Only a few minutes before class," he said.

"I suppose you buried the gull," Grandfather growled to Cordelia. "Doubt if there's much of any use left by now."

"It's not buried, it's frozen."

"You froze it? Here?"

Baptiste, who had opened his own box and was lifting a slice of bacon to his mouth, paused, as if not sure he wanted to eat something that might have come out of the same freezer as a dead gull.

"Not here, you old fool," Cordelia said. "I took it down to our local veterinarian. Between treating poultry and working as a wildlife rehabilitator, he's quite knowledgeable about birds. I wanted him to do a necropsy."

"A necropsy?" Grandfather echoed.

"An autopsy performed on an animal," Cordelia explained. "If—"

"I know what a necropsy is!" Grandfather bellowed. "I've performed enough of them. Why in blue blazes did you ask him to do a necropsy on the gull?"

"Because I wanted to know what killed the wretched thing. Make sure it wasn't anything that would endanger my guests." She paused there, though I could tell she was watching Grandfather with amusement.

"And what did kill the gull, dammit?" he roared.

"Extreme old age. He was almost as old for a gull as you are for a human. Reassuring to know it was nothing contagious, in case any of my guests asked. Anyway, I called our vet yesterday to see if he still had the gull in his specimen freezer, and he does. We'd already discussed the fact that it was an unusual and interesting specimen, and were planning to try to identify it when we had some time. If you ask him nicely, maybe he'll let you have it."

Grandfather sat for a few moments, scowling at her.

"It doesn't change our need to find rest of the flock," he said. "But it might be useful."

Cordelia cocked her head to one side as if waiting for something.

"Say thank you," I said, nudging Grandfather. "Unless you want to annoy Cordelia badly enough that she tells the local vet to dispose of the dead gull."

"Thank you," Grandfather managed—though if I'd been a non-English speaker, his tone would have convinced me that he was uttering a savage curse.

She nodded once, tossed a business card on the table, and strode away. Looking annoyed. Well, if she expected the prospect of possessing the dead gull to sideline his pursuit of the live ones, she really didn't know him as well as she thought she did.

Grandfather picked up the business card and began patting his pockets. Looking for his cell phone, no doubt.

Baptiste reached over, took the business card from his fingers, and pulled out his own cell phone.

"I will call the gentleman," he said. "Let's go to our classroom before our students rebel and defect to one of the other instructors."

Grandfather grabbed his coffee and headed for the door, leaving Baptiste to juggle both carryout boxes along with his phone and the business card.

"Why don't you let me negotiate with the vet?" I said. "You have your hands full with Grandfather. Not to mention Grandfather's breakfast."

"That would be excellent." Baptiste handed over the card.

"Not only will I be rather busy assisting the good doctor, but very soon we will be heading into the mountains for today's shooting expedition, and my cell phone will be useless. Evidently I do not have the optimal carrier for this area."

"There is no optimal carrier up in the mountains." I turned and headed for the studios, and he fell into step beside me. "Except maybe a carrier pigeon. Cordelia had to install some kind of special cell phone signal-boosting equipment for us all to get a signal here at the center."

"And we are all grateful to her," Baptiste said. "I must say, the lack of cell phone signal does enhance our shooting expeditions. No one can check their e-mail or their Facebook status—there is nothing but us and our cameras. It focuses the mind wonderfully. On our way back, I can tell the moment the bus comes within range of the signal. Suddenly conversation ceases, and everyone bows their head over their devices, as if in prayer to the gods of the Internet." His face fell slightly. "I only worry about how we would cope if something happened to one of us up there, with no way to call for help."

"A good point. I'll speak to Cordelia about that. Maybe there's something that would work up there. A shortwave radio, perhaps."

"An excellent idea." We had reached the door of his and Grandfather's studio. "May you have a productive day." He bowed slightly before entering the room.

"You, too," I said, as I headed for my own studio. Then I paused in the hallway, took out my phone and dialed. The veterinarian could wait—8:00 A.M. might be a little early to call him about something that only Grandfather considered an emergency. It was also a little early to call my brother, Rob, but what I wanted to ask was a lot more urgent.

"Meg? What's up?" He didn't even sound all that sleepy.

"You, surprisingly," I said. "I was actually just going to leave you a voice mail."

"I'm a reformed character. In bed by ten, up at six to jog. It's amazing how much energy you get when you start the day right."

Yes, it was about time for another of Rob's periodic forays into healthy living. I'd give it a week or two if he'd come up with it on his own, and maybe a few months if he was being egged on by some new lady love. I made a mental note to see what Mother knew on the latter front.

"Great," I said aloud. "I have a request from Grandmother Cordelia that requires your technical expertise."

"My technical expertise? She wants a game invented?"

Well, yes, that was Rob's actual expertise—coming up with odd but successful game ideas.

"The technical expertise of all those minions whose paychecks you sign every other week," I said. "Cordelia and I want a way to communicate with the bus when it's up in the mountains where there's no cell phone reception. What if Grandfather got mauled by a bear when they're out there in the woods?"

"Cordelia would give the bear a medal."

"Okay, what if Dad was the one getting mauled? She'd mind that. So we need something like—I don't know. Maybe some shortwave radios. Can you send us someone to set up whatever we need? Preferably today?"

"Sure," he said. "I have no idea what's involved, but I'll figure out who does and send them up pronto."

"And if whoever you send also happened to have the equipment and know-how to start installing some kind of security system at the center, maybe we can finally talk Cordelia into it. Or maybe just install it while she's not looking and present her with a useful fait accompli."

"Roger. I'm on it."

And if Cordelia objected, I'd point out that the cameras wouldn't just be protecting her craft center. They'd be protecting her family. Particularly her great-grandsons.

I dashed into my studio a few minutes late for the start of class, but feeling so much calmer that it was worth it. Tech help was on the way.

Chapter 19

My good mood survived for maybe half an hour. Yesterday morning my students, while easily distracted, had still seemed essentially cheerful and interested in their work. Today everything and everyone seemed heavy and slow. Was it worse for my class because Victor had been, however briefly and annoyingly, one of our members? Or was everyone at Biscuit Mountain feeling the strain? I found myself wishing I could be a fly on the wall in some of the other classrooms.

When, shortly before lunch, one of the students accidentally fractured a fireplace poker she'd been working on all morning and burst into tears, I did my best both to comfort her and turn it into a teachable moment. I started a discussion about working past failure and through negative times. Not something I'd ever seen in any of the blacksmithing classes I'd taken, but then I'd never taken a class next door to a crime scene. Or maybe hanging out so much with Rose Noire was having an effect on me. We talked about striking a balance between working even if you weren't in the mood and knowing when you needed to stop and fill the creative well. The fine line between working through discomfort and recognizing when you had an injury. The joy of being able to vent anger and frustration and fear on your anvil and the importance of maintaining control when you were working with white hot iron and massive hammers. No one actually came out and mentioned what was on all our minds—the weirdness of trying to carry on as usual, learning to make ornamental ironwork when for all we knew we might be the murderer's next victim. But we didn't have to. Quite possibly the strangest, most touchy/feely blacksmithing class ever taught, but when the bell rang for lunch, I realized that people were smiling again—perhaps a little tremulously, in some cases, but smiling. They trooped off to lunch in small groups, calling back to me to join them if I could. I lingered in the studio wing until all the classes had broken up and did what had now become my usual lunchtime routine, making sure all was well in the studios before heading for the dining hall.

All six upper studios secure. Two of them still barred with yellow crime-scene tape, but I checked those doors as well, on the off chance that Horace or one of the Riverton officers had been careless. All three lower ones locked up tight, along with Cordelia's office and the storage rooms, including the one Chief Heedles was using as her headquarters. And no one lingering behind.

Well, almost no one. When I came up the stairs to the upper floor again, I found Dante Marino, the woodworker, standing in the hallway, staring at the door to Prine's studio. He had a strange look on his face.

"You okay?" I asked.

"I'm fine." He shrugged slightly. "Any idea when the police are going to finish with Prine's studio and let that new painter lady move in? Because I think that would go a long way toward getting us back to normal around here."

"No idea. And frankly, I don't think anything's going to get us back to normal until they find out who killed Prine and Victor."

"Point taken."

He continued to stare at the studio door. I waited. I suspected if I waited long enough, just having me there would inspire him to talk, and I was curious to know what he'd say.

"Did your grandmother tell you I almost walked out last week when I found out Prine was teaching here at the same time I was?" he finally said.

"She mentioned that some of the other instructors were less than ecstatic about having him around."

"Less than ecstatic." He chuckled and shook his head. "No, I wouldn't say I was ecstatic. I went all Vesuvius on her. She didn't turn a hair. Tough lady. Smart, too."

I nodded, but didn't want to derail whatever he was trying to say.

"She waited till I'd blown off my head of steam, and then she told me to suck it up and tough it out. Not quite in those words, but that was the idea. Said if I left, everyone— including Prine—would know it was because of him, and did I want to give him the satisfaction of driving me away?"

"So you stayed."

He nodded.

I waited a while before prodding him again.

"What did you have against him, anyway?" I asked. "Was it the whole Dock Street craft center thing?"

"That was part of it," he said. "And it was mostly his fault the damned thing failed, you know, no matter what some of the others would say. He was the one who had the most money to put in, so he thought everything should be done his way. And then at the first sign of trouble he ran away."

Dante pounded his right fist into his other hand and scowled at the door of Prine's studio.

"I can see how you'd be mad at him," I said. "Especially if you're still feeling the financial impact after all this time."

"Oh, you've heard those rumors, have you?" He tried to smile and it came out as a grimace. "Sad to say, the rumors are true. My credit's so bad I have to buy my tools and supplies with cash, and get my brother to cosign for me to rent an apartment."

"Ouch."

"Yeah. But seeing Prine here, day after day, for the past week, I realized it wasn't because of the money that I was still so mad. There was a while—a long while—when I thought he'd broken up my marriage."

He stopped for so long that I practically had to bite my tongue to keep from asking questions. Some smarter part of my brain told me to shut up, and eventually he went on.

"He didn't, of course. Not for lack of trying. He hit on my wife the way he does—did—with any halfway attractive woman who comes within a mile of him. Tried to get her to pose for one of his sleazy pictures. I tend to be a little old-fashioned and hot-headed about that kind of thing. And when I thought the same guy who was ruining me financially had also stolen my wife—"

He closed his eyes and shook his head slowly.

"But he hadn't?" I asked.

"No. She didn't leave me for him, or even because of him. She left me because of me. I was a jealous, controlling, hot-headed jerk." He opened his eyes and half smiled. "Still am, I guess, but not nearly as bad as I was. I've learned a little. Long way to go, but . . . seeing him here, day in, day out, I realized I needed to work on not letting him get to me. Needed to stop blaming him for everything that had gone wrong in my life. Maybe even needed to talk to him and see if I could get some closure. In case you haven't guessed, I've been doing a lot of therapy for the past decade."

He chuckled slightly, and then it faded into a sigh.

"It's weird, but you know what's bugging me most now?" he said. "I was just getting to the point where having him around didn't bother me so much. I could usually ignore him as if he was a tree or a fire hydrant or something, or even look at him without sending my blood pressure into the stratosphere. And he goes and gets himself killed, and dammit, I wasn't finished working through all that. And before you say it—yes, I told Chief Heedles all about my history with Prine. She'd have found out from someone else anyway—a whole lot of someone elses if she did enough digging—so I thought it would sound better coming from me."

"That was smart," I said.

"I manage smart sometimes," he said. "Not often, but enough. So maybe it's selfish of me, but I want the lady painter in there teaching her class as if Prine had never used that studio. And I want Chief Heedles to have already found Prine's killer, and I want the killer to be someone hateful and despicable, not some basically nice person who was driven over the edge by something nasty that Prine did. I want it all over with."

"Amen," I said.

"And even when it is, now I'll never really know whether I could ever have gotten past it all and had a civil conversation with him. Stupid, selfish reason to wish he was still alive, but there it is."

He flashed me a melancholy smile and ambled off down the hallway toward the great room and the dining room beyond.

I stood looking after him for a few moments. I wasn't sure how far I believed in the new, mellower, therapy-enhanced Dante. I kind of missed the old, foot-in-mouth Dante, the Dante who'd erupt in bellows of anger one minute and gales of laughter the next. I had the sinking feeling that the chief might find this new, philosophical Dante a lot more suspicious and I wouldn't exactly disagree with her.

And why was I so focused on my fellow instructors, anyway? I pondered it as I strolled toward the dining room. Maybe because they were a lot more likely to have known Edward Prine well enough to have a motive to kill him. The majority of the students had little contact with him, and even the ones in his class mostly seemed to shrug off his unpleasant personality or excuse it on the grounds of artistic temperament.

But there were so many of them, I thought, with a sinking feeling, as I stepped into the dining room and surveyed the assembled crowd. Nearly two hundred students, not counting the kids in Michael's class. So even if very few of them had had enough contact with Prine to inspire homicidal urges toward him—it only took one.

"There you are." Cordelia and Chief Heedles strolled up, both holding trays with carryout boxes on them. "Get your lunch and join us in my office. Chief Heedles wants to consult us about something."

So much for having a quiet lunch with my students and enjoying their improved mood. I filled my own carryout box, nodding to Marty, who was standing on the other side of the buffet today, alternately glowering at his employees when they raced in with new supplies of the more popular dishes, and peering over our heads to see how the people out in the dining room were reacting to their meals.

"Looks great, as usual," I said in my most cheerful voice.

He uttered a noise that was probably meant to be "thanks," but only came out sounding like "unk," and stared at me under knit brows, as if trying to decide if I was being sarcastic.

Well, we hadn't hired him for his personality.

Cordelia and Chief Heedles were seated across the desk

from each other. Cordelia seemed to be studying some papers in front of her.

"Come in," the chief said through a mouthful of meatloaf.

"The chief has gotten into Prine's computer," Cordelia said.

"Actually it was Horace and Lesley Keech," the chief said. "And they found out that in addition to the phone calls, Prine was also e-mailing Calvin Whiffletree at the Jazz Hands Art Academy."

"The jerk," I muttered.

"On the surface," the chief went on. "It would appear that these are merely friendly e-mails reporting on events here at Biscuit Mountain. Including, of course, the vandalism."

"In fact, primarily about the vandalism," Cordelia added. "Which strikes us both as rather suspicious. So the chief wants to know if any of Prine's e-mails reveal details that he wouldn't have known if he wasn't himself the vandal."

"Which would mean that under the guise of sharing news, he'd actually be reporting on what he'd done."

"Precisely. For example." Cordelia handed me a sheet of paper so I could read Prine's message to Whiffletree:

I'm sure you'll be happy to hear that all's not well here at La Montagne des Biscuits. *Someone turned a bunch of slugs loose in the clay buckets in the pottery studio, and it was hours before all the lady potters stopped screaming "Eek! Eek!" and washing their hands over and over again. The Duchess tried to laugh it off, but I can tell she's worried.*

"The Duchess?" I said aloud.

"It suits her." The chief smiled at Cordelia. She handed me another e-mail:

Things continue to go downhill here. It would appear that the idiot woman who's teaching watercolors downstairs from me left her studio windows open overnight, and a thunderstorm blew in enough rain to turn all her students' work into papier-maché. If you ask me, whoever did it should be given a medal for his service to the art world. A more talentless crop of nitwits you've never seen. Not much better in my class, either.

"The jerk never comes out and says 'I put the slugs in the clay' or 'I opened all the windows when I knew a rainstorm was coming,' or anything like that." Cordelia was visibly fuming.

"But he was smart enough that he wouldn't," I said.

"So let's figure out if he wasn't quite as smart as he thought he was," the chief said. "If he revealed a detail that you didn't make public, or reported it before you'd made it public . . ."

So the three of us spent most of the two-hour lunch break eating with one hand while working. Cordelia and I sorted through the dozens of texts, e-mails, phone calls, and voice messages we'd sent to each other, Chief Heedles, or anyone else about the vandalism, trying to come up with some detail Prine shouldn't have known, or at least shouldn't have known so early. But if there was a smoking gun in these e-mails we weren't finding it. Prine's e-mails reported on each incident, but did not claim or even imply that he could take credit for it, and didn't reveal anything that couldn't have been known by anyone at the center. Whiffletree's replies were even more terse and equally noncommittal. There was one in which he congratulated Prine for not being one of the targets and added, "Of course pretty soon they might suspect the lucky ones are actually guilty." The next e-mail from Prine reported on finding his studio splattered with red paint. That one went on ten times as long as any of the others, and completely lacked the snidely ironic tone of the rest.

"It's a cry of outrage," Cordelia said.

"That doesn't mean he didn't wreck his own studio," I said. "By Thursday, when it happened, even if Whiffletree hadn't hinted at it, Prine would have figured out that we were looking much more closely at anyone who hadn't been targeted. He'd have realized that his best chance to avoid detection was to make himself look like one of the targets. He'd do it— but he'd be mad as hell at having to do it, so maybe he vented his rage at the person he blamed for getting him into this situation—Whiffletree."

"It's possible." Cordelia didn't sound convinced.

I glanced up at the wall clock. Only half an hour of our lunch break left. I pushed back from the table and rubbed my eyes, which were tired from spending so much time peering at paper and screens.

"So, maybe Prine didn't commit any of the vandalism." I waved at the stack of e-mails. "Maybe he just enjoyed gloating over them to his friend Calvin."

"Fat chance," Cordelia said.

"Theory number two is that he committed some of it," I went on. "But was genuinely outraged to find out not only that friend Calvin had a second vandal working for him but also that the second vandal had targeted him."

"More plausible," Cordelia put in.

"But a little on the complicated side," the chief said.

"And finally, behind door number three," I continued. "We have the theory that Edward Prine was the one and only vandal, and smart enough to fake anger and outrage when reporting on the damage he did to his own studio."

"My money's on that theory," Cordelia said. "The more I learn about that man, the more sneaky, devious, and unpleasant I find him. I know it's a terrible thing to speak ill of the dead, but that's how I feel."

"Three excellent theories," the chief looked glum. "A pity we don't have a shred of evidence to prove any of them."

"Not yet," I said. "But we'll keep our eyes open."

"And keep your fingers crossed that some of those dozens of evidence bags Horace and Lesley hauled out of here bear fruit," the chief said. "Meanwhile, I've officially declared myself over my head and put in another request for help to the State Police."

"I suppose it's necessary," Cordelia said. "But what if they want to shut us down?"

"By rights I should be shutting you down myself. Two murders in as many nights."

Chapter 20

My stomach tightened at the chief's words. I wanted to pro-test, but I didn't think it would do any good. And if the chief shut the center down, I wouldn't have to agonize over whether it was crazy to stay here with Michael and the kids. We could all hurry back to Caerphilly, taking Cordelia with us.

Of course, if we did, it would probably be the end of Cordelia's craft center.

"I'd understand if you have to shut us down." Cordelia sounded calm—probably calmer than she felt. "I suspect it'll kill the center if you do, but maybe that's inevitable. And we don't want any more troubles."

" 'By rights,' " I echoed. "Does that mean maybe you're not going to?"

"Right now I've got all my witnesses and suspects here where I want them," the chief explained. "If I shut Biscuit Mountain down, they're going to scatter to the four corners of the earth."

"Well, not quite the four corners of the earth," I said. "I've been studying the student lists, remember? The majority of them are from here in Virginia, and almost all the rest from adjacent states."

"Still might as well be the four corners of the earth as far as my investigation is concerned." The chief sighed. "I don't have the time or the money to chase them down."

"But won't that change now that the State Police are getting involved?"

"Not really. They're stretched pretty thin themselves. So far, the only resources they've been able to send are one detective to help me with the investigation and two troopers to help patrol. Which reminds me—can we find some rooms for them up here at the center?"

"I'll see who I can rearrange." Cordelia stifled a small sigh and reached for the notebook that held her room and campsite charts.

"That's another reason not to make you close the center," the chief said. "If I did that and then told them all not to leave town, where would they all stay? Every bed-and-breakfast in town is filled as it is."

"So we stay open for now." Cordelia sounded more hopeful. "Provided we can find room for your three state police."

"You stay open with precautions, and it's not just the State Police. I'm borrowing a few officers from neighboring jurisdictions to help secure the center. Well, the building, at least. Nothing much we can do about your camping ground. So we'll have officers patrolling—maybe a dozen of them if I'm lucky."

A dozen officers—I liked the sound of that. Maybe staying wasn't crazy after all.

"Of course, it's not as if we can tell everyone to lock up their tents," the chief added.

"But we haven't had any vandalism or murder in the campgrounds," Cordelia pointed out. "It's all been in the center."

"That was my thinking."

"It would be a lot easier to get at someone in the campground," I said. "But it would also be almost impossible to make sure you weren't seen. Our campers are an observant bunch. One night last week Josh had an upset stomach and we had to take him to the bathroom three times. By the third run we had half the campground asking if he was okay and offering over-the-counter medicines and unsolicited advice. So if the killer thinks he can creep into a tent, off someone, and slink away unseen, then he probably hasn't spent much time in the campground."

"That was more or less how I saw it," the chief said. "Everyone is more exposed in the campground, including the killer, resulting in relative safety. And the news that we'll have law enforcement officers patrolling there should help."

"I hope your borrowed troops aren't trigger-happy." For that matter, I hoped the Riverton officers weren't either, but I didn't think the chief would appreciate my saying so. "You're going to warn them that not everyone creeping about in the middle of the night is a murderer, right? Because this place can be a hotbed of activity at night. Quite apart from midnight bathroom visits, you have Grandfather leading his nighttime nature walks and sneaking out to spread garbage to attract the gulls, the lovelorn herb student sneaking out to meet whomever she's meeting, perhaps other amorous couples seeking privacy—"

"And you checking on every suspicious noise." The chief seemed to be smiling.

"I'll try to restrain my snooping tendencies." Unless, of course, the suspicious noise was anywhere near the caravan, in which case I'd be all over it. "And let's remember to warn Dad. I think if he hadn't been so tired last night from all the nature walks, he might have been snooping around like Victor Winter, and we might be trying to solve his murder."

"I'll talk to him," Cordelia said.

"Good," I said. "Maybe he'll listen to you."

"Don't bet on it."

"I'll be frank with you," the chief said. "Maybe the biggest reason for keeping everyone here is the hope that the killer—or killers—will do something stupid to give himself away."

"Or herself," I added.

"Or herself," the chief agreed. "We're continuing to interview people and probe into everyone's background, but we're not finding much that helps us. Just about everyone who knew him loathed Prine, but that's not really much of a motive for murder. The other people involved in that craft store with him still resent his part in its failure, but it's an old grievance."

"Check on their financial status—I understand some of them could still be broke because of it. That's—"

"You told me. I'm checking on it."

"Good." Not just that she was checking on it, but that she didn't seem annoyed at my asking. "Because if any of them are having financial difficulty, they might still be pretty ticked at Prine, even after all these years. It's not an old grievance if it's still causing you grief."

"So how does poor Victor fit into all this?" Cordelia asked. "Because we seem to be focusing rather exclusively on Prine. Meg and I, at least—I'm sure you're investigating Victor's murder as well."

"Without much luck." The chief frowned and shook her head. "So far I've found no reason for anyone to want him dead. And no reason to believe he was in contact with Jazz Hands or Smith Enterprises or anyone else who might have it in for Biscuit Mountain. He's divorced, no kids, no apparent enemies. Does something bureaucratic at an insurance company. Takes classes and eco-tourism vacations in his free time."

"Mildly annoying but mostly harmless," I said.

"Exactly. So it's looking more and more as if he's collateral damage. He's a mystery reader, like your father. I suspect he was snooping."

"The wrong place at the wrong time." Cordelia shook her head sadly. "Poor man! It's not much of an epitaph, and I have a feeling it was the story of his life."

"Maybe," the chief said. "But I intend to keep on digging. Meanwhile, if it's okay with you, I'd like to have the State Police investigator speak to everyone after dinner. I assume that's the best time to get the whole crowd together."

"There might be a handful missing," Cordelia said. "Most of the people eat here, even if they're staying at a bed-and-breakfast in town, but a few take off right after class."

"Then they're not very likely to have been up here in the middle of the night committing or witnessing vandalism and murder. And I'm not just taking that for granted; I've checked with the owners of all the bed-and-breakfasts in town and your off-campus students seem to be reasonably well alibied." The chief glanced at her phone and stood up. "I should go. Some of my borrowed officers are arriving."

She strode out. Cordelia and I looked at each other.

"The woman who's having the affair," she asked. "Do you know her by sight?"

"Jenni something-or-other," I said. "No, but I'll get Rose Noire to point her out to us. She's in the herb class."

"Good. Let's plan to keep an eye on her when the chief's speaking. See who she's sitting with."

"And who she sneaks glances at." I nodded. "Good idea. It's probably going to be someone who was here last week as well as this."

"That should narrow it down." Cordelia nodded, and glanced at her desk, where she kept a student roster handy.

I suspected she'd be doing some preliminary research on candidates for Jenni's boyfriend.

"And now I've got to run to class." I stood up, leaving her with her roster.

It was a relief to bury myself in the increasingly familiar routine of class. My students weren't quite as focused as last week's class had been by this time in the week, but they were still here, and they were trying. If we didn't manage to get the murders out of our minds for the whole four-hour session, at least we managed it for long stretches of time. I'd settle for that.

Class ended, finally. My students put away their tools and projects and trooped off to dinner, chattering with something more like normal good cheer. I recognized the feeling in myself—relief that we'd gotten through the day without further incidents.

Which was ridiculous if you stopped to think about it, since none of the incidents had happened during the day— not even, as far as we could tell, the acts of vandalism. It was the nighttime ahead we had to worry about.

"Let's hope none of them do stop to think about it," I told myself. And they probably wouldn't—at least not now, with Marty's dinner and several hours of rest and relaxation ahead of them.

When I'd finished tidying up the studio, I sat down to check my phone for texts, voice mails, and e-mails. Nothing important came up except for an e-mail from Rob.

"My guys will be there first thing in the morning," he said. "I was going to send them up tonight, but it would be bedtime by the time they got there, and Granny Cordelia says there aren't any spare rooms, so we rounded up a camper. It's all loaded and they're excited about having a paid camping trip. I'm assuming even if you've solved the murder by the time they get there, you'll still need the shortwave and the security system for next time."

"Next time," I echoed. "Let's hope there is no next time. One set of murders at Biscuit Mountain is more than enough."

But yes, the need for having a way to communicate with the bus wouldn't go away, and maybe if Cordelia had taken Rob's suggestion and installed a security system before the center opened we wouldn't have had any murders to begin with.

"Water under the bridge," I muttered as I stuck my phone back in my pocket and walked over to check that all my windows were secure.

I ran into Amanda and Valerian in the hallway.

"Everything locked up tight," Amanda reported.

"She probably wants to see for herself," Valerian added.

"No, since it's your studio that will suffer if you weren't careful, I'll trust you."

"Could be useless if whoever's doing all this has stolen a key." Evidently Valerian was a bit of an Eeyore. He shook his head lugubriously as he ambled down the hall.

"I prefer to think positively," Amanda said over her shoulder, as she strode off in the same direction as Valerian. "With all these police around, who'd be crazy enough to vandalize anything?"

"Hope for the best, expect the worst." I went in the other direction to check on the rest of the studios.

When I'd finished my inspection and entered the great room, I spotted a bunch of people clustered around the message board. Last week the board had seen heavy traffic on Sunday and Monday, as people tried to figure out where everything was and how everything worked, but it was

Wednesday now. By Wednesday of last week the board had been pretty much ignored.

I worked my way close enough to see what the fuss was all about.

Smack in the middle of the board was a notice written in Cordelia's distinctive printing, so elegant it could almost be classified as calligraphy.

WEDNESDAY EVENING SCHEDULE
6:45 P.M. Children's movie: STAR WARS: A NEW HOPE
   THEATER
Babysitting provided.

8 P.M. Security briefing by Sgt. Abel Hampton of
   the Virginia State Police
Great room
All adult residents requested to attend.

10 P.M. Smudging ceremony
Assemble on the front porch
Wear good walking shoes.

"I call that a step in the right direction," one woman said to her companions—students from Peggy's jewelry-making class I suspected, since they were all heavily festooned with necklaces, bracelets, earrings, and anklets. The others tinkled and jingled as they nodded in agreement—though I couldn't tell whether they were approving the arrival of the State Police or Rose Noire finally going through with her oft-uttered threats to perform a cleansing at the center.

Possibly both.

"Meg! There you are!" I turned to see Cordelia approaching. With the odious Mrs. Venable in her wake. I braced myself. Cordelia gestured, and I followed them out onto the porch.

"So sorry, Mrs. Venable," Cordelia was saying. "I just need to get Meg to take care of something for me, and then I'm all yours. Meg, dear," she went on. "It's about your grandfather."

"What now?"

"Play along," she breathed almost inaudibly. And then, in a low voice that Mrs. Venable could still easily hear, she went on. "He's offering to give up his room to one of the visiting police officers."

"That was nice of him." Was she making this up, for some reason? I couldn't imagine Grandfather volunteering to give up his comfortable room. "But where's he planning to sleep?"

"In one of the bed-and-breakfasts. Specifically, in the bed-and-breakfast I've set up in my house. And quite apart from the fact that I prefer to have my instructors staying on site, I don't want that man to have free range of my house. He's up to something."

Actually, she was the one up to something. And I had an idea what.

"He probably thinks he can find the you-know-whats there," I said.

"At my house?"

"In the fields behind your house. Didn't you hear? They sent a little side expedition down there sometime today, and saw some promising signs."

"Blast the man." Her tone was stern, but her lips were twitching in the effort to fight a smile. Or maybe a giggle. "You need to talk him out of it. He can lurk in the gazebo if he likes, or catch pneumonia crouching in the woods, but I'm not letting him sleep there. I don't care how many rare critters he's looking for."

"Mrs. Mason?" Mrs. Venable stepped closer, with an unctuous smile. "Perhaps I could help."

Cordelia and I both managed expressions of polite surprise as we turned toward her.

"I understand you're looking for a few people to give up their rooms for the visiting police officers. If there really is a room available at your bed-and-breakfast, I'd be happy to make the sacrifice."

"I hate to ask something like that," Cordelia began.

"Nonsense," Mrs. Venable said. "Not a problem. It's so much more important to have the police and staff and instructors staying on site, and I have to admit that I've been a bit nervous about—well, you know. When can I make the move?"

"If you like, I can have a staff member pack your things while you're having dinner," Cordelia said. "And then Meg can drive you down at bedtime."

"Perfect!" she said. "I'll let you have my room key."

She handed it to Cordelia and sailed off, looking smug.

"I can't believe it," I said. "Surely before long she'll come to her senses and realize how unlikely it is that she'll find the seagulls down at your house."

"According to Caroline she's not really a very knowledgeable birder. And by the time she figures out there aren't any gulls down there, we'll have Sergeant Hampton installed in her former room, so she'll just have to like it or lump it."

"So am I also the staff member who gets to pack her up? Because the only other staff we have around at the moment are the kitchen guys, and they're pretty swamped."

"I'll pack her up." She tucked the key in her pocket. "It will give me a chance to snoop in her things."

"If she had anything incriminating in her room, she'd want to pack it herself," I pointed out.

"True," Cordelia said. "But that doesn't mean I can't learn anything of interest. You go have your dinner while I snoop. And don't tell your grandfather about all this."

"Why not?" I said. "He would appreciate your contribution to Operation Gull Quest. It might almost make up for not letting him strew his garbage around."

"I'm not doing this for him." She frowned as if resenting the accusation. "I'm doing it for the gulls. They deserve to be found by a responsible scientist, not some publicity-crazy loon."

She stormed off.

"But maybe just a little bit for him," I murmured.

I joined Michael's class for dinner. It helped my mood to sit in the midst of the happy chaos of two dozen children who'd spent the day having fun and were looking forward to yet another movie night, followed by s'mores and camping.

"I'm going to get the kids settled in for the movie," Michael told me in a low tone. "And then I'll leave Eric and the other counselors in charge so I can come back to hear what Sergeant Hampton has to say. And the chief's leaving a couple of her officers there at the theater, just in case."

"Good," I said. "And check the movie before you leave. Remember the lingerie, and the George Carlin routine? Make sure the vandal hasn't switched out *Star Wars* with *Deep Throat*."

"Will do."

When Michael and the counselors took off to escort the kids to the movie, I looked around to find Amanda. She was sitting at the end of a table with Rose Noire, Peggy, Gillian, and a posse of Rose Noire's herb class students. I slipped into an empty chair beside Amanda.

"So, have they converted you to vegetarianism?" I asked— but softly enough that the others wouldn't hear.

"Luckily they've been too busy discussing the smudging

ceremony." Amanda kept her tone low, too. "Much debate over whether they should just use sage or whether they should add other protective or creativity-boosting herbs to the mix, and figuring how long it's going to take to march around the house."

The smudging posse appeared to finish their discussions— they all rose and scattered in several directions—to gather ingredients, no doubt.

"I do hope no one's allergic to whatever they end up burning," I fretted. "And frankly, I used to love the smell of sage, but lately Rose Noire's been so enthusiastic about her smudgings every time something untoward happens that a mere whiff of it makes me start to expect dire tidings."

"You can borrow my tub and take a long, hot bath in some other kind of smell," Amanda offered. "I've been trading dishcloths and potholders to the herb students, and I think by now I've got a lifetime supply of nice smells."

"I wouldn't want to kick you out of your room."

"Oh, don't worry. I intend to be standing on the terrace with one of Dante's limoncellos, watching the smudgers march by."

"Watching them march by?"

"When they circumnavigate the house. Apparently you get the best results if you march all around the outside of the house. Sunwise, whatever that is."

"They mean clockwise, and they've got to be kidding," I said. "Marching along the front of the house, maybe, but the ground drops off pretty steeply along the left side, and a mountain goat would have trouble marching along the back of the house. One false step and they'll slide all the way down to Biscuit Creek."

"That's kind of what I figured," Amanda said. "Should be quite a show."

"I'll talk to Cordelia. And Chief Heedles. Surely we can come up with some way to confine the smudging to the terrace."

"Oh, you're no fun." Amanda cuffed me lightly on the shoulder. "Seriously, I'm not sure I believe in this smudging thing, but it seems to make a lot of them feel better. Gives them something positive to focus on. We don't want people panicking and deciding that maybe learning how to weave a dish towel or tell St. John's wort from poison ivy isn't worth risking their lives for."

"Or their children's lives, for those who brought them," I said. "So far I haven't heard that anyone's dashed up here to yank their kids out of Michael's class, which surprises the heck out of me. I mean, I'm wondering myself whether it's wise to keep the boys here, even though I know that we've got enough family here to make sure they're never left unguarded."

"Family and friends." She put her hand on my shoulder and gave it a reassuring squeeze. "Over my dead body will anyone hurt Josh and Jamie. Or any of the other kids."

"Thanks," I said. "That makes me feel better. Although I confess, I'm also eager to see the arrival of reinforcements for Chief Heedles. She's a good police chief, but it's a small town, and she doesn't have a lot of resources."

"Can't she call on the sheriff of whatever county we're in?"

"Not if she wants to keep her job in the long run," I said. "From what Cordelia's told me, there's no love lost between the town and the county. The county wants to take over and run things, and the town has always dug in their heels and refused. So turning to the county for help would be like admitting they can't handle their own business. Especially for a crime here on Biscuit Mountain—which, thanks to a bit of gerrymandering by Cordelia's family, is a long, skinny bit of town sticking way far out into the county. Kind of like an upraised middle finger if you look at a map of the town boundaries, and that's certainly how the county sees it."

"How long's that been going on?" Amanda asked.

"Since the Civil War. The town was pro-Union, the county pro-Confederacy, and there's some people still trying to fight that battle. So Chief Heedles will bring in the State Police, and even the FBI if she can get their attention, but I think she'd almost rather let the murderer walk than call in the county."

"Well, the State Police and the FBI are probably a lot more help than some hick sheriff's department anyway. And unless I miss my guess, here comes the cavalry now." Amanda pointed to the door, where Cordelia was standing next to a uniformed state trooper—presumably the promised Sergeant Abel Hampton. "Nice addition to the scenery if you ask me."

Chapter 21

Sergeant Hampton was tall, held himself ramrod straight, and sported the sort of serious high and tight haircut that made me wonder if he'd served in the Marines before becoming a state trooper. And from the way he was looking around at the denizens of Biscuit Mountain—not so much wild-eyed as wary and disbelieving—I suspected no one had told him much about the location of the crime scene he was coming to help out with.

I hoped he had a good sense of humor.

"I'm going to get that limoncello before he starts," Amanda said.

"Before you go—can you point out the herb class student who's supposedly sneaking out to meet someone at night?"

"Jenni Santo. Over there." Amanda pointed to a group of women who were making a second pass through the dessert line. "With the frizzy hair." I studied Jenni, who turned out to be a petite, slightly plump, thirtyish woman with loosely permed brown hair. Far from unattractive, but probably not someone Edward Prine would have been trying to talk into posing.

"Lives in a small town called Crozet," Amanda went on. "And does some kind of office work."

"Crozet?" I frowned at the name. "That's suspicious."

"How come?"

"It's near Charlottesville. Jazz Hands is in Charlottesville."

"We'll keep an eye on her, then. And on whoever she's sneaking out to meet, once we figure out who he is." She stood, picked up her tray, and carried it over to the service hatch.

I followed her example, though I wasn't going in search of Dante's limoncello. I wanted to make sure I got a good place in the great room—a place where I could watch everyone to see their reactions while Sergeant Hampton spoke.

In the great room, my nephew Eric had dragged out the podium we used for formal meetings and was fiddling with the microphone and speakers, while two young men I recognized as the kitchen staff were hurriedly setting up rows of folding chairs facing it. Marty was standing near the head of the room, arms folded, watching. Was he here early for the meeting? Or was he sulking because we'd dragged his staff away from their usual post-dinner cleanup to do the chairs?

As if to answer my question, he sat down in one of the armchairs along the side of the room and proceeded either to fall asleep sitting up or do a very good imitation of it. After all, I reminded myself, he was up before dawn every day, and while Cordelia would have no problem if he had gone off duty as soon as dinner was over, he seemed to prefer staying around until the kitchen was spotless and ready for the next morning's breakfast. Which would happen later than usual tonight, thanks to the meeting setup. From the location of the armchair he'd chosen, it looked as if he was not only planning to stay for the meeting but wanted to gauge the audience reaction—it was not far from the podium and would give a great view of the whole room.

I put my tote bag on another armchair, similarly situated on the other side of the room, and draped a napkin over the chair next to it, to save it for Michael. Then I pitched in to set up chairs. Others who came in followed suit, and in a few minutes we had all the chairs deployed so the kitchen staffers could head back to their dishwashing.

Marty opened his eyes and nodded with satisfaction when they left, then closed his eyes and appeared to go back to sleep. Anyone with any social graces would have thanked the volunteers, but Marty was Marty. I reminded myself of the excellence of his crème brûlée, and wondered if I had time to duck through the dessert line for a second helping.

Why not? People were only just milling into the great room. It would be a few minutes before they took their seats. I saw Eric dash out—heading to the theater to take over for Michael, no doubt. I made my way against the tide back into the dining room and scored not one but two more crèmes brûlées. Not greedy, I reminded myself as I settled myself back in my armchair. After all, Michael liked them, too.

In fact, when he arrived a few minutes later, also carrying two crèmes brûlées, we had very little difficulty dealing with what might at first have seemed like a daunting surplus.

"Attention, everyone." Cordelia was at the podium, calling the meeting to order. Chief Heedles and Sergeant Hampton were sitting in chairs flanking her. "Sergeant Hampton's had a long drive already, so let's get this shindig started and hear what he has to tell us. Sergeant."

"Thank you, Ms. Mason. I have to say, this is a lovely place you folks have up here, and I hope I have the chance to come back and enjoy it under less difficult circumstances."

He had a folksy, good-old-boy style and from his accent I pegged him as a native of someplace a little farther south in the Appalachians—Roanoke, maybe, or Blacksburg. But behind the smile and the affable style, I saw keen eyes studying us, and a sharp brain already sifting whatever bits of evidence his observations produced. I felt reassured. Nice to imagine that the killer or killers did not.

His talk was fairly generic. A reassurance that Chief Heedles was still in charge of the investigation, with him and his colleagues providing technical expertise and additional resources. Strong encouragement—he didn't quite make it an order—for people to go to bed early, stay in their rooms or tents, or if they must go anywhere, to do so in twos or threes.

All fairly predictable, and I got the feeling that the meeting was less about disseminating information than reassuring the public. And also, maybe, to give the sergeant a chance to take our measure as a group. The reassuring part was working. I found my anxiety about staying, and keeping the boys here, was easing considerably, knowing that the steely-eyed sergeant and his fellow officers would be on the case.

After encouraging people to call him or the State Police hotline if they had any information that might be relevant to the case and promising to post both numbers on the bulletin board by the door, he brought his talk to a close.

"Does anyone have any questions?" he asked.

A rustling noise filled the room and people craned their necks to see if anyone was going to stand up and ask a question, especially as the silence dragged on and we began to suspect, from the expression on his face, that Sergeant Hampton was starting to feel slightly disappointed with our lack of inquisitiveness. Then Rose Noire stood up and raised her hand.

"Yes, ma'am."

"Could you tell us what progress the Virginia State Police has made toward making sure that women and minorities are fully represented on the force?"

"Ma'am?" Sergeant Hampton blinked in surprise.

"Because I hope the Virginia State Police understands the

importance of a police force that represents the population it serves."

"Yes, ma'am." Sergeant Hampton made a fast recovery. "We surely do, and from what I can see we're making progress in that area, but while that's a very important issue I'm afraid it's not one I'm very knowledgeable about. I just know about major crimes. Solving them, that is."

"I'm sure Sergeant Hampton can contact his home office to get us some information to answer Rose Noire's question." Cordelia beamed sweetly at Rose Noire, who got the message and sat down. "Does anyone have a question for him about the murders?"

Primed by Rose Noire's question and herded back on topic by Cordelia, others raised their hands. Had Sergeant Hampton heard of any similar crimes in other parts of the state? Was it possible that one or both of the murders were actually suicides? Did the sergeant think that the murders could be the work of terrorists? Was he aware that the murders bore a remarkable resemblance to the plot of a 1977 episode of *Columbo*?

The sergeant answered them all with such tact and charm that it was obvious that either he had a natural gift for dealing with the public or they'd given him considerable training to that end. He didn't even seem to lose his patience when the last questioner kept trying to relate the entire plot of the *Columbo* episode, complete with dialogue.

I focused on studying the crowd, though I'd have been hard pressed to say what I was looking for. If the arrival of the State Police had shaken the murderer's confidence, he— or she—wasn't showing it. For that matter, you'd think at least a few of the crowd would find it alarming that Chief Heedles had felt obliged to call in the State Police—to say nothing of the fact that the State Police had actually shown up. But most of the crowd seemed as carefree and unconcerned as if this was just another part of the entertainment Cordelia had organized for their benefit.

Maybe we were doing a little too good a job of calming their fears.

I particularly noticed the Slacker, who'd found himself a place at the very back of the crowd, where he could keep an eye on everyone.

Or was he sitting at the back out of self-protection rather than nosiness? Maybe he wanted to keep his distance from Sergeant Hampton. Or from Mrs. Venable, who had scored a choice aisle seat in the second row and was studying the sergeant as if he might be an interesting new species to add to her life list.

I studied the Slacker for a while, but if the arrival of reinforcements for Chief Heedles caused him any anxiety, he hid it well. His placid, rather bovine face showed no sign of anxiety.

I also kept a close eye on Jenni Santo.

She was sitting with some of her fellow herb class students, all female. If she was exchanging stolen glances with anyone, she was hiding it well.

Or was she? Like most of us, she glanced around from time to time to see who was asking a question and how others were reacting to Sergeant Hampton's answers. But most of us craned around to see the whole room. She only ever looked right—never left.

Of course, there could be a simple explanation—maybe she just had a crick in her neck and it hurt to turn it to the left. Maybe she was slightly deaf in her left ear and didn't hear the questions from that side very well. But more likely she was was trying to be discreet, never realizing that not ever looking in the direction of her inamorato was almost as obvious as looking at him.

So who was standing to her left?

Not many people, since she was pretty close to the left-hand side of the room herself. Grandfather, Dad, Baptiste, and a couple of male photography students, who weren't exactly the most likely suspects, since during those evening hours when Jenni's romantic outings had taken place they were usually out on owling expeditions. A trio of women from my blacksmithing class—none of them quite tall enough to be mistaken for a man unless whoever had seen Jenni and her lover had pretty bad eyesight. Dante Marino, who held a bottle full of cloudy pale yellow liquid and occasionally filled a shot glass for one of the people standing around him—Amanda, Valerian, and several of Dante's woodworking students.

It suddenly occurred to me that figuring out who Jenni's lover was might require studying where the various suspects were bunking. She was staying in the main building and had been spotted sneaking out of it. If whoever was meeting up with her was also staying in the main building, wouldn't it have been easier to find a rendezvous spot indoors? Especially if you were a faculty member and had keys to a studio?

Unless, of course, you knew that I'd gotten into the habit of checking the studios at unpredictable times. Most of the faculty knew that and probably a growing number of students had figured it out.

Still, knowing where people were sleeping might give us a clue to who was meeting with Jenni. I made a mental note to talk to Cordelia and get a list of who was staying where.

And what if whoever Jenni had been meeting was also the vandal? Or Jenni herself? If I were committing a crime and knew I risked getting caught while slinking about the building pulling off my dirty tricks, maybe I'd find it useful to establish that I had a more innocent reason for being out and about in the wee small hours.

As the meeting approached the two-hour mark, Cordelia stepped forward and took the microphone.

"The kids' movie will be ending pretty soon," she said. "And they'll be arriving for their s'mores. Does anyone have any final questions for Sergeant Hampton?"

It had been a while since anyone had asked a sensible question anyway, so everyone fell silent, no doubt eager to move on to the final part of the evening's entertainment.

"Before we end this gathering," she went on. "I'd like to say that when I started the Biscuit Mountain Craft Center, this is not how I expected the summer to go. I thought I'd be introducing dance recitals, art shows, and children's plays, not briefings on murder investigations. I want to assure you that I and my staff will be doing everything possible to help Chief Heedles and her investigative team solve these crimes. And I want to ask all of you to do the same thing. If we work together, we can get back to having the peaceful, creative summer that I'm sure all of you were looking forward to."

Well, nearly all of us, I thought, as I joined in the applause that followed her remarks. But if one of our number was gloating over our current situation—or studying the enhanced police presence with apprehension—you couldn't tell from their faces. At least I couldn't, and Chief Heedles, who was standing beside Cordelia and Sergeant Hampton, didn't look like someone who was having an aha moment.

Then the kids came pouring in, and most of us turned our attention to the hot chocolate and s'mores. Rose Noire, most of her herb class, and a few other hardy souls were gathering on the front porch, drenching themselves with all-natural mosquito repellent and testing their flashlight batteries. I could also hear that they were squabbling over whether or not to sing as they marched. I hoped they opted for not, because a decision to sing was liable to open up a much more acrimonious debate over what to sing—Christian hymns? Buddhist chants? "Smoke Gets in Your Eyes"?

Eventually the smudging party set off, humming softly and tunefully, though not in unison. Evidently Rose Noire had short-circuited the musical debate by instructing them all to hum whatever fit their musical preferences and personal belief systems.

I sat with Michael and the boys on the terrace, sipping a glass of white wine, methodically toasting marshmallows for the family s'mores, and listening for the sound of humming to appear when the smudgers came around the back of the building. Eventually it did—but it was sounding a great deal more ragged than before, and accompanied by small shrieks and the occasional flurry of language not in keeping with the gentle, positive spirit Rose Noire was trying to create.

I delivered my latest perfectly toasted marshmallow to Josh and drifted over to the railing so I could peer down. I couldn't see much—just a few flashlight beams straggling along the steep hillside.

Suddenly a loud shriek pierced the ambient humming.

Chapter 22

I leaped to my feet and ran over to the far edge of the terrace, where several people seemed to be leaning over to watch something.

"Golly! There goes one!" someone exclaimed.

Yes, one of the flashlight beams had skittered rapidly downhill before landing quite some distance from the building. From what I could see, the unlucky smudger had skidded down the ravine in which first Marty and then Grandfather had been strewing their gull bait. I hoped the kitchen staff had succeeded in removing all traces of garbage, for the smudger's sake.

Things got a little chaotic for a while, as the smudgers tried to rescue their fallen comrade. A few of the men who had been lounging on the terrace, sipping Dante's limoncello, went down to help with the rescue. And once the rescue was complete, Rose Noire decided that while it would have been optimal to completely circle the building with their sage, it would do almost as well if they came in through the kitchen door and smudged their way up the stairs, across the length of the terrace, through the great room, and then out into the night through the door at the end of the studio wing. So we all hummed along when they arrived on the terrace, and waved them on their way when they'd finished.

"Not that I believe overmuch in all this herbal stuff,"

Amanda remarked to me. "But if it does work, this way they'll be waving their torches up and down the corridor where most of the bad stuff has been happening. Can't hurt."

About the time the humming died down, Cordelia came over to talk to me.

"Mrs. Venable's ready to go," she said. "Her suitcases are in the front hall."

"No more s'mores for me, then." I put down my roasting stick and pried myself out of the comfortable deck chair. I filled Michael in on where I was going, and then went to collect Mrs. Venable and her luggage. A good thing I had the Twinmobile, since she had four suitcases, three totes, two cardboard boxes, a giant-sized cooler, and a dozen garments on hangers.

The occasional "Be careful with that!" was her only contribution to the car-loading process.

As we set off, I realized that I should probably at least try to make polite small talk, and mentally scrambled for a topic. Then Mrs. Venable took care of the problem for me.

"I do hope your grandfather wasn't too upset that I took the room he wanted," she said, as we started down the drive.

Okay, this could be fun.

"If he says anything rude about it, just ignore him," I advised. "Though with any luck, by morning he'll be loudly pretending he never even thought of such a thing."

Mrs. Venable giggled with undisguised delight.

"And once you get settled at the bed-and-breakfast, if you see him skulking about the yard, please don't tell Cordelia," I went on. "For some reason that really irks her."

"Of course not." She shook her head vigorously.

I had to struggle to keep from giggling. Had I just assured that Mrs. Venable would stay up late scanning Cordelia's backyard for Grandfather?

"It must be difficult for you, having them not get along," she said. "How long have they been divorced?"

"They were never married," I said.

"Oh, my." She looked expectant.

"Long story," I said.

"And understandably not one the family wants to talk about," she murmured with transparently fake sympathy.

"Actually, we don't mind talking about it," I said. "But it's late and it really is a long story. But if you're curious, once we get to the bed-and-breakfast I can ask Cousin Mary Margaret to show you the feature story the local paper did last year. Cordelia has a copy in her scrapbook."

"I see." Her face had fallen at the realization that what she thought was hot gossip was already common knowledge.

She didn't pursue that line of interrogation, but she did spend the rest of ride trying to pry information out of me—about the police investigation, mostly. I was relieved when I spotted the black wrought iron fence surrounding Cordelia's house.

"So this is your grandmother's bed-and-breakfast," Mrs. Venable said, studying the enormous white frame house as we pulled into the driveway.

"Actually, her house," I said. "She's only using it as a bed-and-breakfast temporarily, to handle the overflow of people from the craft center. The plan is eventually to build more guest rooms up there." Assuming the craft center survived the vandalism, and the murders, and whatever other slings and arrows outrageous fortune was planning to throw at us over the course of the summer. But I wasn't going to say that to Mrs. Venable.

When she answered the door, Cousin Mary Margaret looked hassled. I'd have felt guilty, inflicting Mrs. Venable on her, if I hadn't known that hassled was Mary Margaret's usual mode. She was one of those people who reveled in being just a little overworked, which made her a natural—though willing—target when Mother went recruiting for someone to take on a thankless job. I hoped Cordelia had briefed her on the need to keep an eye on Mrs. Venable.

Yes, no doubt she had. I noticed a brief expression of satisfaction cross her face as she watched Mrs. Venable inspecting the foyer and the living room. They were worth inspecting—clean white walls and woodwork, light-colored oak furniture in Victorian or Arts and Crafts style, and everywhere examples of the brightly colored pottery that had made Biscuit Mountain famous back when it housed a pottery factory rather than a craft center. Cordelia and I had run out of time to execute our plan of decorating the center with some of her pottery collection. Given the vandalism, maybe that was a good thing.

But here at the house, everything was in perfect order, with not a scuff mark or dust mote in sight—as I'd have expected with Mary Margaret in charge. Which didn't stop Mrs. Venable from running a finger over the furniture here and there, and looking mildly disappointed when her finger came away clean.

"I'll show you where to take the luggage," Mary Margaret told me.

We left Mrs. Venable to her genteel snooping and began hauling her baggage to a large, comfortable room at the back of the second floor.

"Cordelia told me to put her in here," Mary Margaret said in an undertone as we set down our first load of suitcases. "She didn't want the nosy old thing in her own room, so I moved in there and gave her this one where I'd been sleeping. And besides, here she'll have a view of the backyard."

"That should keep her busy."

"Especially since we've arranged for a couple of teenagers from town to show up here around midnight and tromp around the back meadow with some flashlights. Why she'd think anyone would go looking for seagulls in the middle of the night with flashlights is beyond me, but Cordelia tells me she's not that bright."

"Not about birds, anyway," I said.

"And I'll keep you posted on what she gets up to."

I could tell that Mary Margaret was really enjoying her new role as Mrs. Venable's keeper and tormentor. Perhaps she'd been finding her role as chatelaine too easy.

I wished her and Mrs. Venable good night and drove back up the mountain. I arrived in time to gobble up the last of the s'mores—the boys had, as usual, fixed more than they could possibly eat—and join Michael, Eric, and the boys in our usual walk back to the caravan campsite.

As we walked, I found myself glancing over my shoulder. Instead of ambling along in our usual relaxed evening mood, we were both hurrying to keep the boys in sight, even though Eric was already watching them. And we hovered like mother hens until the three of them were safely locked away in the caravan.

Michael turned and headed toward our tent. I reached up and tested the caravan's doorknob.

Bad decision. Inside, Spike erupted into furious barking, and Eric unlocked and opened the door to peer out.

"Sorry," I said. "Just being overprotective."

"Don't worry. Last night I think I checked the lock at least five times before I could get to sleep. Tonight I'll probably be still checking it at dawn."

"Do you have your cell phone?" I asked. "If one of them needs to go to the bathroom in the middle of the night, you can wake Michael or me."

"I borrowed a bucket with a lid from Great-Gran. If one of them needs to go to the bathroom in the middle of the night, he can use that."

"Even better idea." I stood there with nothing else to say, but reluctant to leave. "Well, call us if you need anything. *Anything.*"

"Don't worry, Aunt Meg," Eric said. "We'll be fine; we've got a door to lock. You and Uncle Michael take care of yourselves out there in the tent."

I waited as he closed the door and locked it. Then I followed Michael to the tent.

The tent that Michael appeared to be taking down.

"Where were you planning for us to sleep tonight?" I asked. "Because the guest rooms in the center are all full, you know."

"We can sleep in the tent. I just want to move it a little closer to the caravan. And reorient it so we can see the door of the caravan through the front tent flaps."

"I like the way you think."

"Then grab that end of the frame and help me move it."

It took a while to get the tent moved and pegged down again, mainly because there wasn't really a suitable space for it any closer to the caravan than we already were. We finally found a space that would just barely do, though we had to tear out a few small bushes to make room, and we'd be sleeping on some fairly uneven ground that sloped a little more steeply than was comfortable. Eric opened the door again to peer out, nodded when he saw what we were doing, and locked up again.

"Let's call it quits," I said finally. "It won't exactly be the most restful campsite we've ever had, but I think this is as good as we're going to get it by flashlight."

"Yeah." Michael sounded beat. "We'll do some more improvements in the morning."

We inflated the air mattress. We tried the sleeping bag in several positions and decided that feet downhill was marginally less uncomfortable than feet uphill. Then we settled into silence—but not into sleep. I lay as quietly as I could, trying not to toss and turn—not just to avoid waking Michael, but also because every time I moved the sleeping bag seemed to slip a little farther down the air mattress, and my toes were already hanging over the edge.

"It's not that I feel insecure sleeping in a tent," Michael murmured finally. "We can defend ourselves. But it's a little unnerving to think that there's a murderer running around loose when so many more vulnerable potential victims don't even have doors they can lock."

"So far all the problems have been in the center," I pointed out.

"So far. But if the vandal—or worse, the killer—decides to branch out, it'll kill Biscuit Mountain."

He paused, and I suspected he was thinking the same thing I was—that maybe the killer had already dealt Biscuit Mountain a death blow.

"There's just no way we can possibly secure this place," he went on.

"We shouldn't have to secure it." I sighed. "It's supposed to be an open, welcoming place where people can mingle freely to share artistic ideas and encourage each other's creativity. Not an armed fortress."

"Much less a reenactment of *And Then There Were None.* Did you know a few of the students are making bets on who's next?"

"That's horrible!"

"Yes."

We fell silent for a few moments.

"So who does the smart money think is next?"

"I didn't ask."

I decided maybe I'd rather not know anyway.

"From what I overheard, I gather there wasn't a clear consensus," Michael went on. "After all, there was no one nearly as disliked as Prine. Victor the Klutz was a very distant second. I'm not sure who else even comes close."

"Makes sense."

"Your grandfather and Marty, the cook, were mentioned as kind of annoying," he said. "But the general consensus on both was that their usefulness far outweighed their nuisance value, so if the killer was operating with some kind of deranged Darwinian plan, they'd be pretty far down the list."

"That's a relief," I said. "But if— What's that?"

Chapter 23

I'd heard a faint sound coming from the direction of the main building.

"Door, I think," Michael whispered.

Yes, it could have been the sound of a door being stealthily opened and closed. We both lay straining to hear.

A faint clinking noise.

"The gravel path," I breathed.

Followed by rustling.

"Someone slipping through the shrubbery."

In near-perfect unison we put on our shoes, grabbed—but did not turn on—our flashlights, and slipped out of the tent.

We turned to the left—heading away from the caravan, and from the campground beyond. We could hear faint noises ahead as the intruder encountered more bushes. Although *intruder* might not be the right word—we'd heard someone leaving, not trying to break in. Extruder? Fugitive? Well, with luck we'd have an actual name before too long. Whoever it was appeared to have exited the building through the door at the far end of the lower floor of the studio wing, and was headed through the rose garden to the woods beyond, probably planning to intercept the road at a spot that was below—and out of sight from—the campground. If I'd wanted to escape the building unseen that was the route I'd take. The theater wing and the whole rear side of the building looked out on the steep slopes on which the smudgers had come to grief, and the front was clearly visible from the campground.

We were slinking through the rose garden when we heard a voice, low but clear, behind us.

"Whoever you are, stand up straight and show me your hands."

Michael froze and held up his hands. I shot my hands up, but I also whirled around to see who was giving the orders. A flashlight beam suddenly appeared, blinding me.

"Meg? And Michael?"

I recognized that voice.

"Vern?" I said. "Is that you?"

"In the flesh." The flashlight went off again, though it had been on long enough to cloud my night vision. But I could hear footsteps approaching.

"Vern Shiffley?" Michael asked. "What are you doing here in Riverton?" Vern was a deputy in Caerphilly.

"Chief Burke sent a couple of us down to help out. Sounds as if y'all've been having quite a time up here."

"We heard someone sneaking out of the building—going thataway." I pointed. "Toward the woods and the road," I added, since Vern might not see my finger.

"I'll check it out." Vern was suddenly all business.

"I think I know where he's going," I said. "I'll show you the way."

"I'll lead." Vern was already on his way. "You tell me if you think I'm off track."

I remembered that Vern was an expert hunter and tracker, so I fell in behind him and concentrated on not sounding like a herd of elephants galumphing through the rosebushes—which got easier as my eyes readjusted to the dappled moonlight. I could actually see Vern. And odds were he'd scouted the terrain before going on patrol. He seemed pretty sure of where he was going, and he was heading just the way I would have, following a faint path that led toward the woods.

We stealthily crossed the rose garden and entered the woods. A few moments later, Vern stopped and held up his hand.

I inched forward so I could peer over his shoulder. A faint rustling to my left indicated that Michael was doing the same on the other side.

There wasn't much to see. We were at the edge of what Cordelia called the Storytelling Glade—a clearing set up with a circle of benches around a fire pit. We could see a large shape on one of the benches. Then the moon came out from behind some wisps of cloud, and I could see that the shape was actually two shapes, intertwined.

Suddenly Vern's flashlight beam shot through the night and lit up the shapes. They broke apart, turned their heads toward the light, and froze.

"Stand up and show me your hands," Vern commanded.

The two stood up and sprang apart. Jenni Santo, of course. But the identity of the man surprised me.

"Isn't that what's-his-name?" Michael breathed in my ear. "Valentine? The leather guy?"

"Valerian," I murmured back. "Yes. It's always the quiet ones you have to watch, isn't it?"

"I ain't gonna ask what you two are doing out here." Vern was exaggerating his usual drawl, and probably fighting back laughter. "I think we pretty much got it figured out."

Michael erupted in a small coughing fit.

"And frankly, the whole campground's probably figured it out by now," Vern went on. "So you might want to find a less isolated place to carry on in. 'Cause if I can find you, the killer sure as heck can."

Jenni and Valerian looked at each other.

"The nerve!" Jenni snapped. She drew herself up to her full height—only about five four, but she made the most of it—and strode out of the clearing. She missed making the perfect dignified exit by stumbling over a root about the time she left the circle of light from Vern's flashlight, and from the rustling noises I could hear disappearing into the distance, she wasn't having much luck sticking to the path.

Valerian just shrugged sheepishly and shambled off. Though he didn't make nearly as much noise as Jenni. We could tell, because as soon as he left the clearing, Vern turned off his flashlight, and the three of us stood there, listening as we let our eyes adjust to the darkness again.

"You're not going to interrogate them?" Michael asked softly, when he was reasonably sure Jenni and Valerian were out of earshot. "Find out whether they alibi each other for the times of the murders, or saw anything while they were sneaking around?"

"I'll leave that to Chief Heedles," Vern said. "She wouldn't thank me for butting into her case like that. My job's to make sure we don't have a third body come morning."

"You didn't even take their names," Michael persisted.

" 'Cause I knew Meg could tell me who they were."

"Jenni Santo, student in Rose Noire's herb class, and Valerian Eads, who teaches the leatherworking class."

"You see?" Vern said. "I bet you also know if both of them are unattached."

"They're neither of them unattached." I probably sounded pretty disapproving. Well, I was. "I have it on reasonable authority that Jenni's married, and I've met Valerian's wife."

"That could account for the sneaking around." Vern nodded as if I was confirming his suspicions.

"Then again," I said. "If I were planning to vandalize the craft center or kill people, maybe it would be useful to start an affair so I'd have a cover story in case I'm caught sneaking around in the middle of the night. People would be so busy gossiping about the affair that they wouldn't suspect them of anything else."

"Except for people like you, with suspicious minds," Michael said.

"She has a point, though," Vern said. "And even if they alibi each other for a big chunk of time, they're on their own when they're sneaking out and then again on the way back. None of the crimes I heard about would have taken all that long to commit."

"When you put it that way, I guess finding them out here together makes them more suspicious, not less," Michael said. "But it doesn't prove anything, does it?"

"No, but I expect Chief Heedles will be taking an interest in them tomorrow. Gives her a reason to have a closer look at both of them."

"Not just a reason, but probable cause, I expect."

Vern just chuckled.

"You want me to see you two safely back to your tent?"

"We can manage," Michael said.

We picked our way through the rose garden and back to our tent. I went on past the tent, climbed the caravan's two back steps, and tried the door. Still locked.

Inside, I heard a low, fierce growl.

"Good dog, Spike," I whispered.

The growl subsided and I went back to the tent.

"Everything okay at the caravan?" Michael asked.

"Fine," I said. "Normally Spike's bloodthirsty nature gives me pause, but I think I'm going to sleep better tonight, knowing that in the unlikely event anyone gets past Vern Shiffley and us and the locked door, they'll have the Small Evil One to contend with."

"Good," Michael muttered. I shut up, because I could tell he was already half asleep. Nice if at least one of us got a good night's sleep. He'd probably had an even more stressful day than me, trying to keep the boys in sight every minute. I'm sure he was relieved to know they were safe behind the locked door of the caravan.

I positioned myself so I could see that door and settled down for what I hoped would not be a completely sleepless night.

Chapter 24

Thursday

This waking up at dawn was getting old very fast. I lay quiet for a few moments, listening, but all I could hear were birds. Immense numbers of birds, chirping away with such annoying enthusiasm that I despaired of getting back to sleep. I wasn't sure which were the most annoying—the ones like the blue jays that just squawked, or the ones that seemed to be saying something over and over, like "Doom-doom-doom," or "Get-it-right! Get-it-right!" If Grandfather were here, he could have identified every single bird by its distinctive call, of course, and would feel obliged to describe their diet, range, and mating habits. There was a reason I always declined his invitations to early morning birdwatching expeditions.

"Doom-doom-doom" and "Get-it-right" seemed to have settled in right over the top of our tent. Fat chance getting back to sleep. So I got up, checked to make sure the caravan door was locked tight and, after hearing the reassuring sound of Spike's growl, grabbed some clean clothes and my toilet kit and headed for the main house.

No one stirring in the campground. When I entered the great room, a uniformed State Police officer appeared.

"Quiet night?" I asked.

"Yes, ma'am."

He must have decided that I didn't look suspicious, since

he nodded, touched his finger to the brim of his hat, and headed into the studio wing with a gait that looked relaxed but covered a lot of ground pretty quickly. I waited a few moments—it was about this time of day that I'd discovered the two bodies. If there was anything to discover this morning, I was perfectly content to let him do it. I heard his footsteps proceeding down the hallway, stopping every few steps—checking studios. As the minutes ticked by, I felt myself relaxing, little by little.

I decided my own inspection could wait, so I headed for the stairs that led to the staff and faculty shower rooms on the floor below.

I emerged feeling—well, rested would be an exaggeration. Less disheveled and frazzled. A few other early birds had appeared, including Cordelia. I waved, and headed for the studio wing. Not that I didn't believe everything was okay. The state trooper would have sounded the alarm if there were any problems. I just wanted to see it with my own eyes.

No problems in the studios. The theater wing was also unencumbered with bodies or signs that the vandal had returned to work. I began to feel downright cheerful.

Of course, we couldn't expect both the Riverton Police and the State Police to stay around and baby us indefinitely. Sooner or later they had to catch the bad guy or guys, so life at Biscuit Mountain could go back to normal. Or if they didn't catch the bad guys, we'd have to adjust to an uncomfortable new normal.

But at least for the time being, we were safe. The adrenaline-fueled state of alertness and anxiety that had kicked in the moment I opened my eyes began to ease a little.

Which wasn't necessarily a good thing. It was the adrenaline that had been keeping me awake and vertical.

I sat down in one of the most comfy chairs in the great room, leaned back, and closed my eyes. Not that I expected to get any sleep here—soon the great room and the dining room beyond would be swarming with people. Even if I did manage to drop off, someone would notice and wake me in time for breakfast and my class.

But it wouldn't hurt to close my eyes. Just for a minute. . . .

"Meg?"

I was arguing with Grandfather again.

"No," I was saying. "I don't think it's a good idea at all to film a remake of *The Birds* here at Biscuit Mountain."

"But it's the only way we're going to catch the Ord's gulls," Grandfather was saying. "They're too shy to come on their own, but if all the other birds show up for the filming, there's a good chance they will, too."

"Meg!"

I wished whoever was calling me would be quiet, just long enough to let me talk Grandfather out of his movie idea. All I needed was—

"Meg!"

"Just a minute," I said. Mumbled, actually. I opened my eyes, and instead of Grandfather and the circling flocks of starlings, sparrows, swallows, chickadees, cardinals, blue jays, titmice, and maybe even gulls, I saw Cordelia.

"Were you having a nightmare?"

"Yes," I said. "About Grandfather."

"That's understandable." She looked angry. No, make that upset.

"What's wrong?" I asked.

She glanced around. There were a couple of people sitting or standing on the terrace, sipping coffee and enjoying the sunrise. Not nearly as many as usual, though.

"I need to show you something."

I heaved myself out of the recliner and trailed behind her, back into the building.

"What's wrong?" I asked as soon as we were out of earshot of anyone.

"You have to see it."

So I followed her to her office. She unlocked the door, marched in, and then stepped aside and gestured at her desk.

"That was on my desk when I came in this morning." She pointed to a sheet of paper covered with brightly colored splotches.

"One of Josh's paintings." I smiled at the sight. Jamie's paintings were more precise and detailed, but Josh had a more dramatic flair for color. The combination of a red wagon against green grass with a yellow sun, orange flowers, and a bug-eyed purple monster throwing a blue frisbee to a boy wearing a red Caerphilly Eagles t-shirt—definitely Josh.

"Check the other side. Here." She handed me a couple of tissues. "Use these to pick it up. My fingerprints are already on it, and I suspect whoever left it was careful to wear gloves, but just in case."

I took the tissues and used them to pick up the painting. I turned it over and saw words, evidently cut out of a magazine or newspaper and pasted onto the paper: CUTE KIDS. I'D HATE FOR SOMETHING TO HAPPEN TO THEM.

My stomach clenched with anxiety. And then the anger kicked in.

"They've crossed a line," Cordelia said. "Pranks and minor vandalism's one thing—threatening children is quite another."

"I'd have said they crossed the line with the first murder." I was trying to keep my hand from shaking as I studied the note. "And left it way behind with the second. But yeah. Threatening children. We need to show this to the chief." I put the paper back down on the desk, art side up.

"Already put in a call." We exchanged a look. I wondered if my face looked as stern and grim as hers.

There was a tap on the door.

"Cordelia?" The chief.

"Come in," Cordelia and I said in unison.

The chief studied Josh's painting for a few moments. She looked up at us, slightly puzzled. And maybe also slightly annoyed—after all, she was still in the midst of two murder investigations, and probably still a little edgy about the possibility that a third murder might turn up after all.

"Does this have something to do with the murders?" she asked.

"Turn it over," Cordelia said.

The chief reached into her pocket, pulled out a set of plastic gloves, and put them on before doing so. Her face hardened into a stern expression as she scanned the paper.

"You already touched it, I expect."

"Unfortunately," Cordelia said. "When I came in, I just thought Josh had brought it to me as a present. And then I turned it over and saw the threat."

The chief nodded, a little absently, her eyes fixed on the paper. The note seemed to anger her—even more than the murders. I suddenly realized that I knew nothing about the chief's private life. Was that sudden extra fierceness there because she could imagine how she'd react to a threat pasted to the back of one of her own children's paintings— if she had children? Or did most police officers feel just a little more angry when the bad guys targeted children?

She pulled out her phone and tapped on it.

"Horace?" she said. "More evidence. Mrs. Mason's office."

Either Horace uttered his usual "on my way" very quickly or she didn't wait to hear it. She hung up, stuck the phone back in her pocket, and turned back to Cordelia.

As she took Cordelia through the predictable questions—when was the last time she had been in her office? Was it locked? Who had keys?—I took deep breaths to calm myself.

I was angry—so angry I was glad I didn't know who had left the note, because if I had known, I'd want to hunt them down and hurt them. And from the look on Cordelia's face, I was pretty sure she felt the same way.

And I was scared. They weren't just threatening Cordelia—they'd involved Josh and Jamie.

But to my surprise, my voice was steady as I answered Chief Heedles's questions.

"As far as I know, as of last night that painting was hanging on the clothesline in the children's activity room. Michael and Eric might know for sure."

"I'll ask them," she said. "And I'll have Horace check this out. You realize, though, that he might not find any evidence to help us determine who left this."

"I realize that," I said. "And also that you can't yet tell whether or not this has anything to do with the murders."

"Correct," Chief Heedles said. "Although I'm not a big fan of coincidences. Riverton's a small town. We don't get a lot of vandalism, and we just used up this decade's quota of murders in two nights. I'd be pretty surprised if all these crimes didn't have something in common."

She looked a little grim. Stressed.

"You'll figure it out." Cordelia patted the chief's shoulder encouragingly. "But in the meantime, we need to protect the boys."

Chapter 25

Yes. Protecting the boys was the priority.

"You could send them home," the chief suggested.

"If we sent them home they wouldn't have Michael and me to protect them," I said. "Not to mention Cordelia, and Grandfather and Horace and Rose Noire and Caroline. If we sent them away, we'd need to go with them, and I'm not doing that to Cordelia. We'll find a way to protect them here. I like our odds better here anyway."

"I'll call Stanley." Cordelia had already taken out her phone. "I'm not sure whether personal protection is one of his talents as a private investigator, but if it isn't, he'll know who to call."

"I'm calling Mother." I had my phone out as well.

The chief looked mildly puzzled. She'd met Mother, and probably didn't consider her a particularly useful asset to our mission of protecting the boys. Cordelia, who knew Mother well by now and saw eye to eye with her, nodded in approval.

Just then Horace arrived.

"I'll leave you to it, then." The chief handed the note to Horace, and the two of them went across the hall to the chief's temporary office.

Cordelia and I focused on our phones.

"Meg, dear," Mother said. "You haven't had another murder have you? I know your father would be excited by it, but really, this is getting out of hand."

"No new murders."

"Then is everything all right?"

"No, it's not all right—not by a long shot. We need your help to fix it. The boys need bodyguards. Who do we know who can do it?"

I explained as succinctly as possible our sudden need for bodyguards. As I expected, Mother didn't waste much time panicking. A badly decorated room could send her to bed with a cold cloth over her forehead, but a threat to her grandsons brought out the warrior in her. After a brief discussion of the available talent, we came up with a list. Our top prospects were Cousin Lydia's son Jason, the Navy SEAL—nearly recovered from being wounded while doing something he wasn't allowed to talk about, but not yet back on active duty—and Cousin Lance, a career Marine who upon his retirement four years ago had opened up a combination gym and mixed martial arts studio.

"I'll start with them and work my way down the list," Mother said. "I'll call you back shortly."

I thanked her and hung up just as Cordelia was ending her conversation.

"Stanley's on his way," Cordelia reported. "Meg—if you want to take the boys away, you should do it. The craft center's not worth anyone dying for—especially not them."

"If we have to, we will." I wondered if she guessed how close I'd been to doing so, at least for a few moments. "But I think maybe we're safer here—with proper precautions. After all, up here on the mountain, we have only a few dozen people to keep our eyes on. Caerphilly's a teeming metropolis by comparison. Someone who's not supposed to be here will stick out a mile away."

"Of course, whoever did this probably is supposed to be here," Cordelia said. "Staff, faculty, or student."

"Yes," I said. "But that's still fewer people than we'd have to watch at home. And with this note on top of the murders, the chief has all the grounds she needs for combing through the background of everyone who's here." And if she didn't we still had Kevin's cyber skills. "If they have some kind of connection with Jazz Hands or with Smith the developer, or anyone else with a reason to want to hurt Biscuit Mountain, she'll find it. And besides—I haven't seen anyone here who could take on Lance or Jason. Much less Lance *and* Jason."

"You have a useful sort of family."

"On both sides." We exchanged a smile. "And now I have to grab a quick breakfast and get ready to teach my class. I'll keep you posted."

Before heading back to class, I let myself into one of the storage rooms so I could call Michael to fill him in.

There was a short silence on the other end of the phone when I'd finished rattling off my hurried explanation.

"Michael? Are you there?"

"Hell and damnation," he said. "Sorry—I had to move to someplace where the kids couldn't hear me, because nothing I can think of to say about this is fit for their ears."

"Should we take them home?"

"And abandon your grandmother? No. We can keep them safe. I like your idea of bodyguards. And I have an idea of my own. When Lance and Jason or whoever your mother recruits gets here—let's take the boys camping."

"We kind of already are," I said. "Or hadn't you noticed that's a tent we're sleeping in?"

"Camping as in someplace away from the center. We pack up some tents and after dinner tonight your father and I can take the boys and the bodyguards up into the mountains— someplace where no one will find us. Everything bad that's happened so far has been right here in the center, and in the middle of the night. So during that dangerous time, we'll be far away from whoever's doing this. And then we'll come back down in time for classes tomorrow."

I thought about it. The boys would probably like it. We might even be able to sell it as a special treat rather than scaring them with why we were really doing it.

"Okay." I felt a little lighter as soon as I'd agreed. "I can't say I'm looking forward to camping under even more strenuous conditions—"

"Which is why you get to stay behind and sleep indoors for a change. If your dad wants to come along, you can have his room. Always possible he might like to stay here and keep an eye on the murder investigation, in which case you can bunk with Rose Noire or Amanda."

"I'm not a wimp about camping," I reminded him.

"But you are the best one to stay here and keep an eye on everyone. To notice if anyone seems overly curious about our whereabouts, or disappears for a long time and comes back covered with cockleburs and mud."

"Okay. Provided Jason and Lance, or whoever Mother rounds up, agrees with your strategy, I'm in."

I texted Mother the bare bones of Michael's scheme, and she texted back "Ted can do that."

Ted? We were talking Lance and Jason. I knew of several Teds in the family, but none of them were prime bodyguard material. The fiercest of them was an IRS auditor, and while I hoped never to meet him in his professional capacity, I didn't think his fiscal expertise would do much to discourage whoever had threatened the boys.

"Ted who?" I texted back.

"We not Ted."

AutoCorrect strikes again. Over the course of the afternoon, she texted me occasional misspelled or completely incomprehensible progress reports. I itched to simply dial her number and talk to her, but that would have been rude to do in the middle of class. Even ruder than looking at my phone every time it dinged.

Luckily by halfway through the morning session, I'd deciphered enough of her texts to know that, yes, Jason and Lance were on their way.

And just as classes were breaking up for lunch, they arrived in a Land Rover only slightly smaller than a semi, the sort of vehicle that could easily climb any mountain they were apt to encounter in the Blue Ridge, or maybe even just snarl and smash through mountains if it grew impatient with climbing them.

Just the sight of them made my anxiety lift a little as I stood at one of the windows in the great room watching their arrival.

Lance, who was driving, brought the Land Rover to a stop right in front of the front porch. Jason hopped out of the rear passenger-side seat and hurried over to open the door for their third passenger—Mother.

Lance raced around to the passenger side to supervise as Jason helped Mother down from the high seat, treating her as if she were made of spun glass. Well, she was getting on, though you'd never guess it from her slender figure, perfect posture, and improbably blond hair.

"Somebody taught those boys manners." Amanda had come up behind me and was peering over my shoulder. "Isn't that your mother?"

"Yes." Had I somehow missed Mother's announcement that she'd be joining us? "Come up to see how we're getting along."

"And to make sure your dad isn't bothering Chief Heedles too much, I expect."

"That too."

Lance had offered Mother his arm and was escorting her up the steps to the porch, leaving Jason to carry her luggage. From a distance, you'd have thought them brothers instead of cousins twenty years apart in age.

"Guess your mother's planning to stay for a while."

"Not necessarily." I had pulled out my cell phone and was texting Cordelia to alert her to Mother's arrival. "She's only brought three suitcases."

"Only?"

Mother was making her entrance, and I hurried over to greet her.

"Meg, dear." She almost landed a kiss on my left cheek. "So nice of your grandmother to invite me. I've missed you all."

"And we've missed you."

Just then Cordelia sailed in, so I decided to leave her to get Mother settled. I went in search of Michael and the boys.

Although they were pleased to see their grandmother, it was love at first sight when the boys spotted the Land Rover. And when Lance and Jason emerged from the main building, resplendent in various bits of military clothing and gear, I stopped worrying that the boys would balk at our plans.

Evidently Mother had rehearsed Lance and Jason on the way up to Riverton. The cover story was that Mother had re-cruited Lance to bring her up to Biscuit Mountain to visit us, and he and Jason had decided to go camping while they were here.

"Hey—if you're not afraid of roughing it, maybe you guys could come along?" Lance made his offer sound remarkably spontaneous. Michael wasn't the only actor in the family.

"What a great idea!" Michael exclaimed. He turned to the boys. "Guys—you want to go camping with the cousins?"

"Cool!" Josh exclaimed.

"Awesome!" was Jamie's verdict.

"I think we can fit you all in the Land Rover." Clearly Lance had noticed the boys' fascination with the humongous vehicle.

Over lunch, the expedition evolved beyond what we'd originally planned. Not only was Dad determined to go along, but Grandfather insisted on joining in. Eric pointed out that as the boys' official babysitter, his place was by their side. Several non-family members showed an inconvenient interest in coming along—inconvenient and maybe even suspicious. I made sure the chief knew about them. But Michael easily vetoed their joining the camping trip by explaining that it was a sort of family tradition.

I made a quick call to Stanley Denton, the PI, to warn him that he'd be passing as Cousin Stanley for the duration.

The one non-family member we made an exception for was Baptiste, who had a great deal to say when he found out Grandfather was coming—most of it in rapid-fire French, so I only caught the occasional word like *imbécile* and *bêtise*. Given Baptiste's long experience in looking after Grandfather, we didn't think anyone would find it odd that we brought him along.

"And if we find my gulls, he needs to be there," Grandfather muttered.

"Gulls?" Jason repeated.

A tactical mistake. Grandfather had a new audience for his latest obsession. For the rest of the meal he regaled Jason and Lance with what little we knew about the Ord's gulls.

"Is this just a cover story?" Jason asked in a low voice as we were dropping our trays and dishes off at the service hatch. "Or does he seriously expect us to split our focus between protecting the boys and chasing after a bunch of missing birds?"

"He's serious, but don't worry," I said. "Once you get him out into the wilderness, Michael and Baptiste will talk some sense into him. Or if they don't, you have my permission to ignore him. The boys come first."

"Absolutely." Jason ambled off for an afternoon of playing watchdog over a flock of six- to nine-year-olds.

Chapter 26

Shortly on the heels of Jason and Lance, three employees from Mutant Wizards, Rob's company, arrived in an RV packed chock-full of electronic equipment. I immediately set them to work installing the shortwave radios in the bus and in Cordelia's office. To my relief, recent events had completely overcome Cordelia's previous objections to installing a security system, and before the shortwave installation was complete she began dragging the techs around the building, pointing out the entrances and exits and trouble spots.

After trailing along behind them for a few minutes, I decided I could stop worrying—luckily, since it was getting close to the time when I should start my afternoon class. So when Cordelia and the techs left the terrace, I stayed behind, perching on the railing and letting the view soothe my jangled nerves. And doing a little more of Rose Noire's deep breathing. Somehow it seemed a lot more useful out here in the mountains, with the fresh air and the smell of pine and spruce.

I was slightly annoyed when my phone rang, interrupting my efforts to regain serenity. I glanced down to see who was calling. Cousin Mary Margaret. I hurried to answer.

"Anything wrong?" I asked.

"Not a thing." She sounded cheerful, so I relaxed. "Just wanted to let y'all know what's up with Mrs. Venable, in case you were worried that she hadn't shown up for her class this morning."

"Actually, we hadn't noticed," I said. "I trust she's making good use of her time."

"Been prowling all over the woods behind your grand-mother's house," Mary Margaret said. "In addition to stomp-ing around at midnight with their flashlights, I had the kids we hired drop a clue back in the woods."

"What kind of clue?"

"An old pith helmet your grandfather left behind when he was here last summer. Soon as she found that, she was off into the woods like a hound who's caught the scent of a rabbit."

"Good job," I said.

"Of course, she could be in for a nasty surprise later today," Mary Margaret went on. "I had them leave the pith helmet in the middle of a big stand of poison ivy. I'll keep you posted."

Mary Margaret's call left me feeling more cheerful. I went back to my breathing in a more cheerful mood.

My phone rang again. I glanced at the caller ID—my nephew Kevin. Okay, maybe another useful, rather than an-noying, call. I answered the phone, heading for a quieter part of the terrace as I did so.

"What's up?" I asked.

"I'm still working on those million-and-a-half names you gave me. The students and the faculty and the staff and the Jazz Hands people and the Dock Street people. And remem-ber Smith Enterprises, that developer that's been annoying Great-Gran? Him too. Looking for connections."

"If you're angling for more brownie points, you're going about it the right way. I know I gave you a completely unrea-sonable number of names. Have you found anything else

interesting about any of them?" Sensing—or at least hoping—
that the answer would be a long one, I made myself comfortable in one of the Adirondack chairs at the far end of the
terrace.

"Well, I'm not sure if it's useful, but I found it pretty interesting that the guy who owns Smith Enterprises isn't really
named Smith."

"He's not?"

"No. His real name's Rahn. Charles Rahn."

"Then why is his company called Smith Enterprises? You'd
think he'd want to use his own name—it's much more distinctive. Did he buy it from the original owner?"

"No, he is the original owner, and he didn't want distinctive. Not all that many Rahns out there, so if you Google it
you're probably going to find him. But using Smith makes it
a lot harder to figure out what he's really up to, because it's
so hard to separate his outfit from the dozens of other Smith
businesses, nearly all of them completely legit and respect-
able."

"That sounds like the kind of sneaky thing he'd do. Anything else?"

"Dunno," he said. "Is it interesting that Jazz Hands and
Smith Enterprises both use the same lawyer?"

Interesting? Yes, though downright implausible. From what
I remembered of Cordelia's recent jousts with the developer's
counsel, he was with a white-shoe law firm with offices on K
Street in D.C. and in the Fan District of Richmond—what
our savvy attorney cousin, Festus Hollingsworth, who was rep-
resenting Cordelia, called a worthy opponent. By contrast, E.
Willis Jasperson, Esq., the Jazz Hands attorney, seemed to be
a one-man show who, according to Festus, would have to
step up his game considerably to be considered a bottom
feeder.

"It could be interesting," I said aloud. "Tell me more. Are we talking about E. Willis Jasperson?"

"That's him. Great-Gran had me do a search on him after he sent her that cease-and-desist letter."

"Just mentioning his name makes me grind my teeth," I said. "Are you telling me he also represents that wretched developer?"

"Not usually. Usually Smith Enterprises uses some fancy outfit out of Richmond. But for some reason they hired Jasperson for something they were doing in Charlottesville two years ago."

"It's called hiring local counsel," I said. "There are reasons for doing it. For example, if they had some kind of court appearance that was required, but really quick and simple, they might hire someone on the spot instead of sending one of their highly paid attorneys to do it."

"Or maybe they hire someone like Jasperson for the kind of job the fancy lawyers don't want to get their hands dirty with," Kevin suggested.

"I see someone else has been talking with Cousin Festus."

"Yeah. He thought it was a kind of weird coincidence, too."

"Did he sound worried?"

"Not really. He still seems to think old E. Willis will run away with his tail between his legs if it comes down to a court battle between the two of them. But he thought it was interesting. He's going to look into it."

"Good."

"And I will, too." His voice was less blasé than usual—clearly the thrill of the chase had gotten to him. "Keep you posted."

With that he hung up.

Interesting. I could imagine how Festus would say it, packing several volumes of meaning to those four syllables. Depending on the tone, *interesting* could mean almost anything. I had a feeling in this case it meant highly suspicious and well worth investigating.

Since the vandalism had started, Cordelia and I had more than once debated whether Jazz Hands was behind it or whether it was Smith Enterprises' latest tactic for pushing Cordelia into selling Biscuit Mountain to them. We generally leaned toward blaming Jazz Hands, because it all seemed so petty—and the developer, while sleazy and unscrupulous, usually didn't stoop to petty.

But what if it wasn't Jazz Hands or Smith? What if all along it had been Jazz Hands *and* Smith? Maybe Smith Enterprises had done some opposition research on Cordelia, found out about the Jazz Hands vendetta against her, and decided to join forces and help them out. What if Jazz Hands, though annoyed by Biscuit Mountain, had only launched its legal campaign—and possibly the vandalism—at the developer's encouragement?

I made a mental note to tell Cordelia—and the chief.

But after class. I put my phone away and hurried inside.

As I passed through the great room, I could see and over-hear that a giant game of musical rooms was taking place, as Cordelia tried to find space for the latest contingent of visiting law enforcement personnel. I went off to teach my class feeling mutinous about the fact that I'd probably be rolling out my sleeping bag on the floor of the room Mother was sharing with Cordelia, the room Amanda was sharing with Peggy, or the room Lesley Keech was sharing with a lanky woman deputy from Goochland County. The happiest people at the center were the ones already ensconced in what Cordelia called the "efficiency singles," rooms so tiny that they were barely large enough for a twin bed and a luggage stand. No one was asking the occupants of the efficiency singles to take in new arrivals. Not yet, anyway. Maybe sleeping in the tent wasn't such a bad idea after all.

But no. Not by myself. And I realized I wouldn't have to. There was still the caravan. The boys wouldn't be using it, and I had the key. I could lock myself inside and sleep as snugly and safely as anyone—and a great deal more comfortably than some of the people in tents, since we were expecting thunderstorms overnight.

And for an added benefit, the caravan was in a secluded location, yet commanded a view of both the front porch and the studio side exit door. If anything happened in the night, prowling around the grounds probably wouldn't be a good idea with so many unfamiliar law enforcement officers patrolling the area. For that matter, it probably hadn't been such a great idea before, when whoever killed Prine and Victor was loose in the house. But if anything happened in the night, the caravan would give me a good observation post.

I dashed into my class in a much better mood.

The afternoon crawled by. Since my studio was on the front side of the building, the enormous windows let me follow at least some of what was happening elsewhere in the center as I roved up and down the studio, checking on what my students were doing at their forges and anvils.

The occasional police officer from some other jurisdiction would arrive. At one point, a Riverton police car drove up in front of the main entrance. Officer Keech emerged, went inside, and came out again, accompanied by Horace and Chief Heedles. All three were carrying cardboard boxes. They loaded the boxes in the backseat, and Officer Keech took off. More evidence on its way to the crime lab in Richmond, no doubt.

The Slacker had given up any pretense of attending whatever class he was supposed to be registered for and sat all afternoon in one of the Adirondack chairs on the front porch, sipping a tall glass of lemonade and watching everything that went on with unabashed fascination.

Rob's tech guys occasionally dashed by laden with tools and electronic equipment, or clumped together on the lawn and held animated discussions with a great deal of pointing and arm waving.

Stanley Denton arrived in his nondescript sedan, and was greeted by Cordelia with the hugs appropriate to his role as another of our cousins.

Frankie led her class outside again to paint *en plein air* for the afternoon. She'd also procured a sheep from who knows where, and tethered him on the grassy lawn. Some of the class were painting the sheep while others were immortalizing the main building—with or without the Slacker in his Adirondack chair, depending on their taste. I couldn't hear what Frankie was saying as she darted from student to student, but I could pretty well guess her advice from her gestures—she was imploring most of them to go bigger, bolder, and stop shying away from color. The students all looked happy and intent, which was certainly a change from what they'd looked like the few times I'd peered into Edward Prine's studio. I found myself wondering if the chief had considered the possibility of Prine's students banding together and assassinating him in the hope of getting a better teacher for the rest of the week.

The afternoon classes finally ended, though it was a while before my students could tear themselves away from their projects and their conversations. Their mood, like that of the painters, seemed to have rebounded during the class. Worrying about the investigation had eaten away at my mood, so mine was the only glum face.

Most of Biscuit Mountain's inhabitants seemed reassured

by the police presence—that and the fact that we'd survived Wednesday night and Thursday morning with no new murders and no new acts of vandalism. But most of the inhabitants hadn't seen the threatening note Cordelia had found on her desk.

When I'd finished checking that the upstairs studios were securely locked up, I went downstairs and found a congenial cadre of glum faces in Cordelia's office. Cordelia, Chief Heedles, and Stanley Denton, the private investigator, were sitting in a circle around the desk. The phone was on speaker, and it only took me a few words to recognize the voice coming over it—Cousin Festus, the attorney.

"Festus, Meg just walked in," Cordelia said. "Meg, we're discussing how to get hold of some phone and e-mail records to figure out who's causing our problems."

"Whose phone and e-mail records?" I took a seat on the edge of a two-drawer file cabinet.

"Jazz Hands, for starters," the chief said. "We already know they were in touch with Mr. Prine—but not who else they might have been in contact with."

"Can you do that?" Cordelia asked.

"Shouldn't be too much of a stretch, given the fact that they were chatting back and forth with my murder victim. I should have no trouble selling that to Judge Klein."

"But Smith Enterprises is a whole 'nother can of worms," Festus said. "The information young Kevin has gathered is highly interesting. But however suggestive we may find it that both Smith and Jazz Hands have chosen to retain the odious Mr. Jasperson, I doubt if the most lenient judge on earth would consider it sufficient probable cause to issue a search warrant."

"Well, let's start with Jazz Hands, then," the chief said. "And see where that takes us. With any luck we'll find a smoking gun in their e-mails or phone records. Any chance you can help me draft this thing? Our town attorney's off taking her mother to a medical appointment in Richmond."

"You can use my computer." Cordelia stood up to give the chief her seat.

Festus and the chief plunged immediately into a discussion of the optimal wording for the search warrant. Cordelia leaned against the wall, fascinated.

I left them to it. I wanted to see my boys before they headed off into the wilderness.

The boys were so excited about the upcoming camping trip that they couldn't sit still long enough to eat.

"Don't worry," Michael said. "I've packed doggie bags. They won't starve."

I managed to finish my own dinner and then left Michael to wrangle the boys while I went and packed backpacks for the three of them with what they'd need for their overnight stay. By the time I finished, Lance's Land Rover and Grandfather's Jeep were standing in front of the main entrance, with the boys hopping into first one vehicle, then the other while the grown-ups loaded their backpacks and other gear.

A troubling thought hit me, and I pulled Jason aside.

"Call me paranoid," I said. "But your vehicle has been here all afternoon, and Grandfather's Jeep has been around for days. What if whoever threatened the boys has had a chance to put some kind of GPS device on one or the other or both?"

"You're not paranoid," he said. "Or if you are, welcome to the club. As soon as we get a mile or so away, we're going to stop and scan both vehicles for unwanted devices."

"I should have known you'd already thought of that."

"And I'm very good at finding bugs and tracking devices.

Among other things." Jason's fierce expression, half grin and half scowl, suggested that unlike me, he was rather hoping for a chance to test his mettle on this evening's expedition.

He saw my expression and misinterpreted it slightly.

"Don't worry," he said. "They'll be fine."

As they were sorting out who went in what vehicle, Stanley Denton pulled me aside.

"I wanted to give you a heads-up about something," he said. "Don't turn and look if you can help it, but you know that guy who's sitting in one of the Adirondack chairs on the front porch, sipping a lemonade? About five ten, medium brown hair cut fairly short, regular features—"

"Hang on," I said. "Let me find an unobtrusive way of glancing over my shoulder. Let's both look up and study the sky as if we were discussing the coming weather."

We did so, and while we were pointing at the gathering clouds and nodding at each other, I managed to glance over my shoulder. There was only one man sitting on the front porch.

"You mean the Slacker," I said. "So-called because he has been bouncing from class to class, never really doing much work in any of them."

"Oh, he's working all right," Stanley said. "I'd call him the Snooper, not the Slacker. He's a colleague."

"A private investigator?"

"Yes, and odds are he's on the job. I couldn't find a chance to talk to him privately to find out what—I'll work on that tomorrow."

"The developer could have hired him," I said. "Or Calvin Whiffletree from Jazz Hands."

"Either is possible—or he could be on a case that has nothing to do with Biscuit Mountain. His bread and butter is doing workman's comp investigations for a couple of insurance companies. And he does the odd bit of domestic work—you know, helping jealous wives and husbands find out if their spouses are straying. I hate those cases, so I've referred a few of them to him in the past. The point is, while he may or may not have the craft center's best interests at heart, I don't see him as a killer or a threat to the boys. If I were recruiting a colleague to help me on a case—well, he probably wouldn't be at the top of my prospect list, but he'd be a long way from the bottom. He could be an ally."

"Do you think he told the chief he's a PI?"

"No idea." Stanley shrugged. "Me, I would. But everyone operates differently. Maybe you should drop a word to her, just in case."

"Yes," I said. "That might keep him from getting shot if his case requires him to prowl around at night."

Stanley smiled, nodded, and headed back to the camping crew.

I studied the Slacker with new suspicion. I'd have to keep my eye on him—and more to the point, figure out who he was keeping his eyes on. Maybe he was on a domestic case—working for Jenni's husband, for example, or Valerian's wife. And even if Jazz Hands or the developer had hired him, I couldn't imagine what information he could possibly be gathering that would be of the slightest use to them. But still . . . I'd keep my eyes on him.

At the moment, he was doing nothing more suspicious than watching the members of the camping expedition pack their vehicles.

"What's eating you?" I started slightly. I'd been studying the Slacker so intently that I hadn't noticed Grandfather coming up behind me. And usually he was about as easy to overlook as a brass band.

"What's eating me? Everything!" I shot back. And then I

realized that it sounded ill-tempered and cranky. Sounded a lot like Grandfather's usual tone, in fact. "Sorry," I added. "The stress is not helping my temper."

"You know what's bugging me?" he said. "Those cousins of yours."

"Lance and Jason?" My tone probably sounded cranky again.

"They don't seem to be taking Operation Gull Quest seriously," he said.

"That's because they're not here to help with Operation Gull Quest," I said. "They're here to keep your great-grandsons alive."

"Keep them alive?" Grandfather had a whole wardrobe of scowls. The one he was wearing right now suggested that he thought I was making a joke in very poor taste—on top of not taking his missing gulls seriously.

So I explained, in a few blunt sentences, the real purpose behind the family camping trip.

"In other words," I concluded, "I frankly don't give a damn if Lance and Jason completely ignore Operation Gull Quest. They've dropped everything on a moment's notice to come up here and protect the boys. They could be putting their lives on the line. Stay out of their way."

Grandfather stood for a few minutes, blinking. His face had gone ashen. Maybe I'd been a little too blunt. He was, after all, in his nineties, and right now he looked every minute of his age and then some. I pulled out my cell phone in case I had to call Dad to look after him.

"I'm an old fool sometimes," he said finally. "Why didn't you tell me this before?"

"I've barely seen you since we found the threatening note," I said. "Not something I could shout across the dining hall."

"And I'm not famous for my discretion. So what do you want me to do? Should I stay home from the camping trip?"

I thought about it for several long moments before shaking my head and patting him on the shoulder.

"No," I said. "As long as you understand why Lance and Jason won't be breaking their necks looking for gulls, I see no reason why you shouldn't go along. You have to promise me you'll follow their orders, no matter what."

"Right." His face was glum. For once, he clearly got it. "Okay if I brief Baptiste? He's a lot more likely to be of use than I am."

"Make sure the boys don't overhear," I said.

Just then we heard a horn honking from where the Jeep and the Land Rover were waiting.

"Great-great, hurry up!" Josh called.

"Time to leave!" Jamie added.

Grandfather stood for a few moments, staring morosely at the waiting vehicles.

"Thanks for telling me." He lifted his chin, squared his shoulders, and marched over to climb aboard the Jeep.

I watched them drive away with mixed feelings. I hated having the boys out of my sight at a time like this. But I also felt very relieved that I was sending them off to a safe place. I'd actually have felt pretty good about sending them off with Michael. Add in Dad, Eric, Baptiste, Stanley, Jason, Lance— and yes, even Grandfather? I could rest easy about the boys.

Chapter 27

"They'll be fine." Cordelia came up beside me as I was watching the Land Rover and Grandfather's Jeep disappearing into the woods.

So much for my attempt to appear calm and collected in the face of danger to the boys. Then again, Cordelia read me better than most people.

"I know they'll be fine," I said. "But I reserve the right to worry about them anyway. At least a little."

"Worry away."

"Although getting them away from here has freed up my mind to think about a few other things as well."

"That's good."

"No, not so good. I'm feeling guilty."

"Whatever for?" she asked. "You're not still thinking you should go along, are you?"

"No, I'd only be in the way of the boys' night out," I said. "It's Grandfather."

"That's the one thing that worries me," she said. "The old fool thinks they're all going to look for his gulls. Maybe you could pass the word to Michael to brief him on what's really happening. Make sure he stays out of Lance and Jason's way."

"I already briefed Grandfather, just now," I said.

"So that's why he was looking so gloomy all of a sudden. You think he gets it?"

"Yes. He even offered to stay behind if I wanted him to."

"You're joking."

I shook my head.

"Well, I'll be." Her face took on a bemused look. "Will wonders never cease. But then why am I surprised? We may disagree on a lot of things, your grandfather and I. And I know we're pretty annoying about it sometimes. But one thing we absolutely see eye to eye about is keeping our family safe."

"I know."

"And I'll try a little harder to stop goading him," she said with a sigh. "Entertaining as it is."

"Maybe I should have told him to stay home." A wave of worry was washing over me. "What can he possibly do if they're attacked? And what if he gets himself killed trying to protect the boys?"

"Don't underestimate him." Cordelia's face wore a look of grudging appreciation. "Remember that old saying—age and treachery will beat out youth and skill every time."

"Here's hoping," I said. "But meanwhile, since he so readily agreed to drop looking for the gulls and focus on protecting the boys, maybe I should do a little work on Operation Gull Quest. It's not as if I've done much so far."

"In your copious spare time, between classes and murders."

"Still. I'm going to humor him."

"Of course." She rolled her eyes and threw up her hands. "Doesn't everyone? Always?"

"He'll be a lot easier to live with if we find those wretched gulls," I said. "And Chief Heedles won't have to arrest him for interfering with a police investigation."

"Has she threatened to?" From the sound of it I suspected Cordelia rather liked the idea.

"It's only a matter of time," I said. "That's one of the reasons I didn't try to talk him out of joining the camping trip. But he'll be back in the morning, and even though he gets that the gulls should take a backseat to protecting the boys, he won't be happy."

"He'll be crankier than ever," Cordelia predicted. "Unless they happen to stumble on the gulls, which seems unlikely."

"And we need the chief focused on the case," I went on. "Cases, actually, since we still have no idea if the two murders are connected, or if either of them have anything to do with the vandalism. She has enough on her plate. She shouldn't have to deal with him."

Cordelia nodded.

"So I'm going to set out some bait for his gulls. Several miles away from here," I added, before Cordelia could object. "I was thinking somewhere over in that direction." I pointed over the roof of the center toward the higher mountains beyond. "Someplace where we could see the gulls from the terrace if they show up."

"Half a mile would do as long as it's off my property. But all around me is Park Service land. They'll charge you with littering if they catch you."

"I don't plan on getting caught," I said. "So where can I find some plastic garbage bags?"

"You could try getting some from Marty."

"I could also try taking a bacon treat away from Spike. But I'd rather not."

"Wise woman. He's been on a tear all day. No idea why."

"Having to feed so many extra people?"

"It's only a dozen, and we're totally set up to handle significantly larger numbers than this week's enrollment. I think it was the police searching his kitchen."

"There's also the whole lack of sleep thing," I said. "He's running on short rations of it to begin with, and Grandfather waking him up an hour or two too early the other night didn't help."

"Another thing to thank the old coot for," Cordelia grumbled. "The way it's going, I might need to hire more kitchen staff again tomorrow."

"So any idea where else I can snag a couple of garbage bags?"

"Try the storage room in the barn. And make sure you're well away from here before you start dumping the garbage."

"Don't worry," I said. "I remember how it smelled around here last week. Oh, by the way—Stanley has shed some light on the mystery of the Slacker." I filled her in on what Stanley had told me.

"I knew he was up to something." Cordelia glowered at him. He didn't seem to notice.

"But not necessarily something that has anything to do with us." An idea occurred to me. "Why don't you mention it to the chief? If he hasn't told her what he's up to, she might appreciate knowing—and if he has, maybe she's found out what he's investigating." Since Cordelia and the chief were old friends, she might have a better chance of gleaning information from her reaction.

"Good idea." Cordelia looked more cheerful, as she always did when she had something definite to accomplish. "You go strew your gull bait and ease your conscience. I'll find out what he's up to."

She strode off. I trudged out to the barn and rummaged in the storage room there. Yes, Cordelia was right—everything I'd need was there. I found a box of black plastic garbage bags. And several brand new pairs of heavy-duty plastic utility gloves. But even with the gloves, the notion of filling the bags by hand and then hauling bits of garbage out of them turned my stomach. I grabbed three plastic buckets and what looked like a large grain scoop—perhaps left over from some previous owner who'd actually kept livestock in the barn. I could fill the buckets with the scoop, and then pour the gull bait out on the field. The plastic bags would still be useful. After I filled the buckets, I could bag them. It would make riding with all that garbage in the back of the Twinmobile more palatable, and reduce the danger of a spill. And then I spotted a long-handled shovel—even better.

I loaded bags, buckets, gloves, scoop, and shovel in the back of the Twinmobile and headed down the road to the trash area.

Cordelia had done her best to camouflage the trash area. It was about half a mile down the mountain from the main building, at the end of a short gravel lane that branched off the main driveway. The lane was lined with graceful crêpe myrtles that would come into bloom shortly, and the fence surrounding the trash yard was covered with honeysuckle and trumpet vine. We'd actually done such a good job of camouflaging its real nature that newcomers frequently mistook the lane for a pleasant byway, and we'd had to put up a sign at the entrance warning "Garbage dump ahead—staff only!" Even with the sign, a high percentage of people coming to the center still found their way down the road. We probably had the most photographed trash dump in Virginia.

Inside the fence were a Dumpster for trash, an industrial-size recycling container, and, around the perimeter, a series of stationary compost bins enclosed with chain-link fencing to discourage raccoons and bears. Various varmints did still show up, so I scanned the area carefully as I approached the gate. Out of the corner of my eye I saw something disappear into the woods behind the crêpe myrtles just outside the gate—probably only a deer, but I wanted to be sure. I had no desire to barge in on a frustrated bear. And a bear was more likely than usual since whoever had been here last had left the gate open. Probably one of the long-suffering kitchen staff. Given what they'd had to endure today from Marty's temper, maybe not the time to complain to Cordelia about them.

The trash yard was bare of bears, so I drove in, parked just inside the gate, and got out. I studied the compost bins until I figured out which one was currently being filled and would contain the freshest garbage. Then I grabbed two of the buckets and approached the bin.

It wasn't actually all that smelly. Which probably meant whoever was in charge of tending it was doing a pretty good job of balancing the ingredients. I scanned the bin's contents—vegetable peelings and fruit rinds and spoiled produce of various kinds. Yes, this would do. I could also peer into the Dumpster to see if there were any fish heads. Gulls would like that.

I set the bucket down and turned to go back to the Twin-mobile for the shovel and the scoop. But as I did, I spotted something sticking over the edge of the Dumpster. A piece of wood. A piece of wood that looked a lot like the one-by-two-inch strips of wood Frankie's assistant had been using in her demonstration on how to build and size your own canvases.

I walked over to get a better look.

It was a one-by-two board, all right. But not one of the brand-new ones the assistant had been using. This one had some nail holes in it—and was that a little shred of canvas?

I looked around for something I could stand on to get a closer look. Nothing came to hand, so I started up the Twin-mobile and pulled it up beside the Dumpster. Then I un-rolled the driver's side window and used the window opening as a foothold to hoist myself up level with the top of the Dumpster.

Yes, definitely a disassembled canvas frame—I'd seen enough of them being built lately to recognize the pieces of one, even though it appeared to have been wrenched apart before being stuffed into the Dumpster. I estimated it had been about two by three feet or thereabouts. There were evenly spaced nail holes all along one side of the boards, and a few stubborn nails. Two of the nails sported shreds of canvas.

I held my breath and leaned closer, studying the edges of the boards. One of them had some dark stains at one end that looked like—could that be blood?

Not my job to find out. I pulled out my phone, took a couple of pictures of the boards in situ, and then called 911.

"This is Meg Langslow up at the Biscuit Mountain Arts and Crafts Center," I began when the dispatcher answered. "I've found—"

"Not another body!" the dispatcher exclaimed.

"No, but possibly some evidence. Could you send someone down to the trash area to secure it?"

"Right away," she said. "Are you in any danger?"

"Not that I know of."

"Stay on the line anyway till an officer gets there."

So I stayed on the line—though I decided I was under no obligation to stay in such close proximity to the Dumpster. Curious that it smelled so much worse than the compost bins. I put my cell phone on mute, climbed carefully back through the window into the Twinmobile, and jumped out the other door. I'd leave the car in place so whichever officer arrived could use it to inspect the Dumpster, but I went over to stand close to the gate, to watch for his or her arrival.

As I stood there, I noticed something else—a black plastic garbage bag caught in the space between the gate and the fence. Had I dropped one of the ones I'd brought? No, the box was still in the back of the Twinmobile, closed tight. And the bag behind the gate wasn't empty, either—the loose edges of it ruffled in the breeze, but there was something weighing it down.

At any other time, I'd have picked it up and stuffed it into the Dumpster where it belonged—after taking a peek inside to see if its contents helped me identify who'd been so careless as to drop it there. But since the Dumpster was probably about to become a part of the chief's crime scene, not a good idea to add to or subtract from its contents.

Still, I could make a start at identifying the litterer.

I swung the gate out far enough that I could retrieve the bag and then returned to my sentinel spot. No one in sight yet, but I could hear the sound of an engine approaching.

I peered into the black plastic bag.

"I believe I've found the missing painting," I said aloud—not that there was anyone to hear, with my cell phone still on mute, but at least saying it gave me some satisfaction.

Of course, I realized that I'd just disturbed a piece of evidence. I should have realized that anything within the fence should be left alone. But since the horse was already out of the barn . . .

I carefully pulled the roll of painted canvas out of the bag—luckily I was still wearing the brand new pair of plastic gloves I'd donned in preparation for loading the buckets, so I didn't have to feel too guilty about touching things. The canvas was about two feet wide and had been rolled up rather carelessly. The edges looked slightly ragged, as if whoever had removed it from its frame had done so hastily, and without worrying much about keeping the painting intact.

I began to unroll it. First I saw a naked foot, graceful and feminine, against the background of a white bearskin rug.

"One of Prine's pinups," I muttered. He could paint a bearskin so realistically that you could almost feel the soft caress of the fur, I'd give him that much, but the whole effect was . . . derivative? Retro? Perhaps just a little bit corny? Or maybe just downright sleazy?

The feet were followed by calves, then thighs. Around hip level I could see several slashes that cut right through the canvas, causing flaps of it to droop down. The slashes continued as I unrolled the woman's belly and breasts. They stopped at about neck level, and I unrolled the final foot or so of canvas to reveal a familiar face.

Gillian.

Chapter 28

Prine hadn't given Gillian a smoldering, sexy look, or a flirtatious one. She stared out of the canvas just as cool and unapproachable as she always looked in real life, as if she couldn't care less who saw her.

Though if that really was so, maybe we'd have found the painting in Prine's cabinet, not disassembled and stuffed into the trash.

I even spotted a small reddish-brown stain on one corner of the canvas—a stain that would probably correspond to the similar stain on the one-by-two frame in the Dumpster. And that no doubt when tested would match Prine's DNA.

Chief Heedles's car pulled up just outside the gate and she and Horace hopped out.

"Meg?" the chief called. "Dispatch told me you found something that might be evidence?"

I held up the canvas. Horace's eyes bugged and his mouth fell open. The chief stared at the painting coolly for a few moments. Then, without taking her eyes off it, she took the radio off her belt and spoke into it.

"Lesley? You still up at the house?"

Officer Keech's answer sounded like static to me, but evidently the chief understood it.

"Good. Find Ms. Marks, the pottery instructor, and detain her until I get back to the house."

She turned back to me.

"Any particular reason you were poking about here in the Dumpster?" she asked.

I explained about our plan to spread out bait for the missing gulls. Pointed out the slats sticking out of the top of the Dumpster. Horace pulled out his camera and his forensic gear and set to work. Photos of the canvas. Photos of the slats in the Dumpster. The plastic bag I'd found the painting in went into an evidence bag. So did the slats, and my gloves. Horace took swabs of the reddish-brown stains on the painting and the slats.

And then he stood staring up at the Dumpster.

"There could be more evidence in there," he murmured.

"Seems unlikely." The chief also studied the Dumpster with a pained look on her face.

"Unlikely, but possible." Horace wore a glum expression.

"Work everything but the inside of the Dumpster for now," the chief said finally. "I'll arrange to have an empty one hauled up, and when it gets here you can process the contents of this one into the new one."

Horace nodded.

"Getting dark soon." He took a visible deep breath as he stared at the Dumpster. "I'll need some lights."

"I'll arrange that," the chief said. "And I'll get one of my officers to help you."

Just then her radio crackled and she toggled it on, eyes still on the Dumpster.

"Yes?" she said.

More static-laden words. The chief frowned.

"Have dispatch put out a BOLO. Include the neighboring counties and the State Highway Patrol."

"What's wrong?" I asked, as she hung her radio back on her belt.

"Ms. Marks is in the wind. Most of her stuff's still in her

room, but her car's missing, and no one's seen her for the last hour or two. Horace, you may have to work this scene by yourself for a while. My officers will be a little busy looking for the fugitive."

Horace nodded absently. Actually, I suspected he was just as happy to work the crime scene on his own. Give him half an hour or so and he'd be so far into his zone he wouldn't even notice the smell.

"Blasted inconvenient timing." The chief was frowning at her watch. "I'm due down in Charlottesville in a little over an hour."

"Visiting Jazz Hands?" I asked. "Sorry—none of my business, actually."

"Not a state secret." She chuckled softly. "Meeting with a detective from the Charlottesville PD, and then he's going to help me pin down Mr. Whiffletree, the owner of Jazz Hands. Even if Ms. Marks turns out to have committed both murders and Jazz Hands had nothing to do with them, there's still the matter of the vandalism."

"You've got good people here," I said. "And a lot more of them than usual, remember? Go tackle Whiffletree. They'll call you if anything interesting happens."

"That's true." She gave me a sharp look. "While I'm gone, try to keep Rose Noire from doing any more smudging. Turns out Sergeant Hampton is allergic to sage. Had to use his epinephrine injector last night."

"Oh, dear." I'd been dreading something of the sort. "I'll do what I can."

She nodded, returned to her car, and drove off.

I stuffed my equipment back in the Twinmobile and silently apologized to Grandfather. Operation Gull Quest would have to wait until after Horace had processed the scene.

I drove back up the mountain and parked the Twin-mobile in the center's main parking lot. I tucked the spare gloves and the plastic bags in my tote and left the rest of my gear in the back. Then it occurred to me that I didn't have to disappoint Grandfather after all. I could probably score some compost in the kitchen if I asked nicely. Or maybe just liberate some from the holding bins outside the kitchen door.

Of course, either option meant dealing with Marty. I took several of the deep, calming breaths Rose Noire would have recommended, squared my shoulders, picked up my gear again, and marched down the stairs to the kitchen.

Marty was beginning breakfast prep while keeping an eye on his underlings as they frantically raced through the post-dinner cleanup. It had been about this time last week that the previous brace of underlings had given notice. This week's set didn't look much happier. Marty glared at me as I entered.

"Just passing through on my way to the trash bins." I felt his eyes on me all the way across the kitchen and out the back door.

I had just donned my rubber gloves and was starting to load my garbage bags when Marty stuck his head out the door. He watched me for a few moments.

"She'll pitch a fit if she finds any more garbage on her land," he said eventually.

"I'm going to take it way off into the mountains."

"Fine, but you're not dragging that mess through my kitchen."

"Okay." I glanced up at the steep path that led along the side of the building. At least if I hurried, I'd be climbing it in daylight. It was the darkness as much as the slope that had tripped up Rose Noire's smudgers.

I'd keep telling myself that.

"Save yourself a lot of trouble if you'd just go down to the trash yard and fill your bags there," Marty said. "Almost as fresh, and you can just shove it in the back of your car."

"The trash yard's a crime scene at the moment."

"Crime scene? What do you mean? There can't possibly have been another murder."

It occurred to me that this was how crazy rumors started. I put a last few bits of garbage in my first bag and stood up to ease my back.

"No new crimes whatsoever, as far as I know," I said. "But I was down at the trash yard, getting ready to fill these bags— because yes, I did realize that would be the easiest place to acquire a supply of garbage—and I found something that could be evidence in one of our existing crimes. Not sure the chief would want me to say any more."

I bent over to fill the other garbage bag. Marty just stood there—although when I glanced over my shoulder I saw, to my relief, that he wasn't still scowling at me. He was staring down at the ground looking lost in thought.

Then he glanced up and scowled, but it was a pretty tame and pro forma scowl compared to his usual menacing version.

"Did this have anything to do with the cops turning the whole place inside out looking for Gillian Marks?"

I shrugged. I tried to convey, with my expression, that it wasn't so much an "I don't know" shrug as an "I really shouldn't be talking about it" one.

"They're crazy, then. Couldn't hurt a fly, that one. Whatever evidence you think you found, I bet it will turn out to have some perfectly innocent explanation."

"I hope so," I said. "I like Gillian."

"You shouldn't have done that to her."

I wanted to protest that I hadn't done anything to Gillian,

that I had called the cops before I'd realized this could be embarrassing to her, but he'd already gone back inside, slamming the door behind him.

I finished filling my second black plastic garbage bag, and then I hiked around the outside of the building until I arrived at the front, out of breath and covered with scratches from all the thorny shrubs lining the vestigial path.

My original plan was to go up tonight and strew the garbage, but finding the painting at the trash yard had eaten up a lot of daylight. I could go do it tomorrow. If recent mornings were anything to go by, I'd be awake at the crack of dawn anyway. I'd have plenty of time for a quick run up into the mountains.

I hauled my trash out to the barn, tied the mouths of the bags securely with the drawstrings, and locked them in the storage room. Then I headed back to the main building.

The kids—minus Jamie and Josh, of course—were still in the theater watching *Toy Story*. Rose Noire's meditation class was in full swing in the library. The bridge players were out on the terrace, three tables strong with several kibitzers. One of the harried-looking kitchen staffers was pulling a cart full of s'mores supplies off the dumbwaiter.

I found I wasn't the least in the mood for s'mores without Michael and the boys. But I probably should go, at least for a while, if only to see whether anyone took an undue interest in their absence.

In the meantime, I was going to do my usual pre-bedtime check of the studios. And then, after a short appearance at the campfire, I was going to guilt-trip one of my relatives or friends into letting me borrow her bathtub for a long, hot soaking bath.

Nothing out of place until I came to my own studio. When I opened the door, a piece of paper went skittering across the

floor. No, not a piece of paper—a pale blue envelope. Someone had probably slipped it under the door. Or maybe
someone had left it on the counter to the right of the door
and then the draft when I opened the door had knocked
it off.

I closed and locked the door. I took a picture of the envelope both close up and from a distance, so it would be clear
where I found it.

"Obviously Dad and Horace are rubbing off on me," I said
to myself.

I went over to the corner where there was a small sink for
end-of-class cleanup. I kept a pair of kitchen gloves there for
when I had to scrub the sink. I put them on, and then picked
up the envelope.

The outside said *To Meg* in an elegant flowing handwrit-
ing. I opened it and found two sheets of pale blue stationery
covered with longhand in purple ink.

Chapter 29

Dear Meg, the letter began. *Please accept my apologies.*

I suspected I knew who it was from but I flipped to the end to make sure. Gillian. I turned back to the first page and paused. I felt curiously reluctant to read the letter. Was it because I didn't want to learn what Gillian had to say? Or was I merely feeling a resistance to reading two pages of cursive writing—who in the world read or wrote that much in longhand these days?

I braced myself and read on.

Dear Meg. Please accept my apologies. If you're reading this, I'll be gone, and the police will be looking for me. I'm sure they think I killed Edward Prine. I didn't.

We had a brief affair, many years ago, just after my divorce. It ended badly, and if I'd known he was teaching here at Biscuit Mountain, I'd never have come. He brought along one of the paintings he did of me during our relationship. He was making inappropriate demands and threatening to hang it in his studio where everyone could see it if I didn't comply.

Inappropriate demands? From what I knew of Prine, I suspected I could guess what those demands were. I shook my head and read on.

I decided I had to do something, so last Saturday, when so many people were leaving and everything was in chaos, I borrowed your grandmother's spare keys and made copies of the ones I needed. I planned to go to Edward's studio, steal the picture of me, and burn it. But when I went to his studio Monday night, just after midnight, I found him lying dead on the floor.

I was afraid the police would suspect me if I reported the murder, or if they found the painting, so I dragged it out of the studio, cut the canvas off its frame, and hid the dismantled frame and the rolled-up canvas in the crawl space under the terrace. The next night I was planning to take it out into the woods and burn it, but I was interrupted by the hue and cry after your discovery of Mr. Winter's body and only just managed to hide it in the trash collection area. I'm going to try again tonight, but if you're reading this, I've probably failed.

I didn't kill Edward. I didn't kill Mr. Winter. And I'm not the vandal. I don't think the police will believe me. But maybe they'll believe you. Make them keep investigating. Or do what you can to solve the murders yourself. Please help me!

The letter ended with her large, looping, elegant signature. I stared at it for a while, then folded the pages together again and stuck them back in the envelope.

I had no idea whether to believe her.

Neither did the chief when I called her and read it to her.

"This doesn't tell us anything we didn't already know," she said. "Or could have surmised."

"True."

There was a long pause. I could hear the faint sounds of traffic. She was probably getting close to Charlottesville.

"But it's interesting," she said. "Can you turn it over to Horace?"

"I'll call him as soon as we hang up. Good luck with Mr. Whiffletree."

Horace, when he arrived, was dubious that the letter would provide any useful forensic clues, although he was properly appreciative of my efforts to preserve any evidence it might contain.

"Wish more people carried gloves around for occasions like this." He carefully placed the letter and envelope in evidence bags.

"If people did, it would mostly be the criminals who used them, you know," I pointed out. "So I guess things look pretty bleak for Gillian. That's a statement, not a question." He was giving me that mournful, disapproving look he always had when people tried to get him to talk about his cases.

"She seems like a nice lady," he said.

"She's a very nice lady. I hope she doesn't turn out to be the killer."

He nodded and left, bearing his evidence bags.

I finished inspecting my studio, locked up, and decided to skip campfire after all. Instead, I went in search of someone who wasn't presently using her bathtub.

I ended up in the bathroom attached to the room Cordelia and Mother were sharing, soaking in a tub full of Rose Noire's best rose and lavender bath salts, while in the bedroom the two of them caught up on news. It made me happy to know that they got on so well, although sometimes it worried me how much they saw eye-to-eye on things. It also made me happy to know that Mother was making plans for coaxing several recipes out of Marty, including the spectacular crème brûlée one—though I hoped it wasn't too difficult, since I knew the odds were I'd be the one making it, not Mother. And because the two of them had been known to stay up chattering until dawn, it made me supremely happy to know that I had some place to sleep other than their floor. After my bath and a little family bonding with the two of them, I could go out to the caravan for a night of peace and quiet.

"Don't worry." Cordelia looked up and smiled at me when I emerged from the bathroom. "We won't stay up much longer. I know you need your rest."

"You need to bring in your sleeping bag, dear." Mother was tucked up in Cordelia's reading chair and looking around with approval at the elegantly decorated room. "We've cleared a nice space for you."

"Grateful as I am for the offer, I will be sleeping elsewhere," I said.

"Where?" Cordelia asked.

"Not out in that wretched tent, I hope." Mother shuddered at the thought. Of course, she usually did at the mention of sleeping in tents. "Even if Michael weren't out in the woods I don't think that would be a good idea at the moment."

"No, I don't fancy the tent by myself. Especially since it sounds as if the heavens are going to open sometime later tonight. Several people have offered me places on their floors, but given all the insomnia I've been having lately I'm not really sure I want to share with anyone."

"Why not set up your sleeping bag in your studio?" Cordelia suggested.

"I thought of that," I said. "But even if I didn't suspect that the vandal might have managed to make a copy of our master key—"

"Oh, my. I hadn't thought of that," Mother murmured.

"The studio's got those enormous windows, and no curtains," I went on. "I like a little more privacy, thank you. I'm taking the caravan."

"What a good idea." Cordelia nodded her approval. "And you can take Spike with you. Let's go get him now."

"Spike?" The idea didn't enchant me, but I followed her out of the room anyway.

"We originally penned him in the barn," Cordelia said over her shoulder as we descended the main stairs. "But we have some of the visiting police officers bunking there, and he just keeps barking at them obsessively. Rose Noire made a bed in his traveling crate, down in the great room, but I'm afraid that's not going to work out, either."

"Why not?" I asked. "It's a perfectly good crate. If he's not used to sleeping in it, he needs to learn."

We heard growling, followed by a shriek. One of the pottery students came running up the stairs.

"Why is that vicious dog loose in the house?" she wailed.

"He's not loose," Cordelia said. "He's crated."

"Are you sure the crate can hold him?"

"Of course, and anyway we're about to relocate him." Cordelia turned back to me. "He's used to sleeping in the caravan. And—"

"Okay." I knew when to stop fighting. "I'll take him."

"Just one thing." Cordelia frowned at me. "Please promise me you're not turning down all those places on people's floors because you plan to go snooping around again before everyone else is up. Because I think that's a bad idea. Finding two bodies is enough."

"Finding *one* body was more than enough," I said. "No matter who finds them. No, now that we've got plenty of police officers to patrol the house and grounds, I'm a reformed snoop. I don't plan to poke my nose out of the caravan before morning. And if anyone tries to poke his nose in, I'll have the Small Evil One." I didn't mention my plan to stay awake and observe whatever events were happening outdoors. She probably wouldn't trust me not to go out if I saw anything interesting. For that matter, I didn't altogether trust myself, but if the temptation arose, I planned to combat it by remembering exactly how Edward Prine and Victor Winter had looked when I'd found their dead bodies.

Cordelia studied me for a few moments. Then she nodded and strode off.

I stopped by the nearest bathroom one last time. The covered bucket Eric had found for the twins' use was probably still in the caravan, but I hoped I could avoid using it. Then I made my way back to the great room, grabbed Spike's leash, and managed to get him out of the crate and attach the leash to him without getting bitten. I wasn't sure whether he was hoping I'd lead him to Josh and Jamie or whether he was just delighted to be out of the crate.

"One nip and you're back in there," I warned him as we crossed the great room toward the front door.

He trotted briskly at my side out to the caravan and stood at the base of its steps, looking cranky and entitled as he waited for me to lift him up.

"No nipping," I reminded him.

He condescended to let me lift him up into the caravan, and then scampered inside, doubtless planning to lie in wait for me there and get in the forbidden nip by pretending to mistake me for a burglar.

I went to the tent to get Michael's and my things. The rest of our things—we were already using the caravan to store a lot of stuff we didn't want to leave lying around in the tent. I checked to make sure Spike was safely out of the way, and then hoisted our stuff inside. I easily found space to tuck everything away, out of sight and, more important, out from underfoot. That was another thing I liked about the caravan—the storage space.

Not for the first time I admired the craftsmanship that had gone into making the caravan. And I didn't mean the painting, gilding, and carving, though they were, of course, fabulous. No, I meant the way the builder had made such efficient use of small bits of space that would otherwise have gone to waste. Caroline's caravan probably had more storage space than most—she'd had it made with much smaller windows, both to leave room for more cabinets and drawers, and also for privacy and security. And then, to ensure ample daylight and ventilation, she'd had the builder install a skylight in the ceiling. Or maybe I should call it a sunroof, since it was in a vehicle and opened up far enough to catch stray breezes.

I'd slept in the caravan a few times on other trips, and had always enjoyed lying in the enormous bed that filled the back third of it, looking up through the skylight at the stars. But I was feeling a little anxious tonight. I wanted to make sure no one could peek in or, worse, get in. Okay, given the small size of the windows and how far they were off the ground, only a reasonably agile and very skinny person could get in, but still. I made sure all the windows were locked and the shades tightly closed; I even pulled the carved wooden cover over the skylight and latched it securely.

"Snug as a bug in a rug," I said to Spike, who had jumped up onto the bed and curled up in the absolute center. He ignored me, as he tended to ignore everyone who wasn't either Josh or Jamie.

I pulled on my night clothes—actually, a t-shirt and some yoga pants, much more presentable than pajamas or a nightgown if I had to make a midnight run to the bathroom. Then I started working on getting Spike to make room for me. Any other dog I would have simply picked up and moved away from the center of the bed, but such a policy was unwise with Spike, unless you liked getting out the first aid kit in the middle of the night. So I used what I thought of as the passive/aggressive approach. I lifted the coverlet ever so slightly, until he was lying on a slope, and held it taut until either gravity slid him toward the side of the bed or he got mildly annoyed and moved to a flatter area. I had to repeat the process five or six times, but eventually I had relocated him far enough away that I had room to get in bed. I curled up in the other side of the bed, being careful not to jostle Spike, who had learned the wisdom of not biting me but sometimes forgot when startled out of sleep. I plugged my phone into the built-in charger, which ran on battery when the caravan wasn't connected to the grid. I turned it on and sent a quick text to Michael, as we usually did when we were separated at bedtime.

"How's the campout going?"

I waited for a few moments, fighting to keep my eyes open. I wasn't expecting an answer, since he was out in the mountains where cell phone service was next to nonexistent. But there was always the possibility that they'd camped in some spot that got a bar or two occasionally. Especially if they were camping near the top of some mountain—that helped, didn't it?

But no reply came, and eventually my phone dimmed, to suggest that if I had no further business with it, maybe I could let it go to sleep. I made sure the sound was on, so I'd hear it if it rang or if Michael replied to my text, and shut it off.

I reminded myself that one of the reasons for installing myself in the caravan was to keep an eye on whatever was happening outside the center. To remain alert and vigilant, ready to spot any threat to the center.

Somehow it had all seemed so much easier earlier in the day. Before I was so tired.

I closed my eyes, ready to drift into sleep.

"Grrr." Spike stood up and walked stiffly over to the narrow little window that ran along the back of the caravan, just above the level of the bed. It was only a foot high and designed to let the bed's occupant keep watch on what was happening outside without sitting up. Unfortunately, this meant it was seriously inconvenient to look out of if you weren't already lying down right next to it. Though it was perfectly positioned to let Spike to see out. He growled softly for a few moments. Then he erupted in furious barking.

I scooted over and bent down to peer out the window. Vern Shiffley, making his rounds.

"Shut up, Spike," I said.

Reluctantly, Spike subsided into silence. But he remained curled up by the window. That didn't bode well.

Sure enough, a few minutes later he began barking again. By the time I'd scooted over to the window so I could see outside, the person he was barking at was disappearing into the distance. Possibly Vern, circling around. Or one of the other visiting officers.

By around 2:00 A.M. I had definitely come to regret the notion of having Spike as a bodyguard. He was taking his job a little too seriously. He barked when campers came and went from the bathrooms, even if they came nowhere near the caravan. He barked whenever one of the borrowed officers passed by on his or her rounds. He barked when a trio of deer strolled by on their way to munch on Cordelia's roses—though at least that bit of barking was slightly useful. He barked at the first few distant rumbles of thunder that signaled the arrival of the promised thunderstorm. And when the heavens finally opened, accompanied by an almost deafening crack of thunder, he nearly went berserk. At least as the thunderstorm ran its course he calmed down—or perhaps he'd exhausted himself.

He was barking again, I realized, as I struggled up from sleep. At the thunder, perhaps. No, the storm was trailing off. I was too tired to peer out and see what had set him off.

"Shut up, Spike," I muttered for what seemed like the hundredth time.

He subsided into growls.

"Didn't anyone ever tell you the story of the boy who cried wolf?" I muttered. We had discussed this before—often.

He growled again.

"I give up." I stuck a particularly fat pillow over my head.

The pillow actually did a fairly decent job of muffling Spike's growls.

"And we're not going through this again tomorrow night," I muttered into the pillow. "I'm going to send you camping with the boys, no matter how much Grandfather protests."

I fell asleep smiling at the thought.

But Spike followed me into my dreams. I knew I was dreaming, because suddenly Spike had grown to the size of a small horse. He was growling incessantly. I was just opening my mouth to say, "Shut up, Spike," when he barked right into my ear with such force that it knocked me off the bed.

I woke up to find that I was still in bed.

But the bed was moving.

In fact, the whole caravan was moving.

Chapter 30

Spike had jumped off the bed and was running back and forth across the floor of the caravan, still growling—but it wasn't his usual confidant, forceful growling. It was a higher-pitched, anxious growl, more bravado than confidence. Not a sort of growling I'd often heard from the Small Evil One. I'd heard him growl like that once when by some oversight he'd managed to slip past us into the bear's den at Grandfather's zoo. And once again when he'd taunted a cousin's Rottweiler mercilessly until the larger dog, ordinarily quite calm and placid, became annoyed and responded with a growl so deep you felt more than heard it. Not happy memories.

"Shut up, Spike," I said, almost automatically.

For once he obeyed. Then he gave one soft bark, sat down in the middle of the floor, and looked up at me with a more familiar expression. The expression that said, "I am displeased with my present circumstances, and I expect you, lowly human, to do your job and fix things."

"Working on it," I muttered.

I crawled to the far side of the enormous bed and peered through the curtains that covered the narrow little window there. The caravan was hitched behind a large pickup truck, and was now moving rather rapidly. Rapidly backward, I thought, irrationally—the detachable shafts that you could use if you wanted a horse to draw the caravan were on the front end, the end with the door, while the permanently installed (though discreetly camouflaged) trailer hitch was on the back, or bed end of the caravan. From what I could see, we were rattling downhill on the gravel lane that led from Biscuit Mountain to the main road. Going a bit faster than I'd have wanted to go on this road, which made the caravan lurch and pitch. But still not going all that fast, probably because the road just wouldn't allow it. Though no doubt the fact that the truck didn't have its headlights or taillights on also discouraged the driver from speeding.

"Sorry, Spike," I said. "You were trying to warn me and I was telling you to shut up."

His look suggested that he'd consider accepting my apology when I'd gotten us out of this mess.

And it was definitely a mess. I couldn't think of a plausible reason for anyone to be hauling the caravan off in the middle of the night unless they were trying to kidnap my boys.

A surge of anger swept through me at that thought. The would-be kidnapper was in for a nasty surprise if I had anything to do with it.

But first I needed to escape.

No, first I needed to figure out who was doing this so I could report them. Then escape. And then sic law enforcement on my kidnapper.

Speaking of law enforcement, how had the officers patrolling the ground missed seeing someone hitching up the caravan to his truck and then hauling it off?

Probably during the thunderstorm. I wouldn't have blamed them at all for taking shelter for a few minutes during the height of the downpour. And even without the thunder, the noise of the heavy rain would have disguised whatever sounds the kidnapper made while hitching up the caravan.

Still—surely sooner or later someone would notice the caravan's absence and come looking for it, wouldn't they?

Well, unless whoever was currently patrolling that part of the grounds was one of the newcomers who didn't know the lay of the land that well.

I'd worry about that later.

I peered out the window again, trying to see if I could read the truck's license plate. Unfortunately, while my perspective through the window was inconveniently low, it was still above the raised bed, which meant from the outside it was too high for me to see down as far as the truck's license plate. And the lack of any illumination meant I couldn't see even the silhouette of the driver.

I glanced at my watch. Four thirty. Later than I expected. So late it was almost early. But not late enough that even the earliest risers would be out.

I took a couple of pictures of the truck anyway. They just looked like dark blurs to me, but maybe Horace or one of Rob's techs would have a way of lightening them to make out any useful details. Though what those details might be I had no idea. It was an ordinary truck, dark blue or black. Nothing in the truck bed. No distinctive marks that I could see. No visible dents or damage. No stickers on the back window of the cab. Nothing memorable about the truck at all.

Well, except for the fact that it was driving too fast down a narrow mountain road with its headlights off, towing a gaudily painted Gypsy caravan.

So, call 911 first or escape from the caravan? I peered out one of the side windows. All I could see was trees, scrolling past the window and sometimes brushing it. Which meant we were still on the lane leading up to Biscuit Mountain. Probably a good idea to escape before the truck hit the main road, where it could pick up speed. And luckily, since the door was on the opposite end from the truck, I could probably do so without the kidnapper seeing me.

I slid off the bed and crawled to the door end of the caravan—given how badly it was lurching, crawling seemed a lot safer than walking. My plan was to open the door, wait until the truck slowed down a bit—going around a curve, perhaps—then throw Spike out and jump after him.

I made sure my phone was in my pocket.

"Here, Spike," I called softly.

He stared at me and continued sitting on the floor.

I crawled back to him, picked him up, and tucked him under my arm. He only made a token attempt to bite me, which meant that he understood the gravity of the situation.

I unlocked the door, turned the handle, and pushed.

Nothing happened.

I shoved harder. Something was holding the door closed. I put Spike down, took a few steps back, and hit the door with my shoulder. Nothing.

Well, not exactly nothing—I bounced back, stumbled, and fell, almost landing on Spike. My bottom hurt almost as much as my shoulder.

"Okay, that won't work," I said aloud. Spike growled softly in agreement.

The caravan lurched suddenly. I thought for a moment it was going to turn over, but it only tipped back and forth several times, slamming me and Spike violently against the cabinets on either side.

I felt a sudden surge of panic. This was getting scary. My initial assumption that I could easily escape from the caravan had given way to a claustrophobic sense of being trapped and helpless. I closed my eyes and took a few deep breaths.

"Grrrrrr."

I opened my eyes and saw Spike staring at me in disapproval.

This was no time to panic. Spike was depending on me.

And for that matter, Josh and Jamie were depending on me to get myself out of this jam and return to them.

Josh and Jamie, who could so easily have been in the caravan. I let anger wash away the fear, and then I tamped down the anger and focused back on making our escape.

I eyed the door. It was a modified Dutch door. The bottom portion was solid wood, elaborately carved and painted inside and out. The top foot or so consisted of two little frosted glass windows with carved and painted frames. I unlatched one of the windows from the bottom part of the door and tried to push it open.

That didn't work, either.

I did manage to push the window open a crack, just enough to peer down and figure out what was wrong with the door. Damn. The caravan's door was flanked by two wooden handholds. When the removable wooden steps weren't in place, you could use the handholds to pull yourself up to the doorstep. And when the steps were in place, the handholds probably comforted anyone who was unsteady on his feet.

Unfortunately, they were also perfect for slipping a two-by-four through if you wanted to trap the caravan's occupants inside. And the ends of the two-by-four were out of reach, even if I got the windows open.

Whatever was holding the windows closed had a little give to it—probably a rope or more likely an elastic bungee cord, tied on either side to the decorative woodwork and pressed tight against the windows.

"Maybe it's time to call the cavalry," I said to Spike. I pulled out my phone and tapped 911.

No service.

"Of course," I muttered. Cordelia's cell signal booster barely reached to the far edge of the campgrounds. As soon as we'd begun rattling down the gravel road we'd entered the vast surrounding dead zone.

Texts sometimes went through with less signal than needed for a phone call. I tried sending a text to Michael. No luck.

E-mail. Sooner or later we'd pass close enough to a cell tower for my phone to get a signal. If I noticed when that happened, I could call or text. But if an e-mail was waiting in my out folder, my phone would send it as soon as it got enough signal.

So I composed an e-mail.

"Help!" the subject line read, and the body continued with "Someone is kidnapping me. They have barricaded me inside Caroline Willner's caravan and are towing it away from Biscuit Mountain with a large, dark pickup truck. No cell phone signal. If you get this, please notify the police."

Then I started filling in the addresses of family and friends. Michael. Cordelia. Caroline. Dad. Mother. Grandfather. Rob. Horace. I didn't have Chief Heedles's e-mail address, but I included Caerphilly's Chief Burke. Kevin. Eric. And then I added my own e-mail address—if the phone found enough signal to send it, I'd probably get the little ding that alerted me to an arriving e-mail—I figured that might also alert me that we were passing through an area with cell phone service.

"Here's hoping." I pressed the SEND button.

Spike growled slightly, as if to remind me that he was still unhappy and I had some work to do to resolve his problems. Yes, even if the e-mail went through right now, it would still take time for help to arrive. I'd better be prepared to help myself.

So—first order of business: find a way to defend myself if my kidnapper stopped the truck and tried to enter the caravan. Second: find a way to get Spike and myself out of the caravan—preferably without alerting my kidnapper that his victims had flown the coop. And third, if possible: either get the truck's license number, or find some way to identify it later.

First, I threw on my clothes. Whether I ended up doing battle with my kidnapper or fleeing through the woods, I'd feel a lot more comfortable doing it with shoes on. And underwear.

Then I began rummaging through the caravan's extensive drawers and cabinets. No luck with the kitchen drawers—we'd removed all the sharp knives when Eric and the boys had replaced Caroline as the caravan's occupants. Then again, did I really want to be waving a knife at my kidnapper?

If I had my tote bag—yes, there it was on the floor in the corner—I might have some useful objects. Because leaving things undone drove me crazy, I'd long ago gotten into the habit of carrying a few tools around in my tote, the better to take care of small maintenance issues when I spotted them rather than having to wait to take care of them. But none of the tools I ever carried would be much of an improvement over a knife—well, with the possible exception of a big hammer.

Aha! The closet contained the boys' baseball gear, including Josh and Jamie's matching bats. I picked up one of the bats and gave it a test swing. It was bright orange and metal, about two and a half feet long. It didn't quite have the same feeling of solid weight that a wooden bat would, but still—a formidable weapon.

Of course, it wouldn't be all that useful against a gun. But better than nothing.

I placed one bat by the door and the other beside the bed,

so there was always one within easy reach, and turned my attention to the escaping part of the program.

I found myself studying all those lovely cabinets and drawers I'd been so admiring before, and wishing a few of them had been left out to make room for more windows. Even one window large enough to make it easy for me to slip out of. The caravan's windows were only about a foot tall, and except for the one over the bed, which would be in full view of the truck's driver, they were placed high up in the walls. The setup was excellent for maximizing both light and privacy but would make trying to wriggle out very difficult. Maybe I was even fooling myself to think it was possible. I held up my hands to measure the height of the windows and then matched that to my own body at hip level. Doable—maybe. If I could suck in everything really well. I wouldn't hesitate to try it if the window was at floor level, but trying to climb up to the window and wriggle out in mid-air? And then add in the fact that I'd be eight feet or so up in the air on the side of a moving vehicle, exposed to the view of my kidnapper.

"Let's try the other options first, shall we?"

Spike growled softly.

I considered, just for a moment, whether I should toss him out one of the windows if the truck slowed down enough that it would be safe. Not that I had any notion that he'd pull a Lassie and go running back to Biscuit Mountain for help, but at least I could get him out of the clutches of our kidnapper. But I vetoed my own idea almost immediately. If I did manage to heave him safely out of the trailer, he'd probably only get lost in the woods, or maybe eaten by some of the carnivorous animals Grandfather and his class had been photographing all week with such enthusiasm. Owls, foxes, coyotes, bears—Spike would look like a very appetizing little hors d'oeuvre to any of them. And while they might not find him quite the easy prey they imagined, you couldn't expect an eight-and-a-half-pound fur ball, however fierce, to survive a trek of several miles through the wilderness.

"Sorry, Spike," I said. "But you're going to have to stay aboard for now."

He had leaped back on the bed and was peering through the window, growling at our kidnapper's truck.

"I agree," I said.

I focused back on our escape. How about the skylight? It only opened about a foot or so, but that would be out onto the flat roof of the caravan—easier to crawl out of than a similar-sized opening in the side of the caravan. And maybe I could remove the inside portion of the skylight's wooden frame and shove out the glass part of the skylight. That would leave plenty of room for me to escape, even burdened with Spike.

I found my tote and rummaged through it. Hammer. Pliers. Phillips screwdriver. Flathead screwdriver. A small folding saw. All of it potentially helpful. Then I rummaged in the drawers in the kitchenette area of the caravan. I could have sworn I'd seen . . . yes! A small battery-operated drill.

"Take that, whoever you are!" I muttered, brandishing the drill at the unseen kidnapper.

The only challenge was going to be getting up to the skylight. A further search of the various storage areas didn't turn up anything like a stepladder. A folding canvas chair? Not much good.

I finally climbed up on the counter and managed to brace myself, one foot on the counter and one on the door of the closet. I began to study the skylight's frame. No visible screws, so it was probably glued in. I could take the hammer, use the big flathead as a chisel and—

Just then the caravan lurched sideways, knocking me off my precarious perch. At least I landed on the bed, missing Spike by a few inches.

"Sorry, Spike," I said. "The Great Escape isn't as easy as I expected."

His disapproving stare spoke volumes.

"But I'm working on it."

Chapter 31

I glanced out a window to see why we'd made such a sharp turn. Damn—we'd reached the junction where the gravel road to Biscuit Mountain met the main road. The truck hadn't even slowed down all that much before turning right.

Now that was interesting. I'd have expected our kidnapper to turn left. Left led to the town of Riverton. Not that I expected the kidnapper to stop in Riverton, but when you were leaving Biscuit Mountain for just about anywhere else, the route led through Riverton.

Turning right would take us up into the mountains. I thought about that for a few moments and decided I didn't like it. I had no idea what the kidnapper was planning to do with Josh, Jamie, and Eric up in the mountains, but it couldn't be good.

Then again, the boys' departure on their camping trip with cousins Lance and Jason hadn't exactly been unobtrusive. So if the kidnapper was anyone staying at Biscuit Mountain, he'd know he wasn't kidnapping the boys.

And not all that many people actually knew I was sleeping in the caravan. Maybe whoever was driving the truck just thought he was stealing the caravan.

No, if he was just stealing the caravan he wouldn't have barred the door. Even if he'd heard Spike bark and wanted to make sure the Small Evil One stayed inside, what he'd done to the door was definitely overkill for any prisoner not equipped with opposable thumbs.

A pity. A caravan thief would have been a lot easier to deal with than a kidnapper. And if it was a kidnapping, I hoped the perpetrator still thought he'd be dealing with two little boys and their mild-mannered babysitter. Little did he know that he'd be dealing with their seriously angry mother—not to mention a small, fluffy, but very evil dog.

Still, in any case, my mission was to escape, and leave him to deal with an empty caravan. And, eventually, notify Chief Heedles and Sergeant Hampton.

But first, I needed to update what I was thinking of as my trail of breadcrumbs.

I pulled out my phone and opened my e-mail program. Unfortunately, my earlier e-mail was still sitting in the out basket, waiting for a signal. I tapped out another e-mail to the same recipients. "Update" the subject line read. "My kidnapper has left the Biscuit Mountain access road and is heading . . ."

Damn. In which direction were we heading? I tried to visualize the map. North? No, probably more like northeast.

Then again, if I wasn't sure, would anyone else be? Did I want them studying maps and compasses or hurrying to my rescue?

"Heading away from Riverton on the main road. If you get this, please notify all authorities!"

I pushed SEND, waited until it gave me the usual message that said it couldn't send now but would when possible, then tucked the phone back into my pocket.

I studied the skylight again. Unless I could find something sturdy enough to stand on, neither crawling out through it nor taking it apart seemed like the easiest way out.

If the caravan fell over on its side, the skylight would be a first-class escape route. I pondered that for a few moments. If I hurled myself from side to side, timing it for when the caravan was going around a curve anyway, could I tip it over?

Maybe. But then my kidnapper would probably come back to investigate. Did I really want to be caught half in and half out of the skylight?

I put the idea on hold. Though given the reckless way my kidnapper was driving he might manage to wreck the truck and overturn the caravan all by himself. I'd make sure I was ready to hit the skylight if that happened.

I turned my attention back to the door. I pushed at the two top panels again. There was some give to them, so whatever was holding them shut was elastic. But not elastic enough to let me get my arm out.

I heard a rumble of thunder. Another band of thunderstorms headed our way. Spike growled.

"Shut up," I said. "This time around, the thunderstorms might be our friend."

I fished the hammer out of my tote. Then I looked back in the caravan's tool drawer where I thought I had seen— yes! A roll of duct tape.

I started with the panel on the right. It consisted of six little panes of decoratively etched frosted glass in a painted wooden frame. I crisscrossed all the panes with duct tape and then, when the next rumble of thunder rolled through, gave one of them a sharp tap. The tape muted the noise a bit and made it easier for me to collect all the shards and deposit them in the trash can under the sink. Not that tidiness counted for much right now, but given the way the caravan was jolting and lurching, I didn't want to litter the floor with any sharp objects that could hurt me or Spike if they became airborne.

After a few more increasingly loud claps of thunder I had all the glass out. I was hoping that with the glass gone I could just knock out the sash bars, but the caravan's makers had built it to last. To get past them, I'd have to saw them out with my folding saw.

But wait! Now that I had access to it, I could cut the bungee cord that held the windows closed. I felt a lot better with both tiny windows open. Although the resulting space was still a little small for trying to crawl through.

"Making progress," I said to Spike. "Now all I have to do is cut through this two-by-four."

Though it wasn't going to be easy. The window opening was too small to fit more than my head and right arm through, and I could just barely reach the two-by-four with my saw. But just barely would do. I began to saw, making my cut as close as possible to the door opening. Eventually I could cut all the way through the two-by-four and the door would be openable.

Just as I was settling in to this task, the truck left the main road and began rattling down a side road. Not even a gravel road—a dirt trail.

What was this creep up to?

Spike didn't like the change, either—especially once the heavens opened and the rain began falling in sheets. I had no idea why Spike was so distraught. I was the one whose head and arm were getting soaked. I'd closed the left side of the door window to keep it from flapping uselessly and I filled the small right side opening so completely that not many raindrops made it into the caravan.

"Shush," I muttered. "We need to maintain the element of surprise." Although come to think of it, if my kidnapper was targeting Josh and Jamie, he'd be expecting to encounter Spike.

And if they knew Josh and Jamie had gone on the family camping trip and were targeting me, they might still be expecting Spike. I didn't like that alternative as much, but I needed to be prepared for it.

My steady sawing was paying off. Only half an inch or so left of the bar. I peered down and decided that I might be able to ram the door and break through the last bit. Then again, my shoulder still hurt from the last time I'd hurled myself against the door. I pulled my head in and resumed sawing.

Just then the caravan slowed. And stopped.

I paused so whoever was driving wouldn't hear the noise of my sawing. I pulled in my saw arm and stuck out my head. We seemed to be in a clearing. The rain was easing, and though the sun wasn't up yet, the darkness was beginning to give way to early morning gray

The caravan moved again. We were turning in a wide circle. Then the truck began to back up.

I twisted my head around to get a better view.

We weren't in a clearing. We were on the edge of a cliff. Luckily the truck stopped with the caravan still on solid ground. But I didn't like the looks of this.

I pulled my head in and scrambled over to the bed end so I could peer out the window.

Someone had hopped out of the truck and was bent over the trailer hitch, unfastening it.

He stood up.

Marty.

I sent another e-mail with the subject line "Marty is the kidnapper!" Though if he was about to shove me over a cliff up here in the middle of nowhere, would any of my e-mails ever reach their destinations?

I opened the window. Nothing to lose by trying to talk to him.

"Marty," I called. "Stop now. It won't work."

"Should work just fine," he said. "And it'll serve you right." He finished unhooking the caravan and gave it a slight shove. It didn't budge. He nodded and turned as if to go back to the cab of his truck. I realized that he was probably planning to push us off the cliff.

"Why?" I called out.

"Because of what you did to her!"

Her? I mouthed it, but didn't say it aloud.

Then I remembered. All those delicacies for the vegetarians. His surprising consideration when Gillian was in shock over Victor's death. How many times had I seen him peering out the service hatch and assumed he was wondering if the diners liked his food. He wouldn't worry about that—he knew his food was superb. But if he was trying to catch a glimpse of someone out in the dining room . . .

"Gillian?" I asked.

"You didn't care that he was harassing her," he said. "You just let him—you and her highness."

"I didn't even know he was harassing her."

He snorted at that.

"You killed Edward Prine because he was harassing Gillian?" I asked.

"He had that embarrassing picture of her." He'd stopped just beside his truck cab. Good—as long as he was talking, he wasn't trying to push the caravan over the edge. "I overheard him tell her that unless she met him in his studio and slept with him, he was going to put the picture on display. He was going to force himself on her! So I made sure I got there first."

Okay, that would have made me mad. And I wasn't besotted with Gillian. And I didn't have Marty's Vesuvian temper.

"Did you have to kill him?"

"The man was a pig."

"You could just have taken the picture," I suggested. "Without the picture, he wouldn't have a hold on her anymore."

"I would have," he said. "But Prine came in and attacked me for trespassing in his studio. We fought, and I killed him in the struggle."

That might sound plausible if I hadn't known Prine was stabbed in the back. I decided not to bring that up.

"And then I heard someone coming," he went on. "So I hid in the closet. When I came out, the picture was gone. I finally figured out that Gillian had shown up, found Prine's dead body, and managed to keep it together enough to take the painting away."

Somehow I didn't think keeping it together had been all that hard for Gillian. But probably not a good idea to tell Marty that.

"And Victor?" I asked instead.

"I figured another death would make them look less closely at people who had motives to kill Prine. I guess he must have been nosing around her studio. And now you." From the way he scowled and clenched his fists, I decided maybe I was lucky to have the caravan walls between him and me. "You wouldn't let it go. You had to find the painting and try to frame her with it."

"I didn't find it on purpose," I said. "And I didn't frame her. If she hadn't run away—"

"Enough talk."

He turned on his heel and began to climb into the truck cab. He started backing up slowly. I could feel the caravan moving—first backward, and then it began to tip downward.

Time for me to act as well. I shoved my phone in my pocket. I emptied out my tote, shoved Spike into it, and slung it over my shoulder. I grabbed the nearest bat. Then I took a deep breath and focused on the door, aiming at it with my shoulder. The one that was already hurt—no sense damaging the other.

"Haiii!" I shrieked, the way my old martial arts teacher had taught me, and hurled myself at the door.

To my great relief, the last shreds of the two-by-four gave way—with a lot less sound than I'd have expected, so with luck Marty wouldn't hear it over his straining engine. But when the door burst open, my momentum carried me out of it.

By this time the caravan was hanging precariously over the edge of the cliff. Luckily it wasn't quite a sheer cliff—at least the first part wasn't—though it was very steep. Spike and I slid for about ten feet and fetched up on a ledge. Below the ledge the cliff was where the sheer part started—looking down made me dizzy, just for a moment.

And then it made me mad.

I looked up to see that about the last foot of the caravan was sticking out over the cliff, and Marty was slowly easing it farther and farther over. No doubt he was going slowly to avoid damaging his truck. But eventually, the caravan would topple over and crash down on whatever was below it.

Spike and me. Even if it didn't kill us, it would almost certainly propel us over the sheer part of the cliff.

I studied the slope between me and the cliff. Luckily it was getting light enough to see possible handholds and footholds. Unfortunately some of the best ones—a couple of tough-looking little shrubs and a small gnarled tree growing out of the side of the slope—were right in the path the caravan would take when it fell. This wasn't going to be easy—especially not with the tote bag containing Spike dangling over one shoulder.

I began carefully moving sideways on our ledge—sideways, and slightly upward. The first priority was to get clear of the caravan's path. And once it fell, I needed to be either out of sight or back on top of the cliff.

Some rocks and dirt spilled over the top of the cliff, landing on us. Spike whined slightly, but had the good sense to keep still.

"I agree," I whispered. "Just hang in there."

I'd managed to make my way clear of the caravan's probable path and about half of the way back up to the top of the cliff when the caravan teetered and began to topple.

It slid until it encountered the scrubby little tree, whose trunk poked in through the doorway I'd shouldered open. And there it stuck, the whole weight of the caravan on that small tree—small, but evidently exceedingly tough.

As I continued scrabbling up the slope, I could see, to my left, the caravan lurching as Marty gunned the engine several times, trying to send it all the way over. The stubborn little tree didn't budge.

I continued to climb, mentally cheering the tree.

The truck door slammed. Apparently Marty was getting out to see what was holding up his murderous plan. Luckily, he was on the opposite side of the caravan, but still, I was running out of time.

"Damn," I heard him say, just as I heaved myself over the top of the slope and lay, panting, on the same level as Marty and the truck. Spike wriggled out of the tote, but luckily had the sense to plop down on the dirt. He lay there panting as if he'd been the one doing the climbing.

Just as long as he had the good sense not to bark.

Marty appeared to be doing something on the other side of the trailer. Something that was irritating him.

"Son-of-a—!" I heard him exclaim.

The truck was still running. And not connected to the trailer.

I began creeping toward the truck. Spike picked himself up and trotted in my wake.

When I reached the passenger side, I raised my head carefully until I could see Marty. He was holding a long branch, poking and prodding at something over the edge of the cliff—presumably the sturdy little tree that was impeding his plans.

"Damn!" He stood up straight and frowned. "Don't get your hopes up." He was looking at the caravan. "If I can't send this thing over the cliff, I'll set it on fire."

Good. He didn't realize we weren't still in the caravan.

No time to wait. I tried the passenger side truck door. It was open. I slowly opened it, and slid into the truck. Spike hopped in behind me. I quickly crawled over the stick shift and was about to reach for the hand brake

Just then Spike, who had been angelically still and quiet, came to life, erupting in furious barks and growls. He leaped out of the open driver's-side window and made a beeline for Marty.

"What the—get out of my truck!" He took a few steps toward me, and then Spike launched himself at Marty, teeth bared. Marty flinched, tried to bat Spike away, and took a few steps backward.

He fell over the cliff.

I eased the hand brake back in place and ran over to the edge of the cliff. Marty was dangling from the sturdy little tree, right below the caravan. He clung to its trunk with both hands as his feet scrabbled in vain for purchase. As I watched, the tree made an ominous cracking noise, but stood firm.

You had to give him points for persistence. Or possibly stubborn, stupid courage in the face of danger.

"Just wait till I get up there!" he bellowed.

Not a man who seemed to feel in need of being rescued,

and under the circumstances I figured playing good Samaritan would be a suicidal move. It occurred to me that he just might figure out how to climb up, and waiting around while he did so probably wasn't the smartest thing to do.

"Come on, Spike," I said. "Let's blow this pop stand."

As usual, Spike ignored me. He was too busy running up and down the edge of the cliff, barking at Marty and occasionally turning his back to the cliff and kicking small showers of dirt and stones down on him. I made a couple of efforts to catch him, and then gave up.

"Okay, suit yourself." I backed away from the cliff. "You can guard him while I fetch help."

As I was heading back to Marty's truck, my phone, still in my pocket, suddenly came to life and began making the various dinging sounds that indicated I had mail, text messages, and voice mail. I fished it out and turned it on.

Evidently here at the top of this mountain we got glorious cell phone reception. My e-mails had gone out. Everyone in the world was trying to reach me. I scrolled through all the missed calls and picked one to return. The one from Michael. I have my priorities.

"Meg? Are you all right? Where are you?"

"I'm fine, but I have no idea where I am," I said. "On top of a mountain somewhere. Marty—did you get my message that Marty was the killer?"

"I got your message that he was the kidnapper," he said. "If he's also the killer—where is he?"

"He's out of commission, at least for the time being," I said. "If Kevin or maybe Chief Heedles has any way to track the current location of my phone, they might want to do that. Meanwhile, I'm going to take Marty's truck and go in search of civilization."

"Just be safe," he said. "You have no idea where you are? What do you see?"

"Trees, and sky, and a very pretty sunrise just beginning. Apparently I'm on the east side of whatever mountain I'm on."

Just then I noticed the birds wheeling around the caravan. Could they be . . . yes! They were gulls.

One landed on top of the cab of Marty's truck and studied me, head cocked. I was no bird expert, but as far as I can see, this gull looked exactly the same as the one in Edward Prine's painting.

"Heading out," I said. "And tell Grandfather that when they find me, I may have a very nice surprise for him."

Chapter 32

As it turned out, I didn't have to go in search of civilization after all. As soon as Michael and I hung up, it occurred to me that if my phone was getting a signal, the GPS app might be working. Sure enough, I was able to call 911 with my longitude and latitude and the knowledge that I was atop something called Oatmeal Mountain. Biscuit Mountain, Oatmeal Mountain—not for the first time, I wondered if the early explorer who had named the local landmarks had been running short on provisions at the time.

So instead of driving back down the dirt road, I sat in Marty's truck with the doors locked and the key in the ignition, watching from a safe distance as Spike continued to taunt his fallen enemy.

In about twenty minutes I heard the first siren in the distance.

Within the hour the clearing atop Oatmeal Mountain was swarming with police officers, including Chief Heedles, back from Charlottesville. Luckily one of the Riverton officers, a dog lover, happened to have a leash and some dog treats in his vehicle, so we were able to drag Spike away from the edge of the cliff before he assaulted too many officers. He was now asleep in the back of one of the cruisers, secure behind the barrier normally designed to protect the officer from violent arrestees. Although I noticed that in spite of the barrier, no one seemed very eager to go near the cruiser.

Once Spike was out of the way, half a dozen of the officers kept their guns trained on Marty as the burliest of the Riverton officers threw him a rope and hauled him up to safety. Then the chief herself handcuffed him and read him his rights before sending him back to town.

"He can cool his heels in a cell till I'm ready to talk to him," she said.

One of the new arrivals was a state trooper who had Gillian in the back of his cruiser. So the BOLO had worked. I deduced that he'd picked her up from wherever she'd been apprehended and had been en route to the Riverton jail when he'd caught the first reports of my kidnapping and joined the hordes rushing to my rescue.

I wondered if he'd told her that she was no longer under suspicion of murder. Or if perhaps she'd overheard enough on the radio to figure it out on her own. Or maybe not. She was sitting in the back of the trooper's car, in handcuffs. I tried to catch her eye, but she was staring down at her feet.

Ah, well. She wouldn't have too much longer to wait. Though I suspect for her, the revelation of her relationship with Prine and his attempt to blackmail her would be almost as bad as jail.

I was relieved when an enormous tow truck arrived and began hitching cables to the caravan to keep it from plunging down the cliff while they figured out the best way to haul it back up.

I was still watching the tow truck's efforts when a nondescript blue sedan pulled up and parked near Marty's truck. A fraction of a second after it came to a stop, all three of its passenger doors flew open. Mother, Caroline, and Cordelia jumped out and rushed over to me.

"Meg, dear." Mother's kiss actually landed on my cheek, a

sure sign that she was less calm than usual. "We were that worried."

"Sorry if I upset you." I gave her a quick hug.

"But I hear you got the bloodthirsty creep!" Caroline thumped me on the back.

"Nearly destroying your caravan in the process," I said.

"I can get another caravan," Caroline said. "I'd rather lose a hundred of them than have anything happen to you."

"Of course, I may never forgive you for costing me my cook." Cordelia's fierce hug belied her words. "Or should I be thankful you unmasked him before he poisoned us all?"

"I suspect Marty would never sully his food with poison," I said. "But I'm sure he'd have found plenty of other ways to dispatch those of us who irritated him, so we'll have to make do with some other cook."

"Your mother is already working on locating someone," Cordelia said. "Though it won't be the same. What that man could do with a soufflé."

"If only I'd come up sooner," Mother said. "Alas! Last night's dinner will probably be the only time I get to try his cooking."

"Meg." Cordelia looked stern. "You should probably go down and get some rest. And let me know if you don't feel up to doing today's class. Under the circumstances, I think everyone would understand."

"Of course I feel up to it," I said. "After last night, I'm really in the mood to whack something with a hammer."

Cordelia studied me for a few moments, and then nodded.

"By the way," I asked. "Do we know where Mrs. Venable is?" I had no idea if the gulls soaring and flapping overhead were Ord's gulls, but I rather suspected they were, and if so, I didn't want Mrs. Venable seeing them before Grandfather did.

"Oh, don't worry," Mother said. "She's out of the woods and should be fine in a day or so."

"Out of the woods?" I echoed. "I just wondered why she wasn't trailing after you. Did something happen to her?"

"Poison ivy." Mother shook her head in sympathy. "Cousin Mary Margaret had to take her to the ER last night. They treated her for anaphylactic shock—apparently she's very sensitive."

I wondered if Mary Margaret felt any guilt about dropping the pith helmet in the poison ivy patch, or if she figured it served Mrs. Venable right. I could ask later.

"Oh, Meg," Caroline said. "Mr. Radditch has something to say to you?"

Mr. Radditch? I'd been aware that the driver of the blue sedan had followed the ladies over to where we were now standing, but they'd been hovering so closely that I hadn't caught a glimpse of him. Now they parted to reveal him.

The Slacker. He smiled and held out his hand.

"Joe Radditch." His handshake was a lot firmer than I'd have expected. "I understand Stan Denton blew my cover last night."

"Only to me," I said. "And I told my grandmother." I decided to play a hunch. "Have you gotten the goods on Mrs. Santo and Mr. Eads yet?"

A look of surprise crossed his face—so quickly that I almost didn't catch it. But he recovered.

"I'm not at liberty to discuss the case I'm working on," he said. "Though I can tell you that I've brought my investigation to a successful conclusion. And let me assure you that my investigation had nothing to do with the craft center, and I hope no one will object if I stay to the end of my week here. I'm overdue to take a few days off, and I can't think of a more delightful place to spend them."

"Of course we have no objection." Cordelia took him by the arm. "Though have you considered signing up for some of the courses we're offering later this summer—the ones targeted to law enforcement and other investigators?"

"What a brilliant idea!" Caroline took Mr. Radditch's other arm, and the two of them led him off, no doubt to experience a full-length sales pitch.

"Oh, good," Mother exclaimed. "They're releasing poor Gillian. I may see if Mr. Radditch can drive her back down to the center." She hurried over to where Gillian was standing, rubbing her handcuff-free wrists and talking to the chief.

When Mother arrived, Chief Heedles left her to fuss over Gillian and joined me.

"Feel like telling me what happened?" she asked. "Or would you rather go back to the craft center and recover a bit?"

"I'm fine." Why did everyone seem to think I was in need of recovery? How bad did I look? "I'd rather stay here a little longer, if that's okay with you."

"Fine with me." She took out her notebook.

"Before you interrogate me, may I ask how your trip to Charlottesville went?" I asked. "I know it probably doesn't have much to do with the murders, but . . ."

I paused, seeing the slight frown on her face. Then she chuckled, and let a broad smile cross her face.

"The trip was very satisfactory. When advised that we were on the brink of obtaining both his personal telephone records and those from Jazz Hands, Mr. Whiffletree became remarkably helpful. He confessed to hiring Mr. Prine to undertake a campaign of vandalism against the Biscuit Mountain Craft Center. But he didn't come up with the idea on his own—he did it at the behest of Mr. Rahn, of Smith Enterprises, and for that matter, with funds that Mr. Rahn provided. And as your grandmother surmised, Mr. Rahn was hoping to discredit the center and drive it out of business so he could purchase the property."

"If he thinks Cordelia would ever sell him Biscuit Mountain, craft center or no craft center, he's delusional."

"No doubt. Unfortunately, however nasty his plan was, there's not a lot we can charge him with."

"Conspiracy?" I suggested.

"No such thing as conspiracy to commit a misdemeanor under the Virginia Code," she said. "If the vandalism had reached felony level, we might have something to work with, but all the damage was relatively minor."

"Except for Baptiste's photos," I said. "He lost half-a-dozen large prints, and he sells those things for four or five hundred a pop. Wouldn't that add up to a felony?"

"It would indeed." The chief smiled slightly as she scribbled in her notebook. "I'll take it up with the town attorney. Thank you. So, getting to your story. Unless—are you sure you wouldn't rather do this over breakfast?"

"Pretty sure," I said. "After all, with Marty in jail, do you know who's going to be fixing breakfast?"

Chief Heedles blinked in surprise.

"I hadn't thought of that. Who?"

"I have no idea," I said. "Cordelia says Mother is already working on finding a replacement for Marty, but even Mother can't produce a chef out of her purse at a moment's notice. People will get fed, but it won't be anything like one of Marty's breakfasts."

"What that man could do with cinnamon rolls," the chief murmured.

"It won't be the same," I said. "But Mother will find someone wonderful—a relative, or an old school friend, or someone who happens to owe her a favor. I'm sure they'll have a replacement by dinner time—maybe by lunch. But for now, I'd just as soon stay here and avoid whatever makeshift substitute meal is going on back at the center."

"Good point. So—"

"And besides, I've been waiting for this moment." I pointed to where the dirt track emerged from the woods. Lance's Land Rover and Grandfather's Jeep were racing up the road, with Michael, Dad, Grandfather, Stanley, Jason, and the boys hanging out the windows, cheering as they caught sight of me.

One of the police officers tried to wave them off, but Chief Heedles stepped forward and pointed them to a parking spot, far enough away from the caravan that they wouldn't interfere with the salvage effort.

The boys had probably broken the rule about never unfastening your seat belt while the car is still moving, but I didn't care at the moment. They reached me a few seconds before Michael did, and nearly knocked me over, throwing their arms around me, each trying to drown the other out in his attempt to be the first to tell me about their camping adventure. Then Michael wrapped the three of us in a bear hug.

"Next time, you can come along and be one of the guys," was all he said.

The rest of the party all came over to shake my hand, hug me, or pat me on the back—all except for Grandfather. He inspected me for a long moment and nodded with satisfaction that I seemed unharmed—not to mention in good hands with Mother, Caroline, and Cordelia at my side. Then he strode to the edge of the cliff, binoculars glued to his eyes.

"It's them!" he cried. "My gulls."

Jason stepped forward, carrying a black plastic trash bag,

and began pouring some rather smelly, evil-looking garbage along the top of the cliff and throwing a few bits over the side. Evidently Grandfather had not gone on the camping trip unprepared for Operation Gull Quest.

Almost immediately a few of the gulls swooped closer, and then a few more. I heard Baptiste's camera clicking away. Before long, Grandfather had to take his binoculars away from his eyes, because he was surrounded by a flock of gulls, swooping down to pluck bits of garbage from the slope and noisily fighting over it in midair, so close that he had no need of binoculars. I didn't think I'd ever seen him look happier.

"See Great-great," Josh called out. "I knew Mommy could find your gulls."